THE KILLER A

Hugh Walpole was born in Auckland, New Zealand in 1884 and as a boy was sent to England to be educated. Bullied and miserable at school, young Walpole took refuge in the library, where he devoured the novels of Austen, Scott, Trollope and others, and he knew from an early age that he wanted to become a novelist. From 1903 to 1906, Walpole studied at Emmanuel College, Cambridge, and it was during this time that he first began to acknowledge his homosexuality. His attention was fixated for a time on A. C. Benson, whom he met as an undergraduate and who helped Walpole enter into a correspondence with Henry James, whom Walpole greatly admired and whose works would influence Walpole's own.

Walpole's first novel was *The Wooden Horse* (1909), but his first success was *Mr. Perrin and Mr. Traill* (1911), which received good reviews and sold well; it also earned the admiration of Arnold Bennett, who would go on to be a good friend. Walpole's career was further aided by a 1914 article by James in the *Times Literary Supplement*, in which he ranked Walpole with D. H. Lawrence and Compton Mackenzie as one of the important young English writers of his generation.

During the First World War, Walpole was rejected for service because of poor eyesight, so he went to Russia and assisted at hospitals, on one occasion single-handedly saving a Russian officer and earning the Cross of St. George. His experiences in Russia helped form the basis for his successful novels *The Dark Forest* (1916) and *The Secret City* (1919) and also earned him a CBE in 1918.

After the war, Walpole continued to write prolifically, usually publishing at least one very long novel each year. His output was diverse and included the popular "Herries" cycle of novels set in 18th-century England, as well as boys' stories featuring the character Jeremy, and what he called his "macabre" novels, including *Portrait of a Man with Red Hair* (1925). In addition to his writing, Walpole toured America extensively as a public speaker, winning great popularity and earning huge sales for his books in the United States.

During the 1930s, Walpole spent time in Hollywood, writing scripts for the films *David Copperfield* (1935) and *Little Lord Fauntleroy* (1936), and in 1937 he accepted a knighthood. At the start of the Second World War, Walpole remained in London and continued to write, working on his final macabre novel, *The Killer and the Slain* (1942), which was published posthumously. Walpole had long suffered from diabetes and his poor health, combined with the strain of his furious writing pace, probably contributed to his early death at age 57 in 1941.

Walpole's reputation had already begun to decline by the 1930s as he was increasingly seen as outdated by many critics, and it took a devastating hit when he was parodied in Somerset Maugham's *Cakes and Ale* (1930). A *Times* obituary that characterized Walpole as a "workmanlike" writer, "ambitious," and "a sentimental egotist" who "was not popular among his fellow-writers" further damaged his reputation, which is only now seeing signs of a revival with recent reprints (and a stage adaptation) of the Herries novels in the UK and this new edition of the book he considered the best of his macabre novels.

By Hugh Walpole

The Wooden Horse (1909)
Maradick at Forty: A Transition (1910)
Mr. Perrin and Mr. Traill: A Tragi-comedy (1911)
The Prelude to Adventure (1912)
Fortitude (1913)
The Duchess of Wrexe (1914)
The Golden Scarecrow (1915)
The Dark Forest (1916)
The Green Mirror: A Quiet Story (1918)
The Shilling Soldiers (1918)
The Secret City (1919)
Jeremy (1919)
The Captives (1920)
The Young Enchanted (1921)
The Thirteen Travellers (1921)
The Cathedral (1922)
Jeremy and Hamlet (1923)
The Old Ladies (1924)
Portrait of a Man With Red Hair: A Romantic Macabre (1925)
Harmer John: An Unworldly Story (1926)
Jeremy at Crale (1927)
Anthony Trollope (1928)
Wintersmoon (1928)
The Silver Thorn: A Book of Stories (1928)
Hans Frost: A Novel (1929)
Farthing Hall (1929) (with J.B. Priestley)
Rogue Herries (1930)
Judith Paris (1931)
Above the Dark Circus: An Adventure (1931)
The Fortress (1932)
Vanessa (1933)
All Souls' Night: A Book of Stories (1933)
Captain Nicholas (1934)
The Inquisitor (1935)
A Prayer for My Son: A Novel (1936)
John Cornelius: His Life and Adventures (1937)
The Joyful Delaneys (1938)
Head in Green Bronze, and Other Stories (1938)
The Sea Tower: A Love Story (1939)
The Bright Pavilions (1940)
Roman Fountain (1940)
The Blind Man's House: A Quiet Story (1941)
The Killer and the Slain: A Strange Story (1941)
Katherine Christian (1943)
Mr. Huffam and Other Stories (1948)

HUGH WALPOLE

THE KILLER AND THE SLAIN

A STRANGE STORY

With a new introduction by
JOHN HOWARD

VALANCOURT BOOKS

The Killer and the Slain by Hugh Walpole
First published London: Macmillan, 1942
First Valancourt Books edition, 2014
Reprinted from the edition published New York: Doubleday, 1942

Copyright © 1942 by Hugh Walpole, renewed 1969
Introduction © 2014 by John Howard

Published by Valancourt Books, Richmond, Virginia
Publisher & Editor: JAMES D. JENKINS
20th Century Series Editor: SIMON STERN, University of Toronto
http://www.valancourtbooks.com

All rights reserved. The use of any part of this publication
reproduced, transmitted in any form or by any means, electronic,
mechanical, photocopying, recording, or otherwise, or stored
in a retrieval system, without prior written consent of the
publisher, constitutes an infringement of the copyright law.

ISBN 978-1-939140-99-9
Also available as an electronic book.

All Valancourt Books publications are printed on acid free paper
that meets all ANSI standards for archival quality paper.

Cover by M. S. Corley
Set in Dante MT 11/13.6

INTRODUCTION

HUGH WALPOLE was a man at war within himself. On one side was the hugely popular author and accomplished speaker who moved in the best circles; on the other was the gauche and insecure boy who had never ceased to crave love and affection. Their struggle usually revealed itself in the depths of his solitude or, sometimes, in the presence of close friends. But they also fought their battles in front of millions—in the pages of his fiction.

Born in 1884 and raised in a loving family, Walpole's years away at school were painful. Sensitive, never confident or at ease, he escaped into an interior world fuelled by literature. But the scars remained. For the rest of his life, despite all his very public successes, he was notoriously thin-skinned. When he felt slighted he could be quick to anger—and as quick to abjectly regret it. Walpole studied at Cambridge, where he also came to terms with his homosexuality, which tended to manifest itself in the desire for deep male friendships and a quest for the "perfect friend".

After university Walpole soon moved to London to pursue his longed-for career in literature. He compensated for his vulnerabilities with a single-minded ambition, not only in writing but in devoting much effort to what would now be described as networking. He came to know many of the leading authors of the day, and formed several enduring and genuine friendships. The most important was with Henry James (1843-1916). Walpole's complex relationship with "the Master" would be of lasting significance.

In 1909 Walpole published his first novel. Over thirty more were to follow with apparently effortless ease. From the outset they often included scenes of almost supernatural intensity, sustaining them within an enveloping gothic atmosphere of physical and psychological menace and dread. In much of his fiction Walpole embraced the "dark theme" with enthusiasm. He knew what he was doing in his "macabres", and did it with easy skill throughout his career.

Five of Walpole's novels deserve special attention for their use of the strange and fantastic. Four of them, *Maradick at Forty* (1910), *The Prelude to Adventure* (1912), *Portrait of a Man with Red Hair* (1925), and *Above the Dark Circus* (1931) were collected in *Four Fantastic Tales* (1932). In his preface to this omnibus volume Walpole stated something his readers already knew: "I have been unable to keep fantasy out of my books. . . . It is not just now the fashion to believe in Good and Evil; at any rate no one pays them the compliment of decorating them with capital letters. . . . It is a matter of reconciling two opposite worlds, a feat possibly too difficult for me, but one well worth attempting."

The fifth attempt came some years later with *The Killer and the Slain*, which turned out to be the most striking of his "macabres". It was a return to the psychological intensity and menace of the earlier novels—only more so. Whether or not Walpole achieved the feat of reconciling two opposite worlds is for the reader to judge; the important thing was that he made the attempt, and in the process put himself "wholeheartedly into the novel, in more senses than one". In doing so, he produced what remains probably his most enigmatic and personal novel. It was also the last he lived to complete, appearing posthumously in 1942.

The theme had first occurred to Walpole as early as 1937, but by the time he set pen to paper in June 1940 Britain was at war. The world in which Walpole had come to maturity and fame was threatened. Nothing and nobody was safe. The novel was largely written in a London living in fear and expectation of air raids, which before long became a reality as the city was subjected to devastating nightly attacks by the *Luftwaffe*. The Blitz left its mark on the book: "all these months of fear, uncertainty, and restlessness are behind it".

Walpole dedicated *The Killer and the Slain* to his early patron Henry James, "the great author of *The Turning of the Screw*". Was the mistake in the title—it was printed as such only in editions published in the UK—merely an uncorrected error, or the younger author's sly comment on a past still alive to him, still able to influence his present? Perhaps Walpole intended *The Killer and the Slain* to be a particularly allegorical fiction. In any case, amidst all the uncertainties of the time, and imagining his own (maybe sudden, certainly premature) wartime death, Walpole formally acknowledged a vitally important relationship at the beginning of an account of other interwoven lives with their profound and ambiguously significant bonds. Although *The Killer and the Slain* does not possess the intricate subtleties of James's story (and what other really can?) it does, nevertheless, share much with it in the way of psychological and physical terror and confusion. Walpole's novel, short by comparison to most of his others, is an intense and headlong work which gains by its brevity. The words count. In those respects at least, Walpole certainly succeeds in emulating his dedicatee.

While Walpole tormented his characters on the page, the real world provided the author with worries and dilemmas to match. At the outbreak of war he had offered his services to the Ministry of Information, but had been rebuffed. Frightened, nervous and irritable in London, he felt guilty when enjoying the tranquillity of Brackenburn, his beloved house in the Lake District, and would soon yield to the urge to return to the capital, with all the danger that posed. Increasingly Walpole used *The Killer and the Slain* as an outlet for his conflicting emotions: "What a lot of nastiness, and pity for my own nastiness, I have in me! It's all coming out in this work." As the story moves toward its inevitable climax, the narrator goes on phantasmagorical wanderings through the blacked-out London streets and relates his struggles with who or what is at conflict within him. When the end finally comes, it seems to be a reconciliation of sorts, and accompanied by welcome peace.

However, peace continued to elude the author. The air raids continued. Walpole's flat in Piccadilly was severely damaged, and the house in Hampstead Garden Suburb where he sometimes stayed received a hit while he was there. Even so, he could never bring himself to stay away from London for very long. It was as if he could not make up his mind about his relationship with death. He began another novel: wherever he found himself, writing remained his only comfort—his "opiate"—as long as he was able to lose himself in the story.

But his stories could not shield him. Walpole had suffered from diabetes for years, and his past carelessness with its treatment, together with the effects of his many wanderings and anxieties, combined to seriously affect his heart. All struggles ended when he died in June 1941. Hugh Walpole never quite found his perfect friend, and the shadows never ceased to interest and lure him. It hadn't only been the outside world at war. Within, at last, killer and slain became one.

JOHN HOWARD

January 9, 2014

John Howard was born in London. He is author of *The Defeat of Grief* and *Numbered as Sand or the Stars*, as well as the short story collections *The Silver Voices*, *Written by Daylight*, and *Cities and Thrones and Powers*. He has published many articles on various aspects of the science fiction and horror fields, especially on the work of classic authors such as Fritz Leiber, Arthur Machen, August Derleth, M.R. James, and writers of the pulp era.

THE KILLER AND THE SLAIN

Dedicated
in Loving Memory and Humble Admiration
to the Author of
THE TURN OF THE SCREW

Part One

I

I, JOHN OZIAS TALBOT, aged thirty-six years and three months, being in my perfectly sane mind, wish to write down this statement.

I do so entirely and solely for my own benefit and profit—in fact, for the quietening of my disturbed mind. It is most improbable that anyone other than myself will read this document, but should anything happen to me and I die without destroying this writing, I wish the reader, whoever he or she may be, to realize fully that no one could conceivably be of a more complete mental sanity and honest matter-of-fact common sense than I am at this moment.

It is because I wish to show this self-evident fact to myself and, if need be, to the whole world (after my death) that I write this down. There will be many minute and apparently insignificant facts and details in this record because *circumstantial facts* are in this matter the thing! I have suffered during these preceding months certain experiences so unbelievable that were I *not* sane, and were many of the facts not so commonplace, my sanity might be doubted. It is *not* to be doubted. I am as sane as any man in the United Kingdom.

Because in the course of this narrative I confess to a crime this document will be kept in the greatest possible secrecy. I have no desire to suffer at the hand of the common hangman before I need. That I do not myself *feel* it to be a crime matters nothing, I am afraid, to the Law. One day, when the important elements in such matters are taken into account rather than the unimportant, justice will be better served. But that time is not yet.

I was born in the little seaside town of Seaborne in Glebeshire on January 3, 1903. I am married and have one son aged ten. I inherited my father's business of Antique and Picture Dealer. I am the

3

author of four books, a *Guide to Glebeshire* and three novels—*The Sandy Tree* (1924), *The Gridiron* (1930) and *The Gossip-monger* (1936). The last of these had some success. I was born in a bedroom above the shop, which is in the High Street and has, from its upper windows, a fine view of the sea and the now neglected and tumble-down little harbour.

I was the only child of my parents and adored by them. Some have said that they spoiled me. It may be so. I worshipped my mother but had always a curious disaffection for my father. This was partly, I can see now, physical. He was an obese and sweaty man and would cover my face with wet slobbery kisses when I was small, and this I very greatly disliked. My mother, on the other hand, was slight and dapper in appearance, and the possessor of the most beautiful little hands I have ever seen on any woman. Her voice was soft and musical, marked with a slight Glebeshire accent. She had something of the gipsy in her appearance, and liked to wear gay colours. I remember especially a dress made of some foreign material—silk of many brilliant shades—that I used to love, and I would beg her to show it me as it hung in the cupboard in the bedroom. My father, when they woke in the morning, would always go downstairs to get breakfast ready (he worshipped my mother), and then my mother would take me into her bed and I would lie in her arms. Never, until I married, did I know such happiness.

My father was successful in his little business—successful, that is to say, for those easier, more comfortable days—and we lived very pleasantly. His great passion was for the buying of old and apparently worthless pictures. He would clean them with the hope that something by a Master might be discovered. He did, indeed, make one or two discoveries—a Romney portrait and an Italian Pietà by Piombo were two of his successes. But his main business was with visitors and tourists. He visited all the local sales and sometimes went quite far afield.

We lived quietly and knew few people. My mother was fastidious about people and I have inherited that from her.

At this point I must say something about my own personality and character because so much of what afterwards happened depends on that. I will try to be honest, although honesty is never easy when we write about ourselves. We naturally incline to our own favour. But I have always trained myself to consider myself objectively and am possibly given overmuch to self-criticism.

I have been always of a reserved nature, careful to say no more than I truly feel and to confide only in those I trust and thoroughly know. My father's sentimentality affected me unpleasantly, and the love that I felt for my mother did not need expression.

From my very early years I have been considered cold and undemonstrative, but in reality I have always longed for affection although I have found it difficult to believe that anyone could in real fact be fond of me—this not because I do not know that there are many things in me worthy of affection, but because I have seen, during my life, so many false emotions, so many bitter betrayals of people by one another, and have realized that most men and women express more than they feel and mean less than they say. I have tried very earnestly to avoid this fault in myself.

I suppose that I must confess myself a prude, and this same prudery has lost me many contacts that I might otherwise have made. The sexual life of man has always seemed to me ugly and dangerous, and only to be redeemed by real and abiding love. The conventional life of man with man regarding the physical side of things has been, and is, repellent to me.

And yet God knows I have longed again and again for friendship and companionship, and have blamed myself bitterly for not obtaining it more easily. Another reason for my reserve is that I have had one ceaseless ambition—namely, to be generally recognized as a good writer. Not a great one—that I long ago realized I should never be. But I have wanted to be one of the writers of my time whose work is generally known. It is *good* work, better by far than the writings of many who have been generally acclaimed, but it has had a quality of rareness and peculiarity that has hindered its general popularity. And then I must regretfully admit that my sense of humour is small. Life seems to me to be altogether too serious, especially during the last anxious twenty years, to admit of much humour!

I have always shrunk from boisterousness, violence and noise. I

love soft voices (such as that possessed by my dear mother), courteous ways, good manners in argument, consideration of others.
The cheerful, hail-fellow, slap-on-the-back sort of man I have never
been able to abide.

I can be exceedingly obstinate and tenacious of purpose. When
an idea is deeply rooted in my mind I find it impossible to reject.
I like to be allowed to go my own way without interference and I
detest enquiries into my personal affairs.

God knows this is not a pleasant self-portrait and I can blame no
one for wishing to see the last of me, and yet I have, I think, quali-
ties of honesty, courage, affection and fidelity that are valuable.

I had better here say something about my personal appearance,
as that is of the utmost importance in these peculiar circumstances.
I will not describe myself as I am at this moment, for reasons to be
seen later, but rather as I was two years ago.

I was, and am, five feet eleven inches in height, I was slender and
yet not meagre. My hair was plentiful, dark brown in colour and
apt to be untidy owing to my dislike of filthy things like brilliantine:
my eyes grey, and my eyebrows faint, my nose neither large nor
small, my lips thin and nervous if I am agitated or worried, and my
chin rather indeterminate. My hands free of hair (my body, apart
from my head, has little hair). Although when clothed I appear
slim, without my clothes I had, two years ago, the evidences of a
slight tendency to stoutness. And here I must mention a possible
overdelicacy as to my being seen by anyone unclothed. I attribute
this to my having been a day boy and, since my school time, I have
mixed very little with men.

I shall never forget my horror when, one morning entering my
room without knocking, an aunt, a noisy careless creature, saw
me nude in my bedroom. I was at that time a boy of about fifteen.

I might have made a good thing of my business had I been able
to put my whole heart into it. My father had trained me well and I
have a natural love for rare and beautiful things. But my mind was
for ever on my writing, and had it not been for my wife, I should, I
fear, have lost everything. I owe her a great deal for this and many
other things.

I am not a religious man although recent fearful events have led me to reconsider many of my earlier views. If there *is* a God I pray Him to forgive my many years of disobedience and to lift, if it may be so, this dreadful present burden from my shoulders.

2

I MET for the first time James Oliphant Tunstall on my very first day at the Seaborne Grammar School. (This was in 1913.) I was a boy of ten years of age and, of course, dreadfully shy and nervous at this, my first day at school. I remember it as though it were yesterday, and indeed because it was the hour of my first meeting James Tunstall, it may be said to be the most important day of my life.

During the morning nothing much occurred. I was placed with several other new boys in a class some way up the school. We were the *bright* new boys and James Tunstall was not among them. He was in a lower form. I remember very well the master of my form—Oxley was his name—for he had a passionate love for literature and was the first human being to make Chaucer and Shakespeare, and even Milton, understandable to me. He was a long, thin man with a long, thin nose, and a habit of sniffing as though an unpleasant odour were somewhere lurking. But how he *adored* Shakespeare!

We were let out for recreation at midday and it was in the play-ground on that sharp September morning that I first saw James Tunstall. Anyone would have noticed him before the other new boys, just as in later life he was always the first to be recognized anywhere. He was exactly my height but even then filled out sturdily and broadly. Whereas I was sallow-complexioned he was rosy and brown in colour, with rounded cheeks. Even then his eyebrows were thick above his bright sparkling eyes.

He was always laughing, joking, calling out, on the move. As a small boy (he was the same age as myself, born in the same month) he was friendly to all the world. I suppose, to use modern rather cheap terms, you would say he was an extrovert. I was an introvert. But there was more in it than that. He used his breeziness and heartiness to cover his secret designs. Even then, at ten years of age, he was plotting how he could use everybody and everything to his own advantage. He was helped, of course, by the fact that he never had any morals whatever.

When I first saw him he was standing in the middle of the stone yard telling some story to a group of other boys, and although he was only a new boy, he had already fascinated them and they were laughing and joking with him as though he had been at the school for years. I didn't want to approach the group but I had to. Even at that very first moment he fascinated me and even at that very first moment I hated him.

He said again and again, in after years, that he had always liked me—even at that first encounter. And I think, in a strange sort of way, that was true—liked me and patronized me.

Now if there is one thing stronger in me than another it is my hatred of being patronized. Patronage of one human being by another seems to me despicable. It is true, I suppose, that the patronizer does not sometimes know that he is patronizing. That makes it worse, for it argues a secret arrogance and conceit, an arrogance of the soul.

In any case, from the first Tunstall patronized and mocked me. This does not mean that he was not pleasant to me. He, as he laughingly said afterwards, from the very first took me under his wing. He called me 'Jacko,' a name that naturally revolted me. "You know, Jacko," he said to me many years later, "I'll never forget how you looked that first morning at the old school—with your anxiety and politeness and helplessness. You were the most tempting object for anyone to rag, and where you'd have been if I hadn't protected you I can't imagine."

Protect me in a sort of way he did, but for me in a very shaming kind of way. He was popular, of course; I was not so much unpopular as negative and colourless. When a boy twisted my arm or kicked my behind Tunstall would come up, laughing, and say: "Stop that. Jacko's under my protection. Didn't you know?" And because he was strong and stoutly built, and everyone liked him, people did let me alone. But the other boys caught up the horrid name, Jacko, from him. How I detested it! It was as though I were a monkey.

I very soon discovered that Tunstall was up to every kind of trick and broke all the rules, but he was popular with the masters as well as with the boys, and he had, then as later, an open, hearty, smiling manner. He was always in good spirits and had great ingenuity in the carrying-out of his secret plans. He was lazy and I often did his work for him. It wasn't as though I were frightened of him exactly, and yet I can see now that there was some sort of secret fear mixed in my feelings about him. Not so much fear, perhaps, as a consciousness of some bond between us. He felt that as well as I.

I have mentioned the word fear. I will admit at once that I am not brave and have never been so. One of the first things to exasperate me in Tunstall was his apparent fearlessness. It seemed that he was afraid of nothing, but I am not really sure that this was so. There was, I fancy, a lot of false bravado mixed up with it.

But I must get on, for I have much to tell—how much I didn't properly perceive when I began.

One summer term at the Grammar School an episode occurred which I fancy affected all my after life—and it changed my nervous dislike of Tunstall into positive hatred. I have spoken already of my sensitiveness to any sort of personal exposure. This was always with me a kind of spiritual passion.

On a certain day in the week the town salt-water baths were reserved for our school. They were formed from part of the sea, but the actual bathing pool was enclosed in an especial pavilion. We boys undressed all together in a long kind of reserved corridor. I was extremely sensitive of undressing before others, and while most of the boys were quite careless about the matter and ran about the place naked, I was always careful to slip on my bathing trunks before taking off my shirt.

One afternoon a number of boys, including Tunstall, were undressing near me when someone mocked me and called me rude names. Then they all teased me. I was standing with only my shirt on when, quite unexpectedly, Tunstall whipped my shirt off, snatched my bathing-trunks away from me, and then pranced round me laughing and gesticulating. The others joined in and formed a ring round me while I stood, trembling all over, my hands folded in front of me. My folded hands annoyed them and they pulled them away, and I don't know what would have happened had not a master been seen approaching. Then, laughing and shouting, they jumped into the water.

It will be difficult for many people to understand the deep and lasting effect that this trivial little incident had upon my character. These things cannot be explained even now when Freud and Jung have done so much to reveal us to ourselves. I felt as though I had been deeply and publicly shamed, and my original shyness and reticence were doubly reinforced.

The affair was, however, made worse for me by what followed. As, after our bath, we walked up to the school, Tunstall joined me. He was in radiant health and spirits. He put his arm round me and drew me close to him. I remember our little conversation as though it had occurred this morning!

"Look here, Jacko!" he said. "You mustn't mind things so much. Why, I thought you were going to blub! It was only a bit of fun."

I hated his touch, the pressure of his fingers against my neck. However, I pretended not to care.

"I didn't mind," I said, "only I thought it was a silly sort of thing to do."

"Yes, you did mind. You know you did. You mustn't mind anything. I don't. If chaps see you mind they'll only do it all the more."

"I don't see why I can't be left alone," I said.

"So you will be if you don't care. I was only ragging. I am awfully fond of you, you know. I am really."

"That's all right," I said sheepishly. Then he ran off laughing, without a care in the world.

Even then I was writing. The only thing I wanted to be in the world was a writer. Oddly enough Tunstall had an artistic side to him. His father was, I should imagine, a ne'er-do-weel. He betted on horses and was always involved in wild-cat schemes to make money. They lived in a little house outside the town, overlooking the sea. His mother was a gentle-faced woman who had, I expect, a pretty hard life. Tunstall could draw like anything. He was always amusing the boys by drawing things for them and often the drawings were bawdy. They seemed to us miraculously clever, although even then I thought there was a certain cheapness and commonness in them. But he showed me one day some watercolours of the sea and coast that seemed to me lovely. It was on that day that most unfortunately I told him about my writing, and under pressure I showed him one or two things.

He professed to like them greatly—especially one, a rather fantastic sort of fairy-story as I remember it. But he did say he wished that they had been a bit more 'spicy.' "Later on, when you're selling things to the papers, put in bits about girls' legs and that sort of thing. That's what sells. After all, it is what men are always thinking of—'a bit of skirt.'"

I remember the phrase 'a bit of skirt' with a very especial horror—it seemed the lowest, most common denominator to which the world could possibly be put.

I suspected then that I had been a fool to show him my writing— very soon I discovered the kind of fool that I had been! Soon everybody was teasing me 'to show my writing.' But I found that I had no need to do so, for Tunstall had informed them fully of the nature of it and especially of the fairy-story, which contained a character called King Dodderer. This became my nickname. How I hated him then! I did have at least the pluck of facing him with it. Trembling with rage, I charged him with betraying my confidence.

"You swore you wouldn't tell anybody"—feeling almost a frenzy at the sight of his round cheeks, his rather coarse but thick dark hair and eyebrows, his rounded but strong and sturdy body. Our conversation was something like this:

"I didn't know you'd mind. Honest, Jacko, I didn't."

"Of course you knew I'd mind."

"Honest, I didn't. And why should you? I've told everybody they're awfully good."

"You haven't. You've made everybody laugh at them."

"Oh, they tease a bit! What does it matter? You *are* a funny chap. You should be like me, bold as brass and not giving a damn for anybody."

"Before I'd be like you I'd drown myself," I answered hotly.

Then he put his hand on my arm, holding it tightly. It was a way that he had. He would stand quite close to me, holding my arm, looking into my face with his bright, bold, sparkling eyes, and I felt as though he absorbed me, took me right inside himself, inside his hateful self, and kept me there a prisoner.

"You know, Jacko, I *do* like you, although you're such a goup. I think you really like me, too, although you're a bit afraid of me. I like that as well."

"I hate you! I hate you!" I cried, breaking away from him.

Then, of course, we grew older. We both left the school when we were sixteen, I to join my father at the shop, he to go into some sort of business in London.

There are other things I remember about the two of us at that school. There was one other thing I never forgave him for. At last I made a friend, the only friend I did make at that place. He was a boy called Marillier, a tall handsome boy, popular with everyone. For some reason or other he took a great fancy to me. I was astonished when I found it was so. He was clever and read books. His great ambition was that one day he would be a publisher. "Then I shall publish your books and we'll both make a lot of money." He was a really charming boy, sensitive and understanding, and, after a while, I poured out my heart to him. He seemed to understand all my reserve and silence and reticence. We went for long walks along the cliffs and bathed in the coves. He made me very happy. I worshipped him and would have done anything for him. Strangely enough Tunstall was jealous of this friendship.

"You like him more than you do me, don't you?"

"Of course I do," I answered. "I don't like you a little bit. I never have."

"Oh yes you do," he answered. "I mean more to you than Marillier does. You can't get away from me. You think you can, but you can't."

Then Marillier began to be a little less intimate with me. He wasn't as frank and easy with me. I taxed him with it and he denied it, but I knew it was true. I was easily hurt and brooded over things. I was sure that Tunstall had said something to Marillier about me. I taxed him with *that* and we had a quarrel. All our intimacy was spoilt. Perhaps if I had been another kind of person I would have broken down the barrier between us, but I was too shy, and our friendship was ruined.

Tunstall said one day:

"You don't see as much of Marillier as you did, Jacko."

"You've put him against me."

"Well, what if I have? I'm the only friend you're going to have here."

"I'm not your friend! I'm not your friend!"

But he only laughed and teased me with his smile, as though he knew everything about me and could make me do as he wished. Other little things I can remember.

There was some sort of an examination and I helped Tunstall with his paper. This was afterwards discovered and we were both punished, but Tunstall, because he was a favourite, was let off lightly, and I, because none of the masters, save only Oxley, liked me, was severely handled.

I brooded long over this unfairness.

There was a master called Harrison, a big, fat, rosy man, rather an example physically of what Tunstall might be when he became a man. Their resemblance was, I think, more than physical. Their natures were of the same kind.

Harrison disliked me very much, and it happened that for a whole year Tunstall and I were both in his form. He seemed to understand the relationship of Tunstall and myself, and fostered its disagreeableness in every way. He had a complete understanding with Tunstall and their eyes would meet and they would smile.

Harrison had a trick of jingling his keys and money in his trouser-pocket which for some reason or other disgusted me. The backs of his hands were covered with dark black hairs, and sometimes, when the weather was warm, he would take off his coat and turn up his shirt-sleeves. His thick strong arms were covered with hair, and this also revolted me.

I was, for the latter part of that year, at the top of the form and the cleverest boy in it, but he would catch me out in a fault whenever he could and would summon me in front of him, before the class. Then he would hold my arm as Tunstall sometimes did and stare at me, smiling contemptuously. I knew that Tunstall, behind my back, was watching with delight, and I felt as though I was held, a prisoner, between these two and that they were, in concert, shaming me.

Harrison had affairs with girls in the town, and at last was involved in some scandal and was dismissed from the school, but I think that he continued to see Tunstall.

During most of these school years the Great War of 1914-18 was, of course, raging and, although we boys had little actually to do with it, I don't doubt but that it affected all our nerves and that the weak nutrition of the last years of the War was bad for our health.

In 1919 both Tunstall and I left.

3

FROM 1919 until March 1929 Tunstall was in London, or in any case did not return to Seaborne. His mother and father died. Their little house by the sea was sold. It seemed that no fragment or memory of them remained.

I worked in the antique shop and, during those years, the boom years that followed the War, we did sufficiently well. In 1924 my first novel, *The Sandy Tree*, was published. I will not now, when my hopes have been so sadly disappointed, say very much of my almost delirious excitement at that time. The shore of the world is scattered with the bones of disappointed artists. I had written several novels before *The Sandy Tree* and sent them to various publishers. They were refused and I destroyed them. But on that morning when I received the letter saying that *The Sandy Tree* had been accepted I knew such joy that I was, for a while, insane. I realized on that morning that with a little luck I might be encouraged to be an entirely different human being—genial, friendly, communicative. My mother and father were almost as wildly delighted and all our friends and acquaintances were told of the event. I corrected my proofs as though they were the very blood of my body. As the day of publication approached I could scarcely sleep and ate almost nothing. Then my six presentation copies arrived in their dark blue covers and I gave the first one that I handled to

my father and mother. They both thought the book wonderful
and looked at me with new eyes. Then came the day of publication. Weeks followed. Nothing happened at all. There were some
reviews, none very rapturous, one or two advertisements. Some
jocular remarks were made by our acquaintances. It was altogether too queer and unusual a book for their understanding. After
a month the book was as though it had never been. I told myself
that this always happened to a first novel of any peculiar merit. I
told myself that I was so unusual that it would take time for me to
be discovered by the people who really understood me.

But in my heart I had been dealt a dreadful blow. All my life long
I had looked forward to the day when I would be an author before
the world. I consoled myself, at moments of bitter loneliness or
disappointment, with this self-prophecy of my future glory. Now
I had tried and I had failed.

In 1926 my father died. He was ill for a week from some sort of
fever and then quite suddenly one evening passed away. On the last
day of his life he spoke to me in a very touching manner.

He lay there seeming to me to be cleansed of all his grossness
by approaching death. His eyes were dim but of a great kindness and even tenderness. I sat beside his bed and suddenly tears
began to fall. I loved him for the first time and learned all that I had
missed. But he himself was gay and even jocular. He had always
been a merry man.

"All our lives together, John, I've loved you and you've not loved
me. You've wanted to get away from me. Something in me has
shocked you. But I've understood that, for I've always seemed to
be both myself and yourself—the rake and the puritan bound into
one body. I've not been physically faithful to your mother and
she has known it and forgiven me. But I have loved her dearly all
through life. Don't be too shocked at things, John. Men are partly
animals, you know, and the animal in man isn't as evil as the devil
in man—the devil's weapons are meanness, treachery, betrayal of
heart, coldness, uncharitableness, not fornication and all lascivi-
ousness. Remember not to judge or you may yourself be judged.
It was the man whose house was swept and cleaned that took in
the seven new devils."

That was the way my father talked, in a kind of scriptural style. He pressed my hand, and that night about ten he coughed and cried out and died.

I took on the business.

I should say something here about Seaborne itself, for I loved it so much until a certain evening and after that came most bitterly to hate it as, afterwards, I will write down. In Elizabeth's day it had been quite a flourishing seaport with a bustling trade. It was well situated between the hills and having in front of it a natural harbour with a strong breakwater. This was needed, for the houses of the little town went to the water's edge and, during three-quarters of the year, the storms could be terrific.

The Upper Town was like any other seaside resort in Glebeshire, with a High Street, a Methodist chapel, a tourist hotel 'The Granby,' a Smith's bookshop with its messenger-boy sign, a hosier's, a grocer's, a china-ware and our own antique shop.

Above the Upper Town, straggling up the hill, were decent villas with pleasant gardens. All this was conventional, but the Lower Town was very unconventional. It reminded one of Polchester *in piccolo*, for Polchester's Seatown on the Pol was at one time—and not so very long ago—as wild and neglected as any place you could find in England.

Seaborne's Lower Town wasn't wild and neglected. It was simply deserted. It had fallen into a still and gloomy sea-green, slimy decay. Any sea traffic there was had moved to the New Harbour, that also boasted a new pier with a hall and a cinema.

So the Lower Town harbour had surrendered to history. The houses that abutted on the sea had still some remnants of Elizabethan architecture, and there were proposals once or twice a year that something should be done with this part of the town. 'The Green Parrot,' a very low sort of pub, hanging right over the water, and with one foot on the old deserted grass-grown landing-stage, was in reality a fine little building with the remnants of an Elizabethan staircase and spy-hole. 'The Green Parrot' had in fact a long and exciting history had anyone taken the trouble to delve into it.

I little thought, at the time of my father's death, that I was, in my own destined moment, to add to that history. Possessing the twisted and restless imagination of a romantic novelist, the Lower Town appealed greatly to my taste and fancy. I liked especially on an early spring or midsummer evening to wander quite alone under the shadows of the warped and tumbled houses, looking upward into a sky faintly green with the piercing silver of a new-born star and then down, beyond the rotting wood iridescent with slime, into the water that heaved as though it were asleep and reflected, a little out of focus, the glass of windows, the tufts of greenery between the window-joints, the pushing eaves, the drunken chimneys, and, behind them all, the line of quiet hill like a smudged drawing, grey and still. That is how it was. Green and grey, still and crooked, waiting, sleepily speculative, on the edge of the Atlantic.

On these evenings there were few passers-by. Even 'The Green Parrot' was not greatly patronized. In the day-time tourists visited the Lower Town and found it 'picturesque.' They bought post-cards of it. But on my evenings I was a solitary, and loved to be so.

4

I HAVE NOW REACHED the point of my marriage. I must say here, for I wish to be completely frank and honest in everything, that my wife was the first woman with whom I had intercourse. I knew no woman of any sort or kind before I knew her. I was twenty-five years of age when I married her. I had, of course, my temptations as every man must have, but I put them always resolutely behind me. I wished to keep myself for the woman I loved.

I think I should say in this place that prayer helped me very much in my struggle against temptation. I was not, I suppose, a very religious young man. I went to church on Sunday to please my dear mother, but the prayers and hymns in the Church of England service seemed to me very empty and hollow. But in my own private prayers I did undoubtedly find strength and assistance. George Meredith has said: "Who rises from his knees a better man, his prayer is answered." I felt a contact which may indeed have been but wish-fulfilment. It had nevertheless its actual concrete effect.

I had fancied myself once or twice in love and always, I can see now, with the same type of woman. We have all of us, I fancy, a type physically of especial attraction to us, but in my own case it must be a woman retiring, virginal, modest, of the kind that Burne-Jones once wonderfully painted. With this character I liked a woman to be also slender, with a face like the heroine of Browning's great poem.

I would lie sleepless, imagining her to myself, her noble brow, her sweet mouth so formed with smiling kindly tenderness, her white delicate hands, her slender virginal waist.

Unhappily, girls answering to this physical appearance had, I was sorry to discover, characters little in common with it, and I began cynically to wonder whether the more virginal the face the looser the character!

One misadventure I had of this kind is too shocking to mention, and I shrank yet further within myself.

Then one evening I was taking a solitary walk in Lower Town when I saw a female figure standing on the decrepit landing-stage looking down into the water. It was a grey misty evening and a very slight rain was falling.

I fancied for the moment that there was something desperate in her poise, and that even it might be that she would throw herself into the sea. So I approached her, but, on standing beside her, found that she was entirely composed and controlled. She was wearing a grey cloak and bonnet and, when she raised her face to mine, I knew at once that the love of my life had, in an instant of fiery ecstasy, been created. Her face was, for me, the loveliest I have ever seen or ever shall see. It was the face of my dreams, the features exquisitely formed, and the expression that of one of the Burne-Jones angels.

She did not seem in the least afraid of me, nor did she move away. She even smiled and said that she thought it would soon rain heavily. I have asked her since whether she was not afraid to speak to a strange young man in such a lonely place, but she said that I looked such a very innocent young man, and that in any case she was well able to look after herself.

So we talked for a little. I was trembling with anxiety lest she should move away and I lose her for ever. She has told me since that she knew from that very first moment that I was in love with her.

She showed, however, no intention of moving away, and told me that she was in Seaborne for a holiday, that she had a job as a stenographer in London. I ventured to ask her, breathlessly, whether she were married.

She said no, that she was an orphan, and lived with a sister in Chelsea. She also told me that she disliked her present employer and hoped to find some other job. She was taking her holiday alone, which she greatly preferred.

I told her something about myself, that I had an antique shop in the High Street, that my mother was still alive, and that I had published a novel. She seemed to be greatly interested when I told her about the antique shop. She said that it was her ambition to own a little business and that she was sure that she could make a good thing of it. I ventured, my heart beating in my throat, to say that she did not look like a business woman but something very much better. She smiled at that and even laughed.

Then, by the mercy of Providence, as it seemed to me, it began to rain heavily. I had an umbrella and she had not. I suggested that I should guard her under my umbrella as far as her door.

After I left her there I could not sleep. A totally new experience had come into my life. I told myself that, when I saw her again, the spell might be broken. But of course it was not. It was rather intensified. I called to see her on some pretext. She came and had tea with my mother and was very charming to her. She was charming to everybody with a quiet virginal tranquillity. Her interest in my antique shop, however, was more than virginal. She handled the articles—the brass, the china, the water-colours, the furniture— with an eagerness that surprised me.

Laughing, she said one day that she would stay and help me, and she remained all the afternoon. She sold a number of things and charmed the customers. I can see her now, standing there in her dove-grey costume with rose-coloured cuffs and collar. One voluble American lady liked her so much that she was ready to buy anything from her.

"I haven't enjoyed an afternoon so much," Eve (that was her name—Eve Paling) said, "for years and years." Her pale cheeks were flushed and she was to me so beautiful, standing there with a cup with yellow flowers marked on it, that I could have fallen on my knees and worshipped her.

The night before she returned to London I asked her to marry me. She showed no surprise. She must have known from the very first that I loved her. She neither accepted nor refused me. How often afterwards was I to recall the words that she said then!

"I don't know, John." She let her hand lie very quietly and passively in mine. "I like you very much. I'm sure I could be happy with you. And I should enjoy immensely helping you to run the shop. All that is tempting to me. But is it fair—fair to you, I mean?"

"Fair to me!" I cried. "Fair! Why, if you marry me you'll be doing me the greatest, most wonderful——"

"Yes, I know. So you think now. But, you see, I'm not in love with you. I know what it is, being in love. The kind of man for me physically is someone big and strong, a little violent perhaps. The kind of man," she added, laughing, "you read about in cheap novels, the cave-man. Now you're not a bit the cave-man, John. You'll give in to me and let me have my way. Even physically you're altogether too thin and too pale. You need fattening up."

I had already made the discovery that she often said things that did not seem to belong to her virginal, otherworldly appearance. She had shown herself very practical indeed about the shop, and had said things once or twice about men that were not virginal at all.

"If you marry me," I said, "I'll get so fat from content that you won't know me."

But she shook her head and looked at me anxiously.

"We've only known one another a fortnight. We don't really know one another at all. You're in love with me now, and later on, when you've got over that part of it, you may not like me. I'm not dreamy and imaginative as you are, John. I see only what is directly in front of me and what I see is very tempting, for I like you and admire you, I hate my present job and want to get out of it. And I think that together we could make a fine thing of the shop."

I did go down on my knees then and laid my head on her lap.
Then I looked up into her face and implored her—oh, how I
implored her!—to take pity on me. I did not mind that she did not
love me. That she liked me was enough. I would serve her, work
for her . . .

"Yes," she interrupted, "that is just what I am afraid of. I want a
man to master me, not to be my slave!"

Yes, I must always remember how frank and honest she was. All
that has happened since has been my fault, not hers. She is in no
way to blame—or only very little. She said that she would write
to me.

A week later I received a letter saying that she would marry
me. Oh, then I went mad with joy! I kissed my old mother again
and again. I walked about the town like a madman; I went into
Lower Town and stood on the very spot where I had first seen her.
I remember that it was a sunny windy morning and that the ocean
was covered with gleaming, glittering white-caps and that at my
feet against the broken landing-stage the waves broke and splashed
and the sun made their foam iridescent.

We were married on April 5th, 1928. We went for our brief
honeymoon into Cornwall. We slept the first night at Penzance.
I would have made a clumsy wooer but for her quiet, humorous
command of me. She slept into the full sun of the morning with
deep surrender, while I lay awake, thinking over and over again
of my wonderful good fortune, but haunted by an odd little half-
formed wish that she had not been quite so well-assured, so ready
for my immature, inexperienced love-making.

5

THAT MARRIAGE is a strange business I suppose every married
man and woman will in their hearts admit. Even the happiest
must realize that incomprehensible mixture of intimacy and non-
intimacy so that at one moment your partner seems a piece of
yourself and at another it is as though you had never seen him or
her before.

So, at least, it was with us, or with myself, I had better more truthfully say. My passionate desire for her remained because she never fully responded to it. This side of our married relationship she treated with a motherly irony, permitting my indulgence, as a mother gives a railway train to her little son. "If you really feel like this," she seemed to say, "the least I can do is to grant you some pleasure. It doesn't hurt me and you like it—so why not?"

I realized, I suppose, from the beginning that I was not, as she had frankly told me, her type. And that was neither her fault nor mine. But I was kept for ever on the edge of unsatisfied desire—so near and yet so far! And I would lie beside her at night, while she slept so calmly, longing, praying, that one day she would of her own accord turn to me and show me that she loved me!

In all other aspects our marriage was for a long time most happy.

My mother and Eve fortunately liked one another from the start, and achieved an underground understanding: it was almost an alliance against myself—a sort of intimation that they were both fond of me, but that I was a poor fish really.

I did not resent this. I was of the type of man who worships one or two women to idolatry. Eve might do anything to me, say anything to me, think anything of me that she pleased. I did not mind how much she ill-treated me (which she never did). There was something masochistic in me with regard to her. And so my old mother very quickly took something of Eve's tone to me. I had always been a devoted son, but now, when she saw that I was on my knees to my wife, she thought that it would be amusing if I were on my knees to her too. She had lost now the use of her legs, and she would sit in her chair, a lace cap that with old-fashioned fancy she wore, on her head, a faint moustache that was often slightly moist, and her dark restless eyes regarding me with love and tyranny. Her hands were still lovely and delicate, her little body taut and straight, and when I saw the two women, the old lady in her chair, and Eve, with always that suggestion of the Quaker in her dress, her beautifully proportioned body, that had been so often in my arms but that never truly yielded to me, then I would tremble, and fire would run in my veins, and I would be happy and miserable both at the same time.

To speak of more practical matters, it was at once clear that Eve had a genius for business. She was better than my father had ever been. She had a real love, too, for the things that she handled and, although when she first met me she knew nothing about antiques, by reading books and studying the things that came our way, she soon was far ahead of me in knowledge.

She quickly became a well-known figure at local sales. She specialized in Victorian furniture, china—so many things that we had all for so long thought hideous. And she had an especial liking for Pre-Raphaelite drawings and paintings. She found water-colours by J. M. Strudwick and Arthur Hughes, and Frederick Sandys and Matthew Lawless, for almost nothing at all.

She said that there would be one day a great revival in these artists, and I can see that already her prophecy is beginning to come true. She would say, laughingly, that she was herself a Pre-Raphaelite, and that the old part of Seaborne was Pre-Raphaelite. Sometimes on a day when the sea gleamed in purple and green, and the old decrepit buildings were coloured by the light in sharp, bright detail, I could see what she meant.

But it was on the business side that she was wonderful. She was marvellous with customers, studying their characters, charming to one, sharp with another, leading them on from one thing higher and higher, until they purchased far beyond their original inten-tion, and all so quietly and with so much grace and friendliness, that they would return to our shop again and again, simply for the pleasure of seeing her.

This all meant that I left the shop more and more to her and devoted myself, with an obsession, to my writing. The novel upon which I was working during the first year of our marriage, *The Gridiron*, became an obsession to me. The theme, very briefly, was this: A wife is tortured with love for her husband, who does not care for her, and is persistently unfaithful to her.

She knows in the depths of her far-seeing soul that he will one day hate her so deeply that he will murder her. She is fasci-nated by the thought that he will murder her, and is like a rabbit before a snake. She does not attempt to leave him. Ultimately he does murder her, and is then tortured on the gridiron—not of his conscience, for he suffers from no regrets or self-reproaches—of his new wife's hatred of himself. He adores her, she hates him. He commits suicide.

This grim story seemed neither grim nor true to Eve, with whom I discussed it. She thought it simply silly. She had a brave and practical mind, was afraid of no one and nothing.

"Women don't just wait to be murdered, however idiotic they are," she said.

"You talk," I answered, "as though I had been writing about you. I've chosen someone exactly opposite—weak, yielding, gentle, loving."

I hoped that this last word would provoke her into protesting that she *did* love me, but she paid no attention to it, only went on:

"Besides, John, you're the last man in the world to write about the feelings of a murderer; you who wouldn't hurt a fly."

"Oh, I don't know," I remember protesting. "If I get an idea into my head, I can be very obstinate."

"What's obstinacy got to do with murder?" she asked.

"A great deal. Don't you remember the other day, when Mr. Fortescue, of Four Trees, had the Burne-Jones drawing for 'The Forge of Cupid' that you wanted? How, for several days, before he gave in, you could think of nothing else, could scarcely sleep?"

"Ah, that was different! What has a Burne-Jones drawing got to do with murder?"

I remember looking at her and thinking that, in some ways, she was a very stupid woman. It was imagination that she lacked, and in that there was a deep division between us.

"Both are lusts," I answered. "Lust of hate. Lust of possession."

And I remember that she looked at me a little contemptuously, saying, "Lust! What an odd word for *you* to use, John. You know nothing about lust—and you couldn't hate anybody for ten minutes together."

Oh, couldn't I? I thought of telling her about Tunstall. But I did not. How strangely little, even after daily and nightly intimacies, two human beings know one another!

I was obsessed by *The Gridiron*. Poor *Gridiron* that nobody knows, nobody cares for. But how real both that man and that woman were to me! How thoroughly I understood their hates and their fears! It seemed to me that they were both part of me, both murderer and murderee!

I had been long fascinated by the life, personality and works of George Gissing; Morley Roberts's life-novel about him, writings on him by H. G. Wells, who had been very generously his friend; novels like *New Grub Street*, *The Odd Women*, *A Life's Morning* (in spite of its false ending), and then his momentary escape into his longed-for world of rest and light—*By the Ionian Sea*, *Henry Ryecroft*—all this touched me deeply. He seemed like a brother of mine. I felt that if I had known him I could have comforted him, brought him perhaps to Seaborne and cared for him. The grey dreariness of his novels was akin to me: his obsession with women I understood. I loved the man and greatly admired his art, which seemed to me a unique thing. I tried to persuade Eve to read *Demos* and *The Odd Women*, but she could not endure these books.

She enjoyed romantic novels. She wanted a happy ending. She repeated the formula as though no one had ever uttered it before.

"There's enough in life that's depressing and difficult, without books being depressing too."

Then came the month of March 1929—a month that I am never likely to forget, however long I live.

Eve was about to give birth to our first child. She was as sensible about this as she was about everything else. She did not especially wish for a child—she had not, I think, very much of the maternal in her—but if there must be one she would do her best by it.

I was meanwhile tortured. I had never loved her so passionately. The mother of my child! The mother of my child! Our child! I imagined, of course, every kind of disaster! She looked as virginal, as slender of body as she had done on the day of our first meeting. It seemed to me an awful ordeal through which she must pass. I tried to conceal my terror, for both she and my mother would despise me for it.

The day approached. On March 10th the pains began. About three in the afternoon I walked down to the Lower Town and strode up and down the old landing-stage. Looking up from the grey-cotton waters of the sea, I saw, standing close beside me, James Oliphant Tunstall.

Yes, it was Tunstall.

It wasn't true that I had ever forgotten him, but now, when I saw him, it was as though he had never left me. And with that sense of his accompanying me came a sudden fear that was almost a sickness.

I stood 'rooted to the spot' as cheap novelists say. Yes, but it's a good phrase all the same. I *was* rooted, staring, terrified. Of what? Of whom?

You must remember that I was in a state of nervous tension on that afternoon, expecting the birth of my child at any moment, thinking of my adored, my beloved, and her approaching torture.

Tunstall stood grinning. Then he held out his hand.

"Well, if it isn't Jacko!"

I shook his hand, which was soft and plump. I saw that he wore on the little finger of his right hand a green scarab set in gold.

He was looking very prosperous, wearing dark red-brown tweeds and a dark-red tie, his face ruddy brown, thick-set, inclined to be stout and, although he was exactly my own height, looking shorter than I because of my slimness. His thick eyebrows stood out from his ruddy face, and there, just as they had always been, were his cheeky laughing eyes and lascivious lips. He seemed to swallow me up, in the old horrible way, as I looked at him.

"Well, if it isn't Jacko!"

"Hallo, Tunstall! What are you doing here?"

"Tunstall be damned! It's your old friend Jimmie come back to you again!" Exactly as in the old way he was close to me, his thigh pressed against mine, his hand on my arm. How I hated that contact! But I couldn't move. I waited until he released me and leant back against the railing that they had put up on the old pier to prevent people from falling into the water.

He leaned back, his hands pressed down on the green metal, grinning at me.

"How are you, Tunstall? Come on a visit?"

"Now Tunstall be blowed. I'm Jimmie to you and always will be."

"Jimmie, then."

"That's better. A visit, Jacko? No, my dear boy. I'm here for keeps."

My heart contracted. I could feel the palms of my hands go damp.

"Yes," he went on. "We shall see plenty of one another. I always said you couldn't ever escape me and you shan't. Now confess— haven't you thought of me sometimes?"

"No. I can't say that I have." (How vivid, how horribly, horribly vivid is this conversation to me now!)

"Oh, come now. That isn't true. You've thought of me often. You know you have. And I've thought of you. You were the boy I was fondest of at school, you know."

"Well, I wasn't fond of you," I said, making at last a movement. "And now I must be getting on——"

"Wait, wait," he cried, his eyes watching me mockingly. "We've been apart so long and you want to leave me? What have you been doing with yourself all this time? As a matter of fact I know. I've been down here three days and you were the first person I asked about. Your father's dead and you run the shop. Or rather your wife does. A very nice practical woman I'm told. I'm keen to meet her. And you've published a novel. You see, I know all about you. As a matter of fact I bought the book. It wasn't my sort of novel— too highbrow altogether—but there was a lot of me in it."

"There wasn't any of you in it," I answered indignantly.

"Oh yes there was! Don't you think you can write a book without my being in it."

All this time he had never taken his eyes off my face and he seemed to get a great deal of pleasure and amusement out of staring at me.

Then he said:

"Don't you want to know what's been happening to me all this time?"

"I don't particularly care."

"That is a rude thing to say. All the same I'll tell you. I'm quite a successful painter. Hadn't you heard? Especially with portraits. I paint people as they'd like to be. That's the thing. That's what you ought to do. What's the use of writing these books that nobody wants to read? Simply wasting your time. I've made quite a bit of money, and, like a wise man, I married a woman with money.

"So I've come down here and taken a house—Sandy View—at the end of Chessington Street. There I'm going to be—half the year anyway. And the sooner you and your wife come to see us the better I'll be pleased."

I noticed then for the first time that he had probably been drinking too much. Not that he was drunk. Certainly not. He was completely in command of his faculties, but there was a slight exalted shining in his eyes, a faint breath emanating from him, a suggested, rather than positive, uncertainty about his body.

Now I have always had, foolishly I am sure, a terror of drunkenness. I am myself a teetotaller, not from any virtuous or health reasons but simply because I loathe spirits and don't really care very much for wine. I am, I must repeat, really terrified of anyone whom drink has deprived of his senses. I have been on occasions in company with men so drunk that they knew neither what they were doing nor saying, and these flushed incoherent creatures reeling and tumbling, clutching at one's body, slobbering in one's face—how I have loathed them, run a mile to avoid them! Tunstall was not, of course, *drunk*, but there was the spirit of drunken recklessness about him. I felt it and trembled.

Meanwhile I must get away. Even now my child might be born. But I had one thing to say.

"Look here, Tunstall."

"Jimmie!"

"Well, Jimmie then. I think we had better be quite clear from the start. If you are going to live here part of the year as you say, I don't want there to be any misunderstanding. I should much prefer not to visit at your house and that you should not visit at mine. I didn't like you when we were boys. I used to tell you but you wouldn't believe me. Too conceited, I suppose. We had nothing in common then. We have nothing in common now." (I am repeating the words as I write them down. "We have nothing in common . . ." Oh God! to whom, to what am I saying them?) "Apart from the way I feel about you," I went on, "we are in different spheres. My wife and I keep a little shop. You are a successful painter with a fine house. You have money. We haven't. We couldn't possibly keep up with your scale of living. So good-bye. Keep to your world. We'll keep to ours."

I held out my hand. He took it, held it, and drew me a little towards him. I tried to draw my hand away. I could not. My whole body trembled. Now that I was close to him I smelt his breath, hot and whisky-tainted, quite distinctly.

"No, Jacko," he said, laughing. "It isn't as easy as that—not nearly as easy. I have you in my hand just as I had when we were at school. You say that you don't like me and never did. That may be. I'm the other side of yourself, Jacko, the side you're not very proud of. Stevenson wrote a story about that once. But this isn't Jekyll and Hyde. That was just a story. This is *real*, Jacko—a real alliance. We're like the Siamese Twins and always were."

He was suddenly serious, patted me on the back, lounged lazily away from me.

"Forget my nonsense, Jacko. I was never able to help teasing you, you know. But to pretend that we won't see one another! *What* a hope! Why, as I've told you, you were the first person I asked about when I came back. And you'll like my wife. She's good, like you, and she's fond of me just as you are. I've a sort of idea your wife will like *me*—even if you don't. And you must see my pictures. I'll paint your portrait. There's an idea! I'll take weeks over it and make a good one. So long, Jacko—see you soon!"

He turned his back on me and walked out to the edge of the landing-stage.

I found my wife in labour. Doctor Wellard, an untidy giant of a man, but a good doctor, said she would do all right. I behaved in the traditional stage-and-novel father manner, pacing the little sitting-room, listening, going to the door, digging my fingers into the palms of my hands, sweating at the brow.

At seven-thirty exactly Wellard opened the door and told me that I was father of a son and that mother and child were doing grandly. My son! Ah! How I had prayed for a son! Perhaps for the first time in my life I was really proud of myself. Later I went up to visit Eve. There she was lying, exhausted, looking more virginal than ever, and as comfortably unagitated as though nothing had happened. How I adored, how I worshipped her! Now not only my beloved wife but also the mother of my son.

Her voice was weak but yet contained that tinge of irony that was always there when she spoke to me.

"Poor John! Have you been anxious? It wasn't bad—I had chloroform. Aren't you proud of yourself?"

"I'm proud of *you*," I said.

"I don't know. Is it anything to be proud of—to bring a son into a world like this? Now go away. I'm sleepy."

Before I went to my bed I saw my son. He was hideous, of course, but my heart went out to him. I had now three persons in the world to love: my mother, my wife, my son. It was enough. If they were happy and cared for me I asked for nothing more.

But that night, in my dreams, Tunstall was standing beside me. He stretched out his hand and held my arm.

6

I HAD BETTER NOW, I think, jump nine years, for I have much to tell and little time to tell it. The sequence of events that led to my present horrible position began, I think, with a party given by the Tunstalls towards the end of January 1938, a party attended by my wife and myself.

What shall I say here about those nine years? There is so much to say and yet so little. On the outside things were little changed in my life and Eve's. During these years I published two novels, *The Gridiron* in 1930, and *The Gossip-monger* in 1936.

The Gridiron, into which I put so much work—a novel, I am still convinced, with something unique in it, something that has never been done before and will never be done again—appeared and was dead as soon as born. And yet not quite so! For it roused the interest of certain critics, and Rose, the famous novelist, wrote me an enthusiastic letter concerning it. Now I consider Rose's novels very poor indeed—old-fashioned, romantic, platitudinous—but he *is* a very well-known writer and when he reviews a novel he helps, undoubtedly, its popularity. I have often enough inveighed against the practice of one novelist reviewing another novelist and have especially criticized Rose in this connection, but after he had said some fine quotable words about *The Gridiron* in *The Message* I felt rather differently about him. His letter to me was kind and enthusiastic, if patronizing, and when I next saw the picture of his high and shining forehead in a newspaper I felt, I must confess, quite friendly towards it.

It was not, however, until 1936 that I published my third novel, *The Gossip-monger*, and this had a considerable success. I fear that on this occasion I compromised. Why go on for ever writing novels that no one wanted to read? I compromised, as Gissing and many another has been forced to compromise. There was in *The Gossip-monger* a certain dry humour and irony and it happened that the public fancied in one of the figures of my story a caricature of Rose himself. This helped its sale, and Rose was very magnanimous, alluding, humorously, in his review to the caricature as though he had enjoyed it; as a matter of fact I heard afterwards from a friend of his that it hurt him very much. It was Rose's great ambition in life, I think, to be considered a noble character without being thought at the same time a prig—no easy ambition.

In any case I made some money from *The Gossip-monger* and my hopes were high. My friends and neighbours in Seaborne when they saw my photograph in *The Modern World* began to take me more seriously and even ordered my book from the library.

Against this success must be set the fact that, during these years, I had withdrawn more and more into myself.

Before my marriage the shop had been an easy way for me to keep in touch with my fellow human beings. All day I was talking to this person or that; often I must visit a house or a sale, and although I was never a character to whom anyone took a very great liking, yet I had my friends and acquaintances. But after my marriage Eve's great business efficiency made my presence in the shop a superfluity and I visited it less and less. This I found Eve preferred, for she was cleverer at bargains than I and liked best to clinch them in her own way.

After my boy Archie's birth she had only two interests in the world—her shop and her son. She continued her kindly tolerance and marital sufferance to myself, but I knew that I counted nothing in her life. My mother had died a year after Archie's birth. I wish, neither now nor later, to compel any pity, if an eye should fall on this, from any reader. But I suffered, after my mother's death, from a desperate loneliness. The boy, delicate, shy, feminine in his sensitiveness, loved only his mother. His mother loved only him. I, most unfortunately, adored them both. No new situation in this world, but a hard and testing one, especially for a man who could not express himself easily and was always frightened of a rebuff.

My shyness to the outside world was greatly increased by the presence of Tunstall in the town. He immediately, of course, made his mark there. It was known from London that he had an assured position there as a portrait-painter. He was well-off and enjoyed entertaining. He was the friend of everyone, had no social exclusiveness and apparently no pride.

After a time certain stories were current as to his character. He was certainly no strict moralist, but people in general did not mind that so long as he had money and spent it freely.

As a matter of fact he was, during these nine years, away from Seaborne a great deal. His career as a portrait-painter became for a year or two quite spectacular. He painted some fashionable ladies, an actor or two, and actually Rose himself, whose picture by Tunstall, bright, shiny, gravely complacent, was in the Academy of 1936.

That, I fancy, was Tunstall's peak year. His popularity began to decline. Why? He lost his head a little, I should imagine. Went to late parties too often, drank perhaps too much, was too familiar with some of his grand ladies.

At any rate he appeared again towards the end of '37 and informed the town that he was 'fed up' with London, that he had made enough money for the rest of his days and that he would develop down here his talent for landscape painting.

I heard all this from Basil Cheeseman, a friend of his, and about Cheeseman, known to myself and some others as 'The Rat,' I must say a word or two. Physically he resembled a rat, for he was a little man with very prominent white sharp upper teeth. He had reddish brown hair and restless whisky-coloured eyes. When he smiled his teeth jutted out over his lower lip.

He was, and is, an evil little man; a journalist by profession who had settled down in a ramshackle cottage near Seaborne and there indulged in shabby orgies with girls from London or visitors to the resort. He made a living by picking up paragraphs and sending them to London and the provincial papers. He had, and has, as malicious and dirty-minded a soul as exists in the world to-day. He was the very man for Tunstall. He was more evil, I don't doubt, than Tunstall and yet I did not hate him half as much. He had no power over me. I thought of him possibly as a kind of emanation from Tunstall. When Tunstall couldn't come to me himself he sent the Rat instead, and I can see him now with a faint shiny stubble on his cheeks, his projecting teeth and false grin, his restless cat-like eyes. "He's come back and he's going to stay," the Rat said, eyeing me curiously. His malicious curiosity knew no limit. He had long ago discovered my hatred and fear of Tunstall, but what was Tunstall's hold over me? I did not look as though I had any vices. And, farther than that, why did Tunstall bother about me at all? What was my attraction for Tunstall?

He never discovered the answer to these questions, and I think at last he decided that the solution was connected with my wife.

And now I must try to explain one of the driving decisive elements in this case—Eve, my wife, from the very first moment, liked Tunstall. At least she did not dislike him. I must say here at once that no one could dislike Leila Tunstall, Tunstall's wife. This was a little round pale-faced woman whose face was almost deformed.

It was *not* deformed, although the face *was* definitely twisted, and yet where the twist was you could never decide. She was as plain as she could be but most terribly nice. Tunstall had married her for her money, of course, and he took everything she gave him for granted, patronized her, laughed at her. She accepted it all with a smile, very quietly.

You would call her, perhaps, a saint—the only one I have ever known. But not at all a prig. Nothing shocked her. She had a strong sense of humour. She liked to mother everyone. She was a very fine woman.

Oddly enough Eve liked Tunstall more than Mrs. Tunstall. "Of course she's a good woman," she said. "When you're as plain as that it's all that's left you." Then she added quickly, "That's cattishness. I'm jealous because she's so much better than me."

She argued with me on the other side.

"I just can't see what you've got against Jimmie Tunstall."

"He's foul-minded and foul-living. He's false and treacherous. Vain as a monkey. Greedy."

"Oh, John, that's jealousy!"

"Jealousy! If I were him I'd shoot myself."

"He likes you most awfully anyway."

"He doesn't. He despises me. He likes teasing me, frightening me."

"Frightening you? What have you got to be frightened of?"

"I don't know. I've always been frightened of him since we were kids."

Nevertheless during these nine years we did not see so very much of one another. His success kept him in London. Then he and Leila went for a year on a trip round the world. When he *did* come to Seaborne he was busy with his painting. To my great relief he seemed for a long time to have forgotten all about me. But can you escape anything that is your destiny? I think not.

That was one of the 'turning' moments of my life when Cheeseman told me that Tunstall had come back and was going to stay. I knew it. My throat contracted.

"Things have been going a bit wrong, I fancy," Cheeseman said with satisfaction. "He's a bit ratty. Been drinking more than's good for him. Leila's a bit worried. By the way, he said something about you this afternoon."

"What did he say?" I asked, my heart hammering.

"Oh, only—how's Jacko?"

7

SHORTLY AFTER this there came an invitation to a Tunstall party: 'Dancing. Bridge.'

"What fun!" Eve said.

"You go. You can go with Jessie Parrott. She's sure to be asked."

Jessie Parrott was a twittering spinsterly gossip with grey hair in ironclad waves, a mole on her chin, and little nervous movements of her head like a thrush on an early-morning lawn.

"I won't go if you don't."

"I'm not going."

Eve was never angry. But she could look at me with contempt. "Why ever not?"

"I detest Tunstall. That being so, I won't accept his hospitality."

But I met him on the high road leading to Shining Cliff. He was at his best, healthy, buoyant and sober, his green scarab ring shining in the sun. He had with him his fox-terrier Scandal. Scandal was a lively merry dog, little more than a puppy, who sprang about as though his thin rough legs belonged to a toy dog.

And wasn't Tunstall glad to see me! I thought for a moment that he would kiss me. He held me with both arms and once again I had that curious sensation that he was drawing me into himself. His breast opened. I was drawn in like a stream of air. The breast closed. I was a prisoner.

The dog jumped up on me, greeting me.

"Down, Scandal, down! The dog is as fond of you as I am, you see. Of course you're coming to the party."

"No. I'm not."

"Certainly you are." He stood directly in front of me, his broad thick-set body impeding my path. We were exactly of a height, but I was a pale shadow, cast by the misted sun, of his health, self-confidence and vigour. "Why aren't you coming?"

"Simply because I don't want to."

"That's very rude. I haven't seen much of you lately. I'm going to from now on. Plenty."

I forced myself to speak up.

"Please leave me alone. It's a small profitless thing the amusement you get out of me. We have nothing in common, nothing at all, we never have had. It's just a whim of yours. You know I've always disliked you. You've pretended I don't, but you know in your heart that I do. And you hate and despise me."

I felt as though this were the last appeal of my life that I was making to him—absurd really, here, on this sunny day with the silver slab of Shining Cliff gleaming not far off and the fox-terrier springing about near to us.

He looked at me, his eyes, now a little bloodshot, staring under the black beetling eyebrows. I could see the faint purple veins in his cheeks, the short black hairs thick in his nostrils.

"That's all right," he said. "You can hate me as much as you like. Love's akin to hate, you know, Jacko!" He laughed like anything at that, shaking all over. "Of course you're coming to the party."

And of course I went. Eve and Jessie Parrott and I.

The Tunstall house was large and glittering. To my taste it was vulgar. In the drawing-room was a portrait of Tunstall himself painted by Walter Eckersley, R.A. It was a regular Eckersley masterpiece, exactly like a coloured photograph. The rooms were bare in the modern manner and yet colours clashed. There was a billiard-room, very elegant, a huge radio-gramophone, a little bar downstairs—and Tunstall was proud of showing us his own private bathroom, a steel and marble affair with dumb-bells and a marvellous shower gleaming with taps.

On the party-occasion we met first round the little bar behind which was a bare floor for dancing. There were some thirty people, I suppose. Eve was, in my opinion, by a great way the most beautiful woman there, in a dress of pale grey, her face nun-like, of a remote and lovely chastity.

I was afraid from the moment I entered that house that night. I had been living more and more by myself. I had had a little quarrel that afternoon with Eve about the boy, Archie, and this had upset

me very much. She had said that it was time that he went to
school. I had a horror of school for him. I had suffered at school so
much myself, and Archie was a sensitive, shy boy, more like a girl
in some things than a boy.

"That," said Eve, "is just why school will be so good for him.
That's what he needs."

When she was determined on something like this she could
look hard and ruthless.

"You've no heart," I said.

"I love that boy more than anything on earth."

"Yes, more than me."

"Oh, John!" She burst out laughing. "Don't be so silly! You're
like a girl yourself sometimes!"

But I was terrified at the thought of Archie at school. He would
suffer as I had suffered. So I was upset when I went to the Tunstalls'
and when I am upset it is as though all eyes are upon me, mocking
me. I detest this self-consciousness, but if you *are* self-conscious
what are you to do about it?

Then, as soon as I was downstairs by the bar, Tunstall made for
me. It was as though I were the only guest that mattered. Now my
ideal at a party (if I *must* be present) is to sit in a corner, quite unno-
ticed, and observe other people. How wonderful to be an invisible
physical presence!

I had hoped on this occasion to find a corner and be happily
undisturbed until Eve had had enough of it and was ready to go
home. How dreadfully otherwise was my fate!

We went, as ordered by a stiff and shining parlour-maid, to the
downstairs bar and dancing-room. There everybody was, but as we
entered Tunstall seemed to detect us before we were announced.
He came forward eagerly, greeted Eve and turned at once to me.
"Dear old Jacko!" he cried, in a voice that rang through the room,
put his hand on my arm and led me forward.

Ah, but he was mocking me! Didn't I know it, and didn't
everyone else know it?

It seemed to me that I was faced with a circle of jeering faces.
I don't suppose for a moment that that was so. Although I had no
warm friends in Seaborne, people on the whole respected me. I

was Seaborne's only author and my photograph had been in the London papers. "A dull dog. How he manages to write those books I can't think," would be the verdict.

I am sure that they did not look on me with mockery, but it was part of the fate that now had me in charge that I should fancy their hostility, that it should be almost as though I were back at school again, back at the baths with my enemies uncovering my nakedness.

So I was at my worst, sulky and uncourteous when Tunstall led me up to the little bar and insisted on my drinking. I refused, of course, a cocktail.

He looked at me humorously and addressed the laughing crowd. "You'd never think, would you," he said, "that Jacko is my best friend? He has all the virtues, I all the vices. He is a very serious highbrow author. I'm a common cheap painter." (His hand was round my neck.) "All the same, the best friendships are between opposites." (He was a little drunk already. I could smell his breath.) "We've been friends all our lives, haven't we, Jacko? And will be friends to the end. Aye, and beyond the end, too. Into Eternity. I drink to you, Jacko, and will forgive you for once for drinking my health in tomato juice."

I look back now to that party and, in the light of later events, feel that it was a kind of phantasmagoria with everyone a little out of drawing, larger than life-size. I've noticed, too (many others have noticed the same), that in any gathering of human beings you can, with a very little exercise of the imagination, see people as animals—the wolf, the fox, the snake, the rabbit, the horse, the parrot, the faithful dog. I had a sense that they were pressing in upon me and soon would begin to bark, to whistle, to snarl.

To one person at least my discomfiture was apparent, for little Leila Tunstall arrived, detached me from the others, led me to two chairs in the corner of the room.

"Don't you worry about me," I said, more comfortable at once. "This is what I like—to sit in a corner and not be noticed."

"It was too bad of Jim," she said. "He's so fond of you, but he doesn't seem to understand you a bit. Then he likes teasing people."

She gave me a sudden quick look: "You know—you mustn't

think me rude—you're *very* like a brother of mine in the East. In looks, voice—it's astonishing!"

But I was thinking of Tunstall.

"He likes teasing *me*, you mean," I answered. "And I don't take teasing well. I get self-conscious and stupid. What I'd *like* would be to sit here and watch people all the evening and not speak to anyone. That's dreadfully unsociable, isn't it?"

She was watching her husband. I could see that she was worried.

"Jim thinks such a lot of you," she said. "I believe you could have some influence over him. He wants a friend just now. He's disappointed with the way things have been going, and then he drinks too much and——" She stopped, feeling perhaps that she was disloyal.

"I wouldn't say all this except to a real friend of his."

I wanted to say that I wasn't a real friend, that I hated him and always had done. But of course I couldn't say that to her, especially when she was so kind and gentle.

It was then that I noticed someone I had never seen before. A woman. She was very handsome, bigly built, a blonde, holding herself superbly, dressed rather nakedly. She had daring laughing eyes, and plainly defied the world.

"Who is that?" I asked.

I saw at once that Leila disliked her. Leila's face had that deformed look now—somewhere a little twisted—was it the mouth, the cheek? When she looked like this you were sorry for her and loved her. You knew she would have been very unhappy had she not been too courageous to allow unhappiness.

"Oh, that? That's Bella Scorfield."

"And *who* is Bella Scorfield?"

"Ah, no. You wouldn't have realized her yet. She and her mother have come to live here. They have taken a little house—Middlewood—not far from Shining Cliff. A desolate, lonely place I'd think it, and Mrs. Scorfield is a permanent invalid. Jim insisted on my paying a call—a strange woman—looks like a corpse—lies in bed all day working at chess problems and reading mathematics. Or so Bella told me. Bella doesn't seem to mind. She has a car of her own. She's—what shall I say?—a bit of a rip. She told me the other day—she likes to confide in me, I can't think why—that she had only a few years to have a good time in and she'd make the most of it. So I asked her why she had chosen this dull little place and a house miles from anywhere. She gave me a queer look and said that you could often have a better time in a dull little place."

"You don't like her," I said.

"No, frankly I don't."

"I hate her at sight," I said.

To that Leila replied:

"What a funny man you are! To look at you one would think you are as quiet as a mouse. But when one gets to know you a little one finds you are full of intense feelings—about people especially."

"I'd say exactly the same about you."

She flushed a little, then answered very quietly: "There *are* some things about which one feels intensely, of course."

I wasn't permitted to keep my quiet corner for long. Tunstall was soon very merry. It would be untrue to say that he was drunk; he was flushed and noisy and reckless. It became, in fact, very soon a noisy party. Tunstall had that effect on people; he shook them out of their caution, and especially if there were drinks there to assist him.

And I that evening was his continuous butt. Why, *why* did I not have the wisdom to slip away and go home? Again and again I was tempted to do so, but I did not wish to abandon Eve (she would not have cared, perhaps, if I had). I loved her that night, it seemed to me, as I had never loved her before. How her unattainability stirred my blood! Ah, could I but have been assured that when I touched her arm with my hand she would turn round and, seeing that it was I, would look at me with surprised love. I have caught that look between man and wife, and oh, have I not envied them!

She would not have cared had I gone—and yet I stayed. They danced. We went upstairs to supper, and it seemed that Tunstall could not let me alone. "Where's Jacko?" he would cry. "Jacko! Jacko! Where's Jacko?"

"Your master wants you," some woman, laughing, said to me. How humiliated I was! How desperately I hated his going with me upstairs, his hand on my arm!

We were pressed about with people, and yet at one moment I had a strong impulse to push him on his soft stomach with my sharp elbow and so send him reeling backwards, losing his balance with a cry, tumbling down those sharp-edged wooden stairs, breaking his fat neck perhaps. . . . At that my heart seemed to stop. It appeared to me that I looked out from the very soul of Tunstall himself and saw that fallen, twisted body and the crowd with faces like cambric masks and sharp clown noses, peering at it. I had indeed stopped. He pushed me up the stairs, his hand pressing the small of my back.

"Come on, Jacko! Don't you want your feed? There's gingerbeer, you know—plenty of ginger-beer!"

They did the thing very well. We all sat down to supper at a long table, lit with candles. He sat me down between himself and Miss Scorfield. His knee pressed against mine. Once he laid his hot sweating hand on the back of mine. He leant across me and talked of me to Miss Scorfield almost as though I were not there. He seemed to me to be already on excellent terms with her. I did not look at her, but, in my senses, I was conscious of her half-bare bosom, her naked back, some rose-scented perfume, the heat of her body, the abandonment of her soul.

"You've got to be friends with Jacko, Bella, or you won't be friends with me. He's my better half, always has been since we were at school together."

"It wouldn't be difficult to be *your* better half, Jimmie."

"Ah, that's what *you* think! It's more than you'll ever be, Bella, old girl."

This seemed to them a tremendous joke, and they laughed like anything, he with his hand on my shoulder, his crimson flushed face staring straight into her body. It was almost as though he possessed her in front of my eyes.

After supper we danced, played bridge, gossiped. The silly Parrott girl insisted on staying beside me. Didn't I think Jim Tunstall really *awful*? He couldn't leave a woman alone. How his poor wife was humiliated! And his drinking. Of course if he went on like that his painting would soon go to pieces. In fact she had heard that in London . . .

I put an end to this, saying that we had just enjoyed a jolly good supper at his hands, and that it wasn't in the best of taste to slander him. She gave me a viperish look.

"You know what you are, John Talbot. You're a hypocritical prig. You know that you hate Jim Tunstall like poison and always have. You wouldn't be past murdering him if you could get away with it safely. He's been laughing at you all your life, and if there's one thing you can't stand, it's being laughed at. And I'll tell you another thing. Watch Eve and your dear host you're so keen on defending. I wouldn't put it past the two of them."

With which she walked away, pleased at having disturbed me. As indeed she had, for, at that very moment, looking across to a window-seat near the piano, I saw Eve and Tunstall close together; Tunstall was talking eagerly. Once he put out his hand and touched hers. Eve sat, quiet, beautifully composed, but quite suddenly, as I was staring at them, she laughed, looking up into his face. She gave him a smile—of impudence, daring, adventurous excitement —how should I describe it? The importance of it was in the fact that she had never, in all our married life together, given me such a smile.

You know how in a second of time you can change from good health to ill. You are perfectly well, buried in gardening or letter-writing or reading. You are comfortably settled in the rational normal world. An instant, and we've changed all that! You are trembling, shivering, heated, sick. So it is, I found then, with jealousy. When I saw the smile that Eve gave to Tunstall I became, in that moment, a jealous lunatic.

I showed my lunacy during the walk home. When one is in love and the other feels friendship but not love, one plays, whatever happens, a losing game. There is no safe time for protests, appeals, tears. The other is securely armoured with indifference.

I behaved like a fool on that homeward walk. Like all jealous people, I knew, at the very moment, the fool that I was! "Say nothing. Be gay, indifferent. Pretend not to care." That was wisdom. But I loved her too dearly, and jealousy is a cataract that rushes one's boat over the swirling falls.

I abused her for flirting with Tunstall. I said that he was a man with a monstrous reputation. I said that she had disgraced myself and our child by behaving so before the Seaborne gossips.

Then she was really angry. For the first time in our lives together she was really angry. Her voice had a hard edge to it that I had never heard before. She said some bitter things, things I don't doubt that she had long been treasuring in her heart but had been too kindly-natured to declare.

She said that I was becoming a useless, stupid old maid. She, like the Parrott, called me a prig, and said that all the world thought me one. What kind of life was it for her, did I think, to live with someone who shut himself off from everyone and wasted his life in writing books that no one wanted? I resented, she said, that anyone should have any fun. I was against all human feeling, no one must flirt, or drink, or dance. She liked Tunstall. I was absurdly unfair to him and in reality was jealous of him because he was everything that I was not—gay, popular, a real man.

I broke in then to cry that I hated him, I hated him, I hated him! He was bad, worthless, false to his wife and everyone else. If she, my wife, could like such a man, then she was no wife for me.

She answered, with a dreadful gravity that struck terror into my heart, that perhaps that was true. Our marriage had been a mistake. She had done all she could. The shop would have closed had it not been for her. Yes. We were not suited to one another. She saw that clearly now.

At that I was abject. I said that she was right to despise me, that I *was* a prig. I begged her to understand (oh, the miserable self-humiliation of jealousy!) that I loved her so terribly that nothing and nobody mattered to me beside her. I was jealous, yes. I could not bear to see Tunstall touch her hand, to see her smile into his face. Ah, if she would only love me a little—just a little. How I prayed for it, longed for it! I would try to improve, to see more people, to help her in the shop. I would do this, do that. If only she would forgive me for my stupid jealousy there was nothing I would not do. But she would not, just then, forgive me. She was cold in my arms that night, not kind as she often was. Alas, I wept. But my tears did not move her. I could feel that she thought of me, just then, with repulsion.

Next morning she was kind again.

Everyone knows what obsessions are. They ride you like demons. They dig their talons into your heart. They accompany you, like slithery fat familiars, in all your daily and nightly doings.

From the night of Tunstall's party I was thus ridden. I saw two things. I saw Tunstall falling backwards down the wooden stairs on to the floor of the room where the dancing was—and I saw my wife laughing up into his eyes.

Then followed the episode of the bathe. These were the early days of summer, the beginning of June. To the right of Shining Cliff there was a little beach, Bateman's Cove. At certain tides it was excellent for bathing, having a hard saffron-coloured sand and a steep shelving descent so that you need not wade ignominiously before swimming. Because the path down to it was long, steep and winding, it was less popular than certain more accessible beaches. All the more reason for my pleasure in it!

One late afternoon I went there alone to bathe. It was an exquisite day of soft milky tenderness, the air warm as a gentle embrace, little movement, the blue glassy water broken quite suddenly with the baby energy of a white-crested wave.

I was quite alone on the beach. I was half-undressed when I looked up and saw Tunstall standing there watching me. Hugging now my obsession as I did, it did not seem to me at all odd that he should be with me, for he was *always* with me. I could hardly tell whether he were real or wraith. But he was real enough. He had his bathing-towel under his arm.

"I saw you from above, Jacko. I was going to bathe on Anstey, but when I saw you all alone down here I wanted to join you so badly that I bothered with all that tiresome path. Now isn't *that* devotion?"

I looked at him almost with friendliness. He had been for some weeks now the constant companion of my mind.

"Well, what have you been doing with yourself? I haven't seen you for nearly a week."

"'The trivial round, the common task.'"

"Don't you talk just like a book? How's your most delightful wife?"

"Very well, thank you."

"Now, there's a woman! Aren't you lucky? We've made fast friends. I hope you don't mind?"

"No. Why should I?"

"Well, if *you* dislike me, Jacko, she doesn't. You like *my* wife and I like *yours*. Isn't that lucky?"

He had thrown off his clothes and stood now in bathing-trunks. His body was a white fat. His breasts were heavy. There was thick hair on his chest and even on his shoulders. On the right arm, high up, there was tattooed a mermaid. I was slim beside him, and this was the more emphasized because we were of exactly the same height. I had fancied that I was growing a little stout, but now, looking at him, I was reassured. His red face and hands were in startling contrast with his pale body. In fact for a moment we stared at one another.

"Do you remember," he said slowly, "when we were kids, and I pulled your shirt over your head?"

"Yes. I remember."

"You minded like anything. You know," he went on, curling his toes into the warm sand, "it has always given me a kind of kick when you mind things. Why is that, do you suppose?"

"I've no idea."

"I get a sort of pleasure in seeing you wince. It's like—it's like—pulling your own hair to hurt yourself."

I tore myself away from him almost desperately. Nothing so curious as the way he held me! I ran down into the sea. He quickly followed me. He was a good swimmer and so was I. The water was indeed lovely, the advancing afternoon perfection, but all my pleasure was spoilt. I wanted to be out and dressed, and away as soon as possible. When I came out, he came out too.

As he was dressing himself, he said: "You didn't stay in long."

"No, I didn't."

"That was because you wanted to get away from me."

"Yes."

"Well, you can't. I shall walk along with you to the bus."

I said nothing. We dressed in silence. We walked up the path in single file.

At the top he said:

"Dear old Jacko. You'd do me a hurt if you could, wouldn't you?"

I didn't reply.

"And I'd do you one. But that's because I like you so much."

He suddenly began to chatter. He talked all the way to the bus, about himself, his painting, his jolly life. One thing he said:

"You remember Bella? You sat next to her at supper?"

"Yes."

"Fine woman, wasn't she?"

"I suppose some men would think so."

"You bet they do. I'll tell you about her some time—all about her and me."

"I haven't the least desire to hear."

"No. That's why I shall enjoy telling you."

Looking back now I can see that it was after this episode of the bathe that I moved into a new world. I was not only obsessed, but I was obsessed with an idea—and as yet I was not certain of my idea. You know how it is when you wake of a morning, and are instantly conscious that there is something overhanging your mind. For a second of time you do not know what this thing may be, then it leaps at you—pleasure or pain, terror or anticipation. It was now as though this second of uncertainty was prolonged.

Something was there, waiting to dominate me. I was not sure yet what it was.

About a fortnight after the bathe Tunstall caught me again. This time down in the Lower Town, outside the pub, from whose stomach proceeded the squeak of an amateur and very discordant jazz band.

Tunstall came out of the pub as I turned homewards. He put his hand through my arm and walked with me. He was a little drunk, and greatly excited.

"Dearest Jacko, do you know the time?"

"Yes. It's nine-thirty almost exactly."

(Of this dialogue I, to my shame and despair, remember every syllable—far, far more than I shall ever wish to record on paper.)

"Good. Splendid. In an hour and a half's time I shall be in the arms of my beloved. Come. We'll take this way by the sea. It's longer, but I want to fill in time."

I had not replied.

"Why don't you ask the name of my beloved? I have no secrets from *you*, Jacko. Bella. Bella. Bella. You remember Bella, don't you? The loveliest woman in England. I am going to Bella."

"I thought she lived with her mother."

"So she does."

"Well—does her mother approve?"

"Her mother doesn't know anything about it. Her mother, fortunately, takes sleeping-draughts. See, Jacko, I'll tell you all about it—the minutest details. You are my other half, my better half, my pure, austere, celibate half. I shall be delighted to stir my better half's virginity."

He went on with all the excited eagerness of a semi-drunk man.

"I know I'm a little drunk, old Jacko, but that doesn't impair my potency, old man. As I'll be proving just two hours from now!" He pulled me a little closer to his side. The sea below us was purring like a cat.

"This is the way of it, old chap. I can see her window from Shining Cliff, and if the old lady is well away, then Bella puts a light in the window. We meet once a week—not more. I like my wife, although you mayn't think it. She's a good sort—she is really. I don't want her to suspect anything. Besides, neither Bella nor I want people to talk. I've a reputation to keep up."

"Not much of one," I said.

"Ah, that's all you know! Anyway, once a week is our rule. Just enough to keep the excitement going. So we settle the evening and at the appointed time I'm out on Shining Cliff. If the light is on I advance. The house is all by itself. No road near it. Only a little path. I get in through a window, take my boots off, go up the stairs in my stockinged feet. Her bedroom door's ajar. In I go, switch on the light. There she is in bed, sitting up waiting for me. Oh, boy! Isn't that a moment! But we don't exchange a word, we just grin at one another. Then I fling my clothes off and, when they're all on the floor, then we just stare at one another. After that, in a jiffy I'm in bed."

I began to tremble all over. I felt nausea.

"Let me go, Tunstall! Let me go!"

"No, you don't." He holds me still with his hand. Once again I am absorbed inside him. I pass between his ribs. I am lodged close to the beating of his heart.

Then he begins to tell me everything, detail after detail. I whisper: "Let me go, Tunstall. For God's sake, let me go!"

At last he lets me go.

8

I AM NEVER likely to forget the smallest detail of that afternoon, August 13th—the half-hour that swung me into the heart of my decision.

It was about four o'clock of a hot oppressive August day. From early morning the sun had been burning sulkily behind heavy clouds. There had been a sniff of sulphur in the air. Dust over the garden where the flowers hung their heads. The sea rolled in heavily as an assistant politely unrolls bales of dark oilskin. We sat in our room, all three of us. Eve was at the table, examining some catalogues. She was considering certain drawings by minor Pre-Raphaelites offered therein. She sat, her thin elbows supporting her sharp, pale chin. Her dress was of grey, with an almost Elizabethan ruffle of rose-colour about her neck.

Archie was sitting in the window, turning over the pages of a magazine, looking out between the clearing of roofs to the sea. The veiled and darkened sun fell on his hair, which was the lightest gold in colour. His face was so pale and delicate, his body so slight, that I could never look at him without a pang of anxiety, but if I ever approached him with any kind of solicitude he always repulsed me. "Oh, I'm all *right*, Father!" He loved his mother, not me—or so I thought then—and I longed, how I longed, to take him in my arms and strain him to my breast, and cover his pale shell-like face with kisses.

There was no human being in all the world to whom I could demonstrate affection without reproach.

Eve had in front of her a large print of J. M. Strudwick's, 'The Ramparts of God's House.' She suddenly turned round to me, the narrow gold ring flashing on her finger.

"Too many angels," she said. "And they all have the same faces. How dark the room is! There must be thunder near."

And so it was. Archie was himself a Pre-Raphaelite figure, seated in the window in that deep plum-coloured air that Burne-Jones so often affected. Details stood out most clearly in that oppressive air, the shining brass of the fire-irons, the rose-colour about Eve's throat, the bright yellow of some roses in a bowl, the dim gilt binding of some books on a shelf.

I was reading Gissing's *Nether World*, that most gloomy and hopeless of all stories, but behind the façade of the book were staring figures of the poisoned world that Tunstall had created in my imagination. Yes, he had created them, and with my loathing of them and their actions went a weak inability to dismiss them. Tunstall himself, straddle-legged, mocking, laughed at me while behind him another Tunstall crept up the stairs on his stockinged feet, while behind him yet another stood, while she watched him from the sheets and he pulled his shirt over his head. . . .

The dark oppressive air, the very faint rumblings of thunder like the warning of a muffled drum, the sense that my wife and son cared nothing for me, the longing to rise and lay the back of my hand against Archie's cheek, the knowledge that if I did so he would quietly move his head while his blue eyes regarded me with a little contempt; all this with the added knowledge that everyone thought me a failure and that indeed I *was* one, and added to this again the uncertain, unhappy state of the world, with Hitler, like the brooding Mephistopheles on the Brocken, planning cold ruin and bitter destruction—with all this I was unhappy on that afternoon, beyond, it seemed, any possible alleviation.

The door opened and Tunstall came in. He had never come to our house uninvited before. He went quickly, beaming, forward to my wife, his hand outstretched.

"There's a terrible storm coming. I'm dying for a cup of tea. I have no other apology."

He was at his most charming; quite sober, most respectful,

serious-minded. The flushed purple undertone was gone from his cheeks; his hair was newly cut and sleek above his brown stout neck. He was wearing a heather-brown light coat and a dark tie, and dark purple corduroy trousers—full of colour, animation, sober restrained impudence.

Do you think that from my corner I did not watch every detail of him, feel the reverberation of his voice against my breast-bone, know that even while he was turning to Eve his broad back was full of eyes that mocked me? And he stood in his bare legs pulling his shirt over his head. . . .

But someone else was observing him, too. That was Archie, who had never seen him closely before, had never seen purple corduroy trousers, had never heard so merry, confident, cheeky a voice.

Tunstall had sat down, his legs spread, and was chatting away to Eve.

"What! The Pre-Raphaelites! You don't really admire them, do you, with all their preaching and the rest of it?"

"It isn't their preaching—it's their colour," Eve said.

"Oh, their colour!" Tunstall answered scornfully. "Anyone can make an effect with colour. Now, I——" Then he stopped, laughing, for she was looking at him in the mocking way that she had. "No. I'm not going to boast. You're too sharp for me."

"Why, what do you mean?" Eve cried.

"You think I'm terribly conceited, don't you? Well, I'm not really. I'll even go as far as to say I might have been a much *better* painter. Oh, yes, I might, and you know it. I've let myself go a bit, and I must pull up. You might help me."

"You've got the best wife in the world. You don't need anyone else."

As she said this her hand came down softly on the table, and her wedding-ring clicked against the board. The little sound, I don't know why, inflamed me with jealousy. Their hands were not touching.

"Ah, Leila!" he said softly. "Yes. She's a good woman."

Eve got up and began to fetch and arrange the tea. I felt that she avoided my eyes. I thought that her cheek was a little flushed and that her voice was raised.

For once Tunstall did not chaff me, scarcely spoke to me. He was grave and serious. He began to drink his tea, when his eyes settled on Archie. Archie had been staring at him, and especially at his broad thigh stretched out in the purple corduroy trousers.

"What are your trousers made of?" Archie suddenly said.

Eve reproached him.

"Hush, Archie—that's rude."

But Tunstall was delighted.

"Nonsense. He isn't rude. Here. Come and see what the trousers are made of."

Archie came over to him shyly, and Tunstall drew him in until he was standing between his legs.

"Here, pinch them!" Tunstall said, laughing. Archie did so. "I say, what a grand-looking boy! What do you want to be, Archie?"

"Oh, I don't know," Archie said, with obvious admiration.

"Ever tried your hand at drawing or painting?"

"I have a little."

"Like it, do you?"

"I do rather."

"Having drawing lessons?"

"No. Father thinks it a waste of time."

"Oh, he does, does he? Well, I tell you what. I'll give you some drawing lessons. Would you like that?"

"Oh, rather!"

"Right! You shall come over to me. We'll have a grand time. Got any drawings to show me?"

But I interrupted here. The rain was now slashing the windows. It was dark. I switched on the light and in the sudden illumination I stood facing the three of them. My voice shook. I wanted to steady it, but I could not.

"I'm awfully sorry," I said, "but I'm afraid not, Tunstall. Archie's got his own work to do and——"

But Tunstall broke into a shout of laughter. He threw his head back and laughed and laughed.

"Oh, dear, I'm most awfully sorry! Oh, Jacko! you'll be the death of me yet. Suddenly switching the light up, and standing there like the Commander's ghost. Why, we'd forgotten all about you. I'm

awfully sorry. It's very rude to laugh. If only you could see yourself!"

Eve was smiling. Archie, nervous, half frightened, half angry,
put his hand on Tunstall's arm as though for protection.

It was with that movement that I suddenly saw. It was a blinding
light of illumination, so that I turned round for an instant and
stared at the wall. I knew what it was that had, for a long time now,
been hanging at the back of my mind, just out of my consciousness.

I turned back and stared at Tunstall. He was like a new man
whom I had never seen before. Everything about him was different,
and my feelings towards him were different. He had a kind of
consecrated air. It was as though I had had sudden secret information that he was suffering from a fatal disease. It did not matter any
more what he said or did, how he behaved. I was not jealous, nor
angry. I was at peace with myself, as one is when at last one yields
to a temptation against which one has long been struggling. Above
all, I felt now a strong bond between himself and myself.

On the afternoon of the second day following his visit to us, I
was standing outside Smith's bookshop. It was August 15th, and
very warm. The High Street was thronged with holiday-makers.
The sun sparkled in splinters of light as though someone were
placing and replacing a screen. Motors hummed like drunken
bees. There was a great sense of movement and bustle. Tunstall
appeared. He was hurrying into Smith's, his eyes a little bloodshot,
his soft hat pushed back from his forehead, on which there were
beads of perspiration.

He saw me, and grinned his wicked schoolboy grin.

"Hullo, Jacko."

"Hullo." I smiled. I was glad to see him.

"You look as though you were pleased to see me."

"I am."

"Well, I never! That's a change, isn't it? I say—are you waiting
for someone? I believe you've got an assignation. Oh, my naughty
Jacko!"

"No. I wasn't waiting for anyone."

"Talking of assignations." He dropped his voice, gripped my arm and pushed his face so close to mine that I could smell the perspiration on his forehead. "Next Thursday's the night. Yes. Rain or shine. Nice for you, Jacko." He chuckled. "You can picture us. Every word. Every movement. Eleven prompt I'm at Shining Cliff. Eleven-fifteen creeping up the stairs. And eleven-thirty. Oh, boy! Eleven-thirty! Nice for you, Jacko. You can enjoy it all by proxy."

"Perhaps I'll be there one night, hiding behind the curtain."

I could see that he was surprised at my jocularity.

"You're growing up, Jacko," he said. "You're certainly growing up."

On the evening of the following Thursday I said to Eve, as we were finishing supper:

"I'm going to the pictures. Last house."

"What's on?"

"*David Copperfield*. A revival. I liked it so much when it first came out, I've always wanted to see it again. It comes on for the last time at nine o'clock."

I had for a moment a really choking fear that she would suggest going with me. She seemed to hesitate. But she didn't enjoy pictures.

"All right. I'm going to bed early. Come in and see me when you come back. I shall be reading."

I went out, the collar of my waterproof turned up. It was raining—a kind of warm, misty rain. There was also a moon. This at times broke through the gusty clouds and illuminated the world with a wet, oily phantasmagoria. It was stuffy and close.

I got to the 'Regal' cinema at a quarter to nine. Inside the foyer, Bob Steele, the proprietor, was standing, with the faded carnation in his button-hole, the ill-fitting dinner-jacket (he buttoned it across the stomach, a large one), his curly black hair and his rather foxy smile. It was his business to be agreeable, and agreeable he was, especially, I believe, to little girls.

"Hullo, Talbot! How's yourself?"

"All right, thanks."

"Rotten night."

"Good for your business, though."

"Yes. Mustn't complain. Remarkable how they're turning up to this, although it's an old picture."

I went to the little glass window and paid for a one-and-sixpenny ticket. Then, with a nod at Steele (he would remember me all right), I went in.

I found an outside seat. I watched the News Reel, and a 'Mickey Mouse.' Then *Copperfield* began. I sat through part of this and then I slipped across the passage and out of the side door, raising the iron bar very silently. I was in the side street—Couper Street. There was no one about and the rain was coming down more heavily.

I reached Shining Cliff at ten-twenty exactly. The rain had stopped, and the pale moonlight was like dust on the cliff top. I went to the edge and looked down. The drop was sheer and terrific. The tide would soon be full, and already waves were licking the boulders far below. For half an hour I sheltered behind a broken wall, for the rain came on again, and it was very dark.

Two minutes after eleven o'clock had struck from Climstock Church, I heard someone approaching. I stood up. I saw someone of Tunstall's build come to the cliff, and pause. There was a faint light now, the white dusky shadow thrown before the moon emerges. I saw that he stared, and I knew for what he was looking.

I came forward to meet him. He *was* astonished!

"Why, Jacko—whatever——"

"Quite a coincidence," I answered. "I've been on a job for Eve—seeing the doctor in Climstock. He's the man we always have—Wellard. An awfully good doctor." Then I added, laughing: "Why, of course—it's Thursday! I had quite forgotten."

I could see that he was impatient. "Yes, it is. There's the light, though." I could see, with him, between the trees a faint flicker like an unsteady star.

"I must be getting. Mustn't be wasting a lady's time."

"Wait a second." For the first time in all our two lives together I took his arm. *I* took *his* arm!

"Wait. It isn't quite true what I said. There was something rather important I wanted to tell you. Something serious."

"Serious! Well, what about to-morrow, old boy? Really, I'm late as it is."

I had been leading him gently forward. We were on the cliff edge. I put my arm round his broad back.

"I say, Jacko!" He turned his head to mine. I urged him ever so slightly in front of me.

"But it *is* serious. It is to do with your Bella. I heard this afternoon——"

Then with my knee I shoved him forward, using all the force in my body. At the same moment I threw him out with my arms.

I could see, in the dim light, that he clutched the air with his hands; he gave a great cry, and he fell. The sea was roaring. I knew that the tide, far down below, was deep up against the rocks. Except for the sea-noise there was no sound. The thin rain stealthily stroked my cheek.

I sat down on a wet rock, and waggled the little finger of my right hand—for the jolt of his flying body had strained it ever so slightly.

9

I SAT THERE for a considerable time waggling my finger and feeling, with a pleasant kind of sleepiness, the soft thin rain upon my face. It was so very still and quiet. Nobody was about. The only sound was the distant rhythm of the sea and the gentle hiss of the rain.

Then sharply I reflected that if my wife supposed that I was visiting the cinema she would be wondering that I should be so late. I hurried home. I felt happy and on excellent terms with myself. When I let myself into the house I found everything dark. Eve had gone to bed. But I had only just struck a match when I heard her voice from above the stairs.

"John, is that you?"

"Yes, dear, I'm coming."

I took off my boots and left them in the kitchen. As I did so I noticed my finger again. I had certainly given it a twist.

I came into the bedroom. She was sitting up in bed and at sight of her my only desire was to take her in my arms. I would, too! I was not going to be denied this night of all nights.

"Why, John, where have you been? You can't have been at the cinema all this time?"

I took off my coat and waistcoat. There was a tear in the lining of the waistcoat.

"Indeed I have, dear. Look! This lining's torn. I wish you'd sew it for me."

"But it's ever so late."

"Not really, dear."

I sat down on the edge of the bed, slipping off my trousers. The ends were very wet and this I didn't wish her to notice.

"It's a long picture, *Copperfield*. Little Bartholomew and Rathbone as Murdstone were as good as ever. Pity they had to get an American for Micawber. The first half of the picture is much the best."

I put on my pyjamas and went into the bathroom to brush my teeth. When I came back I saw that she was looking at me curiously.

"The cinema seems to have done you good. I've never seen you look so pleased with yourself."

I turned out the light and got into bed.

"I don't know why it is," she said, yawning. "I'm as tired as anything."

"Now look here, Eve," I said, with a courage and energy that surprised me. "To-night you're going to do what *I* want, whether you like it or no."

When I woke in the morning I felt a wonderful lightness and relief. Eve was already up. The sun was streaming in at the window. I had had one of those delicious sleeps that are the result of complete physical and spiritual satisfaction. I lay back on the pillow, my head on my hands and dodging a little to avoid the brilliant sunshine. For a little while I could think of nothing but my well-being. Then I remembered. Tunstall was gone for ever and ever and ever.

It was then that I felt the first little prick of anxiety. Suppose that his body had caught in some projecting part of the cliff? Suppose that he had lain on some ledge, bruised and battered, but gradually coming to himself, would recover enough to climb back and find his way home? For a moment my heart contracted and twisted. But I was at once reassured. The cliff fell sheer to the sea and Tunstall's body had been thrown outwards. I smiled to myself as I turned on my side. I had not the slightest feeling of compunction or regret. Tunstall was a bad man. He was no good to anyone. He was beginning to seduce my wife and my son. I had to protect my family. But, behind these reasonings and very much more important than any of them, was the certainty that I would not be bothered with him any more. He was gone from my life. I could hear him saying: "We're like the Siamese Twins, Jacko, and always were."

Well, we weren't. I had settled that once and for ever. No more bother from Tunstall.

When I went down to breakfast Archie was having his. I was as hungry as though I were eating Tunstall's breakfast as well as my own. Eve noticed it.

"Why, John, what's happened to you? I must say you're looking wonderfully well."

Archie had something to say:

"Daddy, when's that nice man with the purple trousers coming again?"

"Soon, I expect."

"I liked him. Do you think he'll really teach me to draw?"

"I expect so. He's a fine artist."

Eve, filling my cup with coffee, let her hand rest for a moment on my shoulder and said: "That's right, John. I thought it wasn't kind of you the other day to refuse him as you did."

"I was feeling out of sorts."

"The cinema seems to have done you a world of good. You're a different man to-day."

Archie went on: "Will I go to his house, Daddy?"

"I daresay that you will."

"Oo-oo! How lovely! He's awfully strong, isn't he, Daddy?"

"Not so strong as he used to be, got a bit flabby."

"But he's stronger than you, isn't he?"

I smiled as I helped myself to a second poached egg. Then I got up to cut myself some ham. As I passed Archie's chair I rested my hand lovingly on his shoulder. I felt the bones wriggle a little.

"I don't know that he *is* stronger. I mayn't *look* much, you know, but I keep fit. That's what you must do, Archie. Make your body stronger."

"He's a wonderful painter, isn't he, Daddy? He's made lots and lots of money, hasn't he, painting pictures?"

"Yes, he's made a lot of money."

I was cutting the ham with a delicacy and adroitness quite new to me.

"Much more money than you've made writing books, Daddy?"

"Oh, much more." I turned round, smiling at him. "Say your grace, Archie, before you leave the table."

Archie said his grace.

"When can I go to the painter's house?"

"Soon."

"Can I go to-day?"

"No, not to-day."

"Oh, why not?"

But his questions were interrupted by Eve entering and saying: "See who's here!"

It was Leila Tunstall. Her face was pale and her coat and hat a little dishevelled, the hat crooked, the coat, a rather ugly seal-skin, too high on one shoulder. (I remember the tiniest details of this conversation—yes, I remember the slime of marmalade on Archie's plate and the shadow on his pale thin face raised to Leila's.)

"Why, Mrs. Tunstall!" I said. I remember that as I looked at her I realized how very, very much I liked her and wished that I did not.

She sat down at the breakfast-table.

"Yes, I know. This is a terrible time to call. But you must forgive me. The fact is I'm very anxious."

Eve said, "Have some coffee."

"Yes, I think I will. Thank you so much. The fact is that Jimmie left the house after dinner last night and hasn't been back since."

"Not been back?" I cried—and the odd thing was that half of me was really amazed that he *hadn't* been back! That cry was quite genuine.

"No, you see . . ." She hesitated. "I'm sure I can speak safely to both of you——" She paused, looking at Archie.

"Archie," Eve said softly, "go upstairs, dear, and start your lessons. I'll be up very soon."

"Yes, Mother." He went.

"The fact is—Jimmie has been drinking too much lately. Oh, it isn't a secret. Everyone knows it. That's what makes me anxious."

"Was he quite happy when he went out?" I asked.

"Oh, most. He was especially gay and he hadn't been drinking then, I know. He only had water at dinner. He laughed and asked me whether I didn't think he was a reformed character. He said I wasn't to stay up. He was going to see a friend. That horrible Mr. Cheeseman, I expect." She added quickly, smiling a little: "Forgive me, I suppose I oughtn't to say that. But I can't abide him."

She looked at me quite urgently and asked: "Were you out by any chance, Mr. Talbot, last night?"

"Yes," I said, "I went to the cinema."

"Because it was wet—a kind of misty rain. I'm worried because I think he might have drunk a little with Mr. Cheeseman or some of them at 'The Green Parrot.'"

"'The Green Parrot'?"

"Yes, you must know it. In the Lower Town. That's where they go often, I believe. Oh, I hate that Mr. Cheeseman! He's responsible for so much. I hate him! I hate him!" She beat her little hands together. I longed to help her in her distress.

"He'd be all right, though," I said.

"No, he wouldn't. Not if he was drinking with them and they came out having drunk too much. It's dark there and it would be slippery——"

"Have you asked Cheeseman?"

"Of course I have. That's the first thing I did—on the telephone. He says he never saw Jimmie last night at all. But I never believe a word he says. But it was he who suggested I should come along and see you."

"Us?"

"Yes. He said, 'Ask the Talbots; they might know.'"

"What a funny thing! Why should *we* know?"

She smiled rather wanly. "Mr. Cheeseman always says that Jimmie is fonder of you than of anyone else."

"Oh, but that isn't true!"

"Well, I don't know——"

Eve hadn't said a word all this time. Now, very quietly, she spoke. "I'm terribly sorry about all this, Mrs. Tunstall. But we know nothing, I'm afraid. I went to bed and John went to the cinema."

Leila looked at her. Her eyes were filled with tears.

"I'm silly. . . . It really *is* stupid, but I'm very fond of Jimmie. I know he isn't all that he should be. Perhaps that's why I'm fond of him. But there it is. We all have our vices and Jimmie's mine. . . ."

Eve went over, bent down and kissed her. "Forgive me. I couldn't help it. I like Jimmie too, you know."

I looked at those two women, so good, so fine, and both of them attached to that dirty scoundrel. Attached! Oh, no, that was surely too strong a word for Eve. But I did not know. What secrets were behind that good, sweet face? I realized two things. First, that my relationship to Eve had in some subtle way changed since last night, and secondly, that it did not matter any more whether she was 'attached' to Tunstall or no. At that thought my heart began suddenly to pound in my breast. I felt a kind of mastery over those two women because they didn't know what *I* did.

Eve sat down beside Leila and they held hands. Leila was looking at us as though she wondered whether she dared go further. She moistened her lips with her little, very bright red tongue.

"There *is* another thing. . . . I didn't mean to say anything about it, but you're both such friends now. Only never let Jimmie have the slightest idea that I spoke of it—you promise?"

We both promised—I well knowing that my promise would be kept!

"You know Bella Scorfield? Of course you do. You've met her at our place. There's been some talk about her and Jimmie. You've heard it, I'm sure. . . . It's justified!" Her eyes flashed. "No use pretending. Jimmie can't be faithful to one woman and I understand that in a kind of way. But whether I understand it or not I have had to put up with it for a long time. He's having an affair with Bella Scorfield."

"Oh, I'm so sorry," Eve broke in.

"My dear, don't be sorry. These affairs never last. And I always think the wife's a bit to blame, don't you? Not that I like Bella Scorfield. It wouldn't be natural if I did, would it? In any case I think, I'm *sure*, that it was to Bella he went last night."

"Why are you sure?" Eve asked.

"He's always especially jolly before he goes. I made up the story about his going to 'The Green Parrot' and drinking. I'm quite sure he didn't, because at dinner he was altogether teetotal. He always is before he goes to see her. It's a certain sign."

A little shiver seized her body, a trembling beyond her control, and I realized that this thing had, for a long time, caused her great suffering. She was revealing her soul to us.

"But," Eve cried, "if he was perfectly sober he couldn't . . ." She pulled herself up.

"All right, Eve, dear. May I call you Eve? I know that Jimmie does. You aren't hurting me, I'm really too used to it to be hurt. Besides, as I've said, I regard it as partly my own fault. But that *is* the point. He was quite sober when he went out and if he went to her he would go by Shining Cliff, but he'd take the inner path. He wouldn't be in any danger, however slippery it was."

"Have you asked Miss Scorfield?"

"Yes, of course. She was the first person I telephoned. And then I was more than ever sure. I could tell that she was herself seriously worried. You could tell from the sound of her voice. She *had* been expecting him. She was distressed. She had been sitting up, I wouldn't wonder, most of the night, waiting for him." There was a vindictive snap in Leila's voice.

Yes, I thought, she *was* sitting up, sitting up in bed, waiting for the sound of his stockinged feet. It was for the moment as though I had been he, climbing up those stairs in *my* stockinged feet.

"What did she say on the telephone?"

"Oh, not very much. I couldn't charge her, of course, with waiting for him. All I could say was that we were worried because he had been away all night and I was asking one or two of his friends whether he had said anything. She begged me to ask him to telephone to her as soon as he came in. I will, too!"

She got up. . . .

"Please, please . . . I know that you are our friends, mine and

Jimmie's. *Please* don't say a word about Bella Scorfield. Even if they all know, I don't want him to think that *I* do."

"Of course not," Eve said.

She turned to me. I knew that I must say something. I wanted to comfort, to console her.

"I'm quite sure it will be all right, Mrs. Tunstall."

"Thank you, Mr. Talbot. I'm sure that I'm making an absurd fuss. I'm going home now, and I know that I shall find him there, although what he *can* have been doing . . ."

She smiled bravely at both of us and went away.

"Well, of all the odd things!" Eve said.

"I don't see that it's odd," I answered. "Tunstall had other female friends besides Miss Scorfield. He——"

"Had?" Eve interrupted me. "You speak as though something really had happened to Jimmie."

"I hate your calling him Jimmie."

"Why not? He's called me Eve from the very beginning." She came close up to me, looked me full in the face: "Why *do* you hate him so, John?"

I answered her quietly, "I don't think I do. You can see him as much as you like. I'll never be jealous."

I took her round the waist and kissed her on the mouth. She didn't resist but when I had finished she looked at me with puzzled eyes. But I didn't care. I remember that I sat in my room that morning swimming in self-satisfaction. This was the small room where I always did my writing. It had very little in it. I believed that a writer should have nothing to distract him when he worked. There was a white bookcase, a plain deal table, photographs of my wife and son, and a drawing that I had stolen from the shop, the study for Burne-Jones's 'Nimuë Beguiling Merlin'—afterwards included in his posthumously published *Flower Book*. There was something in the twisted branches of the Witches' Tree and the heavy figure of the old Merlin that greatly pleased me.

I had come up to work on my new novel. It is called *Mr. Porter's Door*. It will certainly never be finished now. I sat there, my hands folded, and looked through the opposite window to the cleft between the roofs which revealed the sea, plum-gold, and the sky blown like a field of corn above it.

I adored this fragment of sea. It was near but not too near. It could not harm me however wild it became; it could not lash my cheek with ice-cold revengeful spray. But its beauty was never-ending. I was thinking of it now, as I rested my elbows on the table and my chin on my knuckles. I was thinking of it with gratitude: it had received Tunstall's body and had dealt with Tunstall's body. I had every reason to be grateful.

It was strange perhaps that now, on the morning after, I should feel no kind of remorse. For after all I am a gentle-natured friendly man at heart. (I *am*! I *am*! Say what you will, I am! I am! I am!)

It was far from remorse that I felt as I turned my plain wedding-ring round and round on my finger and saw the glint of the gold in the sun. Instead of remorse, I felt an exultant, bursting pride! They had despised me, had they?—all of them despised me? "Oh, John's no good," they'd say. "Even his books aren't any good! Even his books . . ." But now I'd done more than they had ever done. They had none of them thrown a man, twice their size, over a cliff, so that he was drowned! They wouldn't dare! I thought of Bob Steele of the cinema, and Cheeseman and Jessie Parrott and many another. They had all sneered at me for years. They wouldn't sneer now if they knew.

I thought of Bella Scorfield. That had excited me greatly when Leila Tunstall had spoken of her waiting for him. She, Leila, didn't know *how* she waited for him, how she sat up, straining her ears for the sound of the softly-closing door and the thin tread of the stock-inged feet. For her bedroom door would be ajar and all I needed to do was to take two steps inside the room and stand there, grin-ning, while I threw my coat and waistcoat . . .

I? What was I thinking? I remember that I stopped, pushed my ring down into my finger and straightened my back, listening. I? The fact was that Tunstall had told me his story with so beastly a vividness that I could almost fancy that I had been there. He had forced my imagination to such a pitch that I could almost see the furniture, the wardrobe on the left, the dressing-table with its pink lace covering. . . . How did I know that it was pink? Tunstall had told me—and in any case it *would* be pink.

Bella Scorfield's bedroom. Yes, she must have sat up all night waiting for him. She must have been very sure of him; he had never failed her. By his own eagerness as shown to me he would not be late by a minute!

I walked about the room. I was smiling. I might be a poor little devil who had been, until now, a failure. But why was that? Largely because I had, since I was a small boy, suffered from this monstrous incubus, Jimmie Tunstall. Jimmie Tunstall. I had never for a single moment been free of him. I could see now that although I had pretended to mock at his 'Siamese Twins' and the rest of it I *had* been conscious of a bond, and that although I had said again and again that I was free I had known in my heart that that was not really so!

But now I was free! At last, at last I was free! I stood at the window looking out to the golden fleeces of the sky that fell now, in an embracing loom of colour over the pale hyacinth-blue of the sea. My heart was glad. I gave the kind sea my blessing.

It is at this point that I wish in my recollection to be severely accurate. I am trying—no man ever tried harder—to tell the truth and only the truth. Everything depends, for my own peace of mind, on my integrity.

I was standing looking out to the sea. Leila Tunstall came to my mind. I saw her anxious disturbed face, twisted a little—just that suggestion of malformity in the thickening of the skin over the right lip—or was it the tightening of the muscles above the right eye? As I saw her face and heard her voice I realized that she was an absolutely good woman—almost the only absolutely good human being I had ever known, and with a little sigh, a slight flutter of the heart, I realized how deeply I needed her in my life. I was not in the least in love with her but I liked her so very, very much. Liked her and admired and needed her. I needed her especially now, for, let me be self-satisfied as I might, I did now carry a burden and would always carry one—a strange burden, half of pride and half—was I beginning to realize it?—of apprehension. I did not consider that I had done Leila Tunstall any harm. She had loved Tunstall, but only because she had not known him. He would have sunk lower and ever lower. Drink, lechery, at last becoming a sot of an old man loathed and despised by everyone. I had done Leila a kindness, and although she would never know it *my* knowledge of what I had done bound us together and would always bind us. It was then—exactly then, as I watched a thin dark shadow like a fish's fin drop over the sea—that I fancied that I heard a laugh in the room behind me.

I did not turn round. My heart gave a jump and a skip, for the laugh had been a man's laugh—it even reminded me of Tunstall's sneering confidential chuckle.

I did not turn round. I disciplined myself. It was as though I spoke aloud: "You must remember that from now on it will be very natural for you to imagine that you hear sounds or see suspicious things. You must be especially sceptical about what you fancy you *see*. Why, already this morning you imagined that Eve was looking at you in some peculiar way. Of course she was not. You must remember that. You have some knowledge now that nobody else has got and that nobody else must have. Remember that the only real enemy you had in the whole world is gone."

It was at that point that again I fancied I heard the laugh. I stood there, my whole body strung up, my heart stiffened.

"Who's there?" my heart seemed to whisper.

"Turn round and see," something seemed to answer.

At last—and it was as though my body acted against its will—I did turn round. There was, of course, nobody there. The room was quite empty. The sun that had been shining over the sea was filmed now and so the room also was less bright—it was dimmed as though a thin mist pervaded it. But there was nobody there. Of course there was nobody there.

I sat down to my table and began to concentrate on my work. In this novel of 'Mr. Porter' I was trying to draw the full-length character, personality of a really wicked man.

I can see now that I had Tunstall for my sitter, although I would violently have denied it had I been accused. Mr. Porter had the physical properties of Cheeseman, the Rat, but he was laughing, speaking, moving like Tunstall.

I remember that I looked at the page of manuscript, half scribbled on, and felt a sort of disgust for it. What a second-hand thing was this writing of stories when, with your own strong fingers, you could push a big heavy man into the sea! There was a sensuous pleasure in the recollection of that moment when that body had yielded, falling backwards. There had been the cry, the pounding of the waves below. . . . My blood thickened as it does when in recollection one recovers the detail of some past sensuality.

Then, for the second time, I was sure that someone was in the room with me and, for the second time, I refused to turn round. But now I was expecting a touch on my shoulder. Crazy, as I was telling myself, to expect a touch on the shoulder when you know that there is no one there. But so it was. My shoulders were bent a little waiting for the touch. I straightened myself. I turned round.

Archie was there, bringing me the cup of coffee that I always have in the middle of the morning when I am working. He looked at me with that half-nervous, half-doubting look that always exasperated me. I hated that the boy should be afraid of me. "Come along. What's the matter?"

"Nothing," Archie said, putting the cup down very gingerly on the table.

"Don't look at me as though I'd eat you."

"I'm not, Daddy."

"Come here." I smiled. I drew him in between my knees. I remembered how readily he had gone to Tunstall. I drew his slight, slender body close to mine.

"Well, have we been working hard this morning?"

"Yes, Daddy."

"What have we been doing?"

"History, Daddy. Mary Queen of Scots."

Then he added, looking at me with wide-open eyes: "I hate her."

"Hate her—why?"

"Because she killed people."

"They were cruel to her. Her husband was a bad man."

"I don't care how bad he was." I felt his body slipping away from mine, eager to go.

I gave him what was almost a push. "All right. Run along. Daddy's working."

He ran eagerly away.

On the following morning at the top of the road that leads down to the Lower Town, I came quite suddenly upon Bella Scorfield. There are, at this spot, some villas with neat gardens and compact little garages. It was a sunny morning with a light breeze. The leaves of the elms were shivering with delicate pleasure. There was no one about, but I could hear the engine of some invisible car like a dynamo at the heart of the world. "While I go on," it seemed to say, "everything is all right. But let me stop———"

We almost ran into one another.

"Oh, Mr. Talbot!" she said.

"Good morning, Miss Scorfield."

"I wanted to see you. That is———" She looked about her in a distracted kind of way. I could see that she was greatly disturbed. A strong scent of crushed violets came from her in the breeze—(I would repeat here that no detail in my story, however small, is insignificant).

"There is no news of Mr. Tunstall."

"I believe, none."

She looked at me searchingly.

"Walk with me a little. This way, where there are no houses. Do you mind? I am in great trouble."

"I am most awfully sorry———"

"No. No. I'll tell you the truth. You are, strangely enough, the only person I can tell it to."

"I don't understand———"

"Of course you do. You know as well as I do that it was to me he was coming the night before last."

"Really, Miss Scorfield———"

She turned on me indignantly.

"Oh, don't pretend! It's too serious: Jimmie has told me often that you know all about us. I'm afraid he's amused me sometimes by the way he's shocked you. But that doesn't matter now. Tell me, Mr. Talbot———" She put her hand on my arm, looking up into my face. "What has happened to him? Where has he gone to?"

"I assure you, Miss Scorfield," I answered, looking at her very steadily, "I don't know a thing."

"Oh, but you must! He told you everything."

"Indeed he did not!"

"Yes, yes. He has the strangest relations with you. He often talked about it. He says that you are inseparables, that even when you aren't together you are together. Oh, I know that it sounds nonsense, but he really believes it."

"If you want to know the truth, Miss Scorfield, he despises and patronizes me and I dislike him. I dislike him very much. I always have."

"Yes. That's on the surface. But I'm sure it isn't so underneath. I know him too well."

"We are opposite in everything," I said.

"Yes, that's why you attract one another. But we're wasting time. Where is he, Mr. Talbot? Where is he? What has happened?"

"I don't know, Miss Scorfield. I really don't. I didn't see him that evening. I was at the cinema—at a revival of *David Copperfield*."

She went on impatiently, her breath catching her words. "No. No. I'm sure you didn't see him. Leila Tunstall says that he left the house, said good-bye to her, told her not to wait up. He was coming to me. Well, what happened after that? *What* happened?"

"I'm afraid I don't know any more——"

"No, but guess, man! Guess! Have some ideas! He was sober, because he always is when he is coming to me. It was wet, a sort of misty rain. But he wouldn't slip or fall into the sea or anything. I *know* he wouldn't. When he's sober he can look after himself perfectly. The funny thing is—at one moment I thought I heard him cry out. Of course I didn't. It was only imagination, but I sat up in bed listening——"

(Yes, I could see her—I knew just how she would do that!) I saw that she wanted me to say something, so I replied quietly:

"He may have gone somewhere else. He did deceive people, you know. He may have deceived you."

I took great pleasure in saying this, for certainly I hated her. She was part of him. Against my will I knew much more about her and her horridness than I ought to know. I hated her and her violet scent and everything about her.

"That's why I wanted to speak to you," she cried. "Is there someone else? Did he ever tell you there was someone else? He has always sworn there wasn't but then he is an awful liar. I know that well enough. Perhaps he's gone off to someone else. That's what's torturing me."

I was suddenly sorry for her, although I hated her. You can be sorry for people you hate. She looked miserable, forlorn, lost.

"I don't think there is anyone else. He'd have told me," I added. "Shall I tell you what I think?" (For I wanted to console her.)

"Oh, do, do! Please do!"

"I think he set off meaning to go to you. Then, seeing it was early, went in somewhere for a drink, drank too much and did go off with someone—just anyone. And he's staying away for a bit. Too ashamed to come back at once. He'll turn up suddenly with a story."

I could see the relief, the flaming, wonderful relief, that I gave her.

"Oh, do you think so? I believe you're right. It's the only explanation, isn't it?"

"The only one," I assured her, solemnly. "Meanwhile, Miss Scorfield, if I may say something——"

"Please do."

"Don't show other people that you care. It's much wiser not. They might talk."

"Yes, you're right. How right you are! Thanks ever so much."

She smiled and walked quickly away.

It was at that moment, just as I watched her disappearing round a bend of the road, that I thought I heard Tunstall's chuckle close behind me.

Very clearly I remember how I stood, stiffly, without moving, and listening. I can see as though it were now before me that quiet country road, the houses neat, tidy, like toy houses, bright and shining, and each house with its gay-tinted toy garden in front of it. There was not a single soul in the road and the only sound was the distant hush-hush of the sea and the delicate shivering of the trees.

I turned round. There was no one there. I had known of course that there would not be.

Then I spoke to myself something like this: "You must accept

for the moment as part of the condition of things these hallu-
cinations. You must not be surprised at them nor distressed at
them. You have done something that you wanted to do and that
you are pleased to have done, but naturally such an act must have
its mental consequences. Further than that, you were under this
man's influence since you were a small boy. You hated him: you
detested, and still detest, everything that he did, thought, and was.
You were always thinking of his voice, his laugh, his physical body.
Naturally you will still be thinking of these things and for a long
while to come. You must not mind this. He is dead. You know that
he is dead and that nothing can ever bring him back. Even if you
fancied that you saw him with your eyes, it would be sheer hallucination, for you know that the dead do not return. Remember the
old proverb—dead men tell no tales. You must face this and master
it. If you do not, you will be disturbed."

I looked resolutely about me. There was no one at all in sight.
I went home.

I discovered, however, that facing the possibility of hallucina-
tions made me conscious of them. That night as I lay beside my
wife, who was quietly sleeping, I even encouraged them.

"Now, Tunstall," I said almost aloud, "come out and let me see
you."

We always slept with our blinds up and our windows open. We
liked the fresh air and the reassuring murmur of the sea. On this
night there was a shadowed, creamy moonlight. Lying on my side,
I stared into the room. "Come on, Tunstall," I said. "Let me see
you." I imagined him as he would be or as I had last in full light
seen him. He was wearing purple corduroys and was fresh and
strong and confident. "Hullo, Jacko," he said, "I can come now
whenever you want me."

But he was not there, of course. However hard I might stare,
he was not there. His voice was there rather than his body. I even
spoke to him aloud. "You're not there really, Tunstall," I said. "You
can't come back, you know, however hard you try."

But I woke Eve, which was very stupid of me.

"Who's there?" she said.

And I did another silly thing, for I pretended to be asleep.

She jogged my shoulder. I pretended to wake with a start.

"What is it?" I asked.

"You were talking to somebody."

"In my sleep, I suppose. What a thing to wake me for!"

"No. It wasn't in your sleep. You weren't asleep."

"I ought to know whether I was asleep or not," I said angrily.

"You said: 'You can't come back, Tunstall, however hard you try.'"

"Did I? As a matter of fact, I was dreaming of Tunstall. I suppose it's because everyone's been talking about him all day."

She said: "I'm sure you weren't asleep. I know when you're talking in your sleep." With a little yawn she added: "What do you think *has* happened to him?"

"I haven't the least idea," I said, and turned over on my other side.

On Monday morning I was in the shop alone. Eve had some shopping that she must do and I was in charge. I liked the shop. When I had worked with my father every item had been of personal interest and importance to me. Now as I moved about arranging things, dusting a little, moving furniture to its better advantage, I wondered whether in my absorption in my own work I had not allowed Eve to take everything over too completely. I felt a new energy in myself. I had a talent for these things, not Eve's business talent, but a taste that was all my own. I picked up a Waterford glass and held it against the light and thrilled at its solid independent beauty. My fingers lay about it with love and appreciation.

The bell on the shop door tinkled. Someone entered. It was, I saw to my disgust, Basil Cheeseman.

I have already said something about Cheeseman before, but I must now speak of him with more particularity, for it is at this point that he comes into my story. I loathed him, but with no obsession about him because he had no power over me.

Physically he looked what people called him—the Rat. His body was small and delicately, even effeminately, made. His face was pale and his hair a reddish brown. On the back of his hands there were reddish-brown hairs, and he had a little reddish-brown moustache. His eyes were mean and pale. He was as false as hell. He was all smiles and urbanity, a most friendly soul. But while he smiled his little eyes darted about taking in everything that might be useful.

He smoked for ever a pipe and, while he rammed the tobacco down into it, he would look at you with the eye of an adder over the top of it. He loved to tempt you into unguarded talk, and months after would say: "You're a one to charge me with spreading stories. All your friends know the things *you* say! Remember what you said to me that day in your shop about——?"

But his profession, beyond that of journalism, was quiet, genteel blackmailing. I don't know how many of the more important people in our town were terrified of him. There was our Vicar, Mr. Thomas, for one. A fat, white, oozy, kindly man with not a grain of vice in him. But he did like his choir-boys and his Boy Scouts, although most innocently. Cheeseman had the whip-hand of him. There was old Miss Chamberlain, a rich virgin with a figure like a battle-horse. A good-natured, generous soul with a liking for young men, shop-assistants, public-house young men, *any* young man who wasn't of her class.

Here again I am certain that there was nothing more than amiable, generous good-nature, but the filthy Cheeseman had a horrible hold over her all the same.

Then there was fat, greasy Bob Steele of the cinema, already mentioned by me. The less said about *his* morals the better, and Cheeseman held him in a steel trap.

Cheeseman was not only no fool: he was really clever about some things: quite an authority on gardening, for example. He worked in his garden all hours and loved it.

He was sitting now on a nice eighteenth-century chair, sitting forward, his little body held together as though he were about to spring. His russet hair had a strange glowing quality against the pallor of his skin. His eyes were everywhere. He saw me treasuring the Waterford glass. "You like beautiful things, don't you, Talbot?" (He had tried once to call me Jacko and I very quickly stopped it.) He was smiling in a would-be friendly fashion and his prominent white teeth stuck out over his thin lower lip.

"Yes, I do."

"Of course. One can tell that from your books. But now, for instance, what is there about that piece of glass you're holding so carefully? To me it's just a piece of old glass."

"It would be," I answered scornfully. Shy though I was by nature, I never attempted to disguise my contempt for him. "It's of no use explaining to you if you can't feel it."

"No," he said, still smiling, "I suppose it isn't. Flowers, now. A really fine rose—there's a lovely thing. And it doesn't stay alive so long that it bores you. Now all that old furniture, those cabinets and tables, I call that junk."

"Do you call *that* junk?" I said, standing beside a little inlaid escritoire. "Can't you *see* its delicacy, the loveliness of its lines, the richness of its colour?"

"Yes," he said, "and when you sit down to try and write on it, it wobbles and there's no room for your elbows. I call it silly."

"I'm sure you do," I said.

"Never mind," he said quietly. "We all have our own tastes— and very peculiar some people's are."

He added in the same casual tone: "You know Tunstall's body has been found?"

His flickering whisky-coloured eyes were on me. My heart stopped a beat. I put down the piece of Waterford glass carefully on the table. I decided that it would be quite natural for me to be interested and even astonished.

"No!" I cried. "Where?"

"On Rotherston Beach—five miles away."

"Well I'm damned!"

"Not a shred of clothing on it. The body badly knocked about but the face scarcely damaged."

"When was it found?"

"Yesterday evening by some fisherman. Leila Tunstall went at once to identify it."

"That settles *that*!" I said almost to myself.

"Poor Jimmie!" Cheeseman went on. "I was fond of him and he was fond of me."

There was a pause. I was wiping some plates with a duster.

"You hated him, didn't you?"

"Yes, I did."

"And yet he was fond of you."

"Oh, no, he wasn't. He pretended to be because it amused him."

"Maybe." He leaned forward a little.

"What is odd to me is how it happened. He was going to see Bella Scorfield. Everyone knows that."

"Perhaps he wasn't," I answered.

"How do you mean?"

"He may have lied to Miss Scorfield. He may have had some other girl as well."

"Did he tell you so?"

"Why should he tell *me*?"

"I believe that he told you a sight more than he told most people."

"Well, he didn't. He never told me anything."

"Come on, Talbot. You know something. Let me in on it. I swear I won't tell a soul."

I smiled. "You're good at that, Cheeseman."

He laughed. "All right, you've won. But this time I mean it. What makes you think he had another girl?"

"I tell you I know nothing—nothing at all. But Tunstall was a rotter in every possible way—false to his wife, to Miss Scorfield, to anybody, everybody. He probably had heaps of women—a different one for every night of the week."

Cheeseman sat back, drawing his two thin legs together like the closing of scissors. He patted down the tobacco in his pipe, looking at me over the top of it.

"As a matter of fact, he hadn't. I'm quite sure he hadn't. He was in love with Bella Scorfield. It was physical, of course, but that seems all kinds of other things as well while it's on."

"You're quite a philosopher, Cheeseman," I said. "And now is there anything else I can do for you? I'm sorry, but I'm busy." He got up, came close to me, knocked his pipe on the heel of his shoe.

"Yes, there *is* something. Tell me—it isn't cheek, I really want to know. What were *you* doing that evening—the evening he disappeared?"

"I think it *is* cheek," I answered. "Why do you want to know? What have I got to do with it?"

"I'll tell you why. Don't be angry with me. My idea, Talbot, is that you and I together can solve this mystery. I'll go further than that and say that I don't think anyone can solve it *without* you."

"Why?"

"Because you were closer to Tunstall than anyone was. You say you hated him and he despised you. But there can be a relationship between people much deeper than hate and scorn and love. So deep that those feelings and emotions simply don't count—a relationship where two people belong to one another, have always belonged to one another, *will* always belong to one another——"

"You don't believe in that nonsense, Cheeseman?"

"Certainly I do. I've seen it several times. But I've never seen it as I have with you two. Now I was a friend of his. He really liked me——"

"He didn't!" I broke out. "He loathed the very sight of you!"

The moment I had said those words it seemed to me as though someone else had spoken. I looked blankly about the room. How did I know that Tunstall disliked Cheeseman? I had always, in fact, thought exactly the opposite. Until this very moment of speaking I had thought that Tunstall liked Cheeseman. What—or who?—had made me cry out those words? For it had been a cry as though from the very heart—so deep-felt, so sincere that Cheeseman himself was affronted with the sincerity.

"It's a damned lie," he said. "Jimmie and I were the best of pals. He showed it in a thousand ways. He said often: 'Basil—if I can't trust you, old man, I can't trust anyone.'" Then, more suspiciously, his white teeth shining Carker-like at me, he said:

"How do you know, anyway? Did he ever tell you he disliked me?"

"Never." I was suddenly weary. All the virtue had gone out of me.

"What made you say that, then?"

"I don't know. Perhaps I had no right to."

He gave me a vicious look.

"You'd better be careful what you go about saying." His hand was on the door. "Oh, and you haven't told me. Where *were* you that evening?"

"I went to the pictures—*David Copperfield*."

"Oh, did you?"

"Yes, if you don't believe me, ask Bob Steele. He saw me go in."

"Yes, and did he see you go out?"

"Really, Cheeseman—one would think that you imagine I pushed Tunstall into the sea with my own strong arms——"

He came back towards me.

"No, I know you didn't do that. You haven't the physical pluck. The point is that you know more about Tunstall's death than anyone alive. You know more about Tunstall in every way. For instance——" He came quite close to me. "You were perfectly right. Tunstall didn't like me. We were useful to one another. But he didn't like me. But no one knew that except Tunstall and me. How did *you* know?"

But I didn't answer.

Eve came in. And as Eve came in Cheeseman went out. And so, as I see it now, this first period after Tunstall's death was almost closed—closed except for one visit. The visitor was Leila Tunstall. The time was the middle morning. Eve was upstairs giving Archie his lessons; I was seated in the window of our dining-room reading a selection from the poems of Thomas Hardy, for which I have a great affection.

I remember the poem that I was reading—'The Dark-Eyed Gentleman.' The bell rang. I went, and there was Leila looking pale and young in her mourning. As I brought her into our sunlit little room I thought her almost beautiful, for the slight deformity seemed to have been smoothed away. She began oddly:

"May I call you John?"

"Of course."

"And you must call me Leila. I think Jimmie would like it."

I felt a movement of revulsion. Was she going to be now the sweet, idolizing-the-departed widow? I did indeed hope not.

I need not have feared. She went on:

"I hope you won't think that sentimental."

"Of course not."

"The fact is, Jimmie had very few real friends. I want them to be mine. Even that isn't sentimental. For the truth is that I was, and am, deeply in love with Jimmie. I don't think him any more than I did, good and fine and noble. On the contrary, he was false and greedy and lecherous. But I don't see that that has anything to do with loving him, do you?"

"Yes, I do," I said. "I can't love someone I despise."

"Oh, can't you? Well, then, you've a lot to learn." She laughed quite gaily. "I despise myself for a thousand things—and yet I rather love myself. The fact is that Jimmie was Jimmie and *is* Jimmie. When I saw him at Rotherston lying there covered up and his face scarcely touched I *knew* that he had escaped somewhere. Knew it as surely as I know that I'm sitting here. Tumbling into the sea wouldn't finish Jimmie!"

She cried this out almost with pride.

I said very seriously: "Please, Leila. I like you too much. I want you to trust me. So you *must* believe me. I was *not* Jimmie's friend. Everyone seems to think I was. I distrusted him. It isn't too much to say I detested him. I hated the things he did and said, but it was more than that. He mocked me. He derided me. I was his butt. From our very earliest schooldays together. I must be honest with you about this."

She put her hand for a moment on my arm. "You're one of the most honest men I've ever known. I'm sure you *believe* that about yourself and Jimmie. I know he teased you. I know you disapproved of him. But all the same—there was something between you that goes deeper than being teased or disapproving of someone's morals. You and Jimmie had that sort of relationship."

As she thus echoed Cheeseman's words, I could only look at her with a sort of stupid dumbness. What *was* this conspiracy to force me into union with this man? As though I hadn't, by my own act, union with him enough!

"In any case," she went on, "perhaps you'll feel a little about poor Jimmie now as I do. He can't do anything wrong or foolish any more. We can think of Jimmie always at his best now."

"But he can!" I cried. "If, as you said, drowning can't kill him,

why shouldn't he be still here, doing wrong, teasing me, breaking
your heart——"

"Oh, I didn't mean that!" she answered. "He's free of his body
now. All his troubles came from his body, which he didn't know
how to control."

"Perhaps not," I answered. "It may have been his spirit that was
evil. And if so——"

She smiled on me as though she were my mother.

"It wasn't his spirit that was evil—he was a child. A naughty,
mischievous, selfish, self-destroying little boy. Now he will begin
to grow up."

She held in her hand a little parcel.

"What I really came for, though, was to give you something.
All his clothes—were gone. His body was badly hurt. But still on
his finger, deeply embedded, was his scarab ring. You remember
it, don't you? The green scarab he always wore. I want you to have
it."

I drew back. "Oh, no! No!"

"Yes, please. I would like it and I know he would. He was very
fond of it. He used to say that the colour changed according to the
way he behaved. The green was very bright when he was doing
wrong. That was one of his jokes."

I stammered. "Oh, but please—I would rather not—I——" She
put the little parcel into my hand.

"Please take it. You can't be so unkind——"

I took it. She said good-bye and left me staring at it.

As though I had no free will I tried it on my finger. The gold ring
was too large. I went to Bettany's and had it fitted. As though I had
no free will I wore it from that time.

10

I count the giving to me of that ring by Leila Tunstall as the end
of the first development in this terrible affair.

I may say that up to the moment of putting that ring on my
finger in the jeweller's shop I had known neither fear nor compunc-

tion. My main feeling had been one of relief. Now the next stage begins and I pray to God (if I dare pray to Him) that everything I now write may be true and may prove the sanity of my brain and the clear accuracy of my memory.

I stood in Bettany's shop, and Mr. Bettany himself, a tall naked-faced man with wide-open staring owl's eyes, attended me.

"I think you will find, Mr. Talbot, that the ring fits you exactly."

"Thank you, Mr. Bettany," I said, putting it on.

"I know, of course, whose ring it was," he said, in a soft, unctuous voice.

"Yes," I said gravely. "Mrs. Tunstall wished me to have it and to wear it."

"A sad and strange business. We all thought so much of Mr. Tunstall."

"Yes," I said.

"Most mysterious his death was. However, there's no doubt, after the finding at the inquest, that in some way his foot slipped on that wet night and he fell over."

"Yes," I said again.

"Might happen to any of us, of course."

But I could not attend to him. I was looking at the ring with a kind of stupid amaze—for I felt that I had had it on my finger before. The gold circlet had been strangely little damaged and the scarab itself not at all. The green of the scarab was astonishingly fresh and bright when you realized that the ring was two or three thousand years old. The carving on the inside of the ring was broken, as Tunstall had once shown me, and I remembered how difficult it was for him to get it off his finger. The horrid sensation that I now had was that *I* had pulled it with difficulty off my finger to show to somebody! I remember that I thought of the absurdity of this and that my thinking it was a proof that my nerves were anything but what they ought to be. But more than that. As I looked at the thing I both hated it and was proud of it. I hated it seeing it on my finger for the first time and I was proud of it as an old treasured possession. Well, it wasn't an old treasured possession! But what a thing to do! To wear the ring of the man I had killed, to wear it flauntingly in the face of all the world. I

remembered that old murder case when Ethel Le Neve had worn
the jewellery of Crippen's wife a week or two after the murder. I
had always thought it a curious and reckless thing to do. But Leila
had herself given me this ring so that it was in a way a confirma-
tion of my innocence. Then a great emotion of loathing the thing
with its green and white squatness came over me. It was almost as
though it were alive. I had to muster all my energies not to tear it
off and throw it down there on the shop floor.

Bettany was looking at me, so I thanked him and paid him
and went away. By this time I was altogether accustomed to my
hallucination of Tunstall's continual presence. I took it that this
was probably the experience of most murderers during the weeks
immediately following the deed. But now, walking home through
the rain from Bettany's, I was aware of this new sense of fear. It
was perhaps the rain. I had noticed already that I was more uncomfortable when it was raining than when it was fine, especially if
the rain was thin and misty. I talked to myself *inside* myself. I had
fallen into the habit of doing this and my anxiety was lest I should
sometimes speak aloud.

"You know that this is all nonsense. Tunstall is dead and no one
in the world has the slightest suspicion of you. Even Cheeseman
is sure that you have nothing to do with it. Clear your brain of all
supposition. Think only of facts. There is nothing to be afraid of—
nothing whatever. The fact that you feel obliged to wear this ring is
simply because you wish to please Leila Tunstall, whom you like.
After a while you can put it away. She will not notice that you are
not wearing it."

But there was something stranger still. I was not *sure* that I had
killed Tunstall.

When I write that, it looks like complete nonsense. Of course
I *knew* that I had killed Tunstall. I knew that I had pushed Tunstall
over the cliff and that his body had been found, there had been an
inquest and the body had been buried. The proof that I had killed
Tunstall was in this scarab ring that I was wearing.

Nevertheless, beneath these undoubted facts was another layer
of consciousness, the consciousness that I had *not* killed him and
that he was still alive. I was, indeed, now entering into that world

known to many perfectly sane and normal people, that world in which material facts are no more facts than non-material facts. I could, for instance, finger my ring and know that it was a fact: I could also *think* about Tunstall and feel that he was not dead.

People live in one's imagination. If they continue to live there after their physical death, then in a sense they are not dead. But I must write more of this later.

I was also now deeply concerned with three women—my wife, Leila Tunstall, and Bella Scorfield.

My wife's attitude to me had changed. I could see, although she at present said nothing, that she was greatly puzzled by me. Puzzled rather than suspicious.

She seemed physically closer. I had seen myself that I was now more masterful with her—a thing that I had always wanted to be— and that she liked this. I was altogether more masterful at home. I had taken a strange and quite unreasoning dislike to her telling me that this morning, or this afternoon, I would not be needed in the shop.

"You can keep away, John," she used to say. "I shan't need you." And now I would say:

"Who does the shop belong to? You or me or both of us?"

"Both of us, of course."

"Well, then—we'll both run it."

"But what about your writing?"

"That's my business."

She was always good-tempered. She would look at me, smiling and puzzled.

"I'm glad to see you're putting on flesh, John."

I looked at myself in the glass. It was true. My cheeks were fattening out. There was sometimes a new, almost audacious look in my eyes.

Another little thing was that I was taking a new, almost excited interest in Archie's passion for drawing and painting. I sat beside him at the table, watching him and encouraging him. One day I pulled a piece of paper towards me and drew quite a little picture— some hills, a house, and some fields.

"Why, Daddy can draw!" Archie cried. I looked at my drawing

rather sheepishly—the first of my life. It wasn't very good, of course. But it wasn't very bad either. Then I tried to draw Archie sitting at the table. I made something of it. It was recognizably Archie.

"Well I'm damned!" I cried, and showed it to Eve.

"You don't mean to say *you* did that!"

"I did," I said, laughing.

"But I didn't know you could draw."

"I didn't myself. You never know what you can do till you try."

Leila Tunstall had gone to London. Her house was up for sale. She was staying with relations in Surbiton. I found that I missed her quite absurdly. It wasn't that I was in love with her. I had no physical feeling about her at all, but she seemed to me now the one really *good* human being, beside my mother, I had ever known. It was her *goodness* I wanted—near to me, so that I could realize it and feel reassured by it. I felt as though I could confess everything to her, pour everything out to her, my loneliness, unhappiness. I wanted to talk to her and say to myself: "You have gone far from goodness. If it weren't for Leila you would doubt perhaps that there is any goodness in the world. But look at her, listen to her voice, touch her hand, and you will know that one good person in the world is enough to convince you that goodness exists."

Yes, I missed her quite desperately.

I was aware that Bella Scorfield was very unhappy and found some strange companionship in me. I have said that I disliked her very much. So, on one side of my nature, I still did. The puritan in me shrank violently from the sensuality in her. She couldn't help it: she was animal in all her being. Tunstall had supplied her with what she needed and now that he was gone she was unsatisfied and lonely. On the other side I began to find that her physical presence had a kind of excitement for me. It was, I suppose, because I knew so intimately of her behaviour with Tunstall.

We had tea together one afternoon at the 'Paradise,' a tea-shop in the High Street.

"It was nice of you to come," she said.

"Why shouldn't I?"

"Because you dislike me and everything about me. But I don't care. When I am with you Jimmie seems closer to me. Perhaps it's that ring."

"Do you mind my wearing it? I only do because Leila Tunstall asked me to."

"No, of course I don't. I like to see it. It reminds me of so many things. And I'll tell you another thing. You may dislike me very much, but not so much as you did. Before Jimmie died you would never have dreamed of having tea with me. Now would you?"

"Perhaps not."

"You don't like me, but you like to be with me sometimes because you want to be reminded of Jimmie."

"But I don't want to be reminded of Jimmie."

"Oh, yes, you do. You were so close together, you two. Why, sometimes now the way you say things makes me think of Jimmie. Almost the same intonation."

"You imagine that."

"No, I don't. . . . But tell me. Do you have at all the sort of feeling I have—that he isn't really dead? I can't believe he is. With all his faults, he could look after himself, and that was such a silly way to die."

"Why, of course he's dead!" I cried out sharply. Then pulling myself in as though I were dragging back into my very entrails some lithe animal with sharp, white teeth and red hair, I said quietly, smiling: "Aren't I wearing his ring?"

"Oh, I know! I know! . . . Of course he's dead. Oh, I miss him! John—— Oh, I beg your pardon. It slipped out——"

"That's all right," I said carelessly.

"May I? Fine! And you must call me Bella. Funny, isn't it? At one time I wouldn't have dreamt of it, but now—Jimmie has drawn us together a little, hasn't he? Or don't you want me to say that?"

"I think he has."

"Well, what I was going to say is that you have no idea how dreadfully I miss him! That house is horrible to me now! Oh, you don't know how horrible it is! I have to play chess with Mother. She always wins. She likes to win. A cat with a mouse, that's what she is when she plays me. She just lets me go on. She likes to make me think I'm winning. And then she pounces! But now—she looks at me over the chess-board. I'm sure now that she knows all about Jimmie and me. I didn't think so before. But now I'm sure that she knew all the time. And she's pleased that he's dead. Horribly pleased. She hasn't mentioned his name."

"You're imagining all this," I said.

"Oh, no, I'm not. You can't imagine things with someone like Mother if she wants you to be sure of something. She can make anything definite without saying a syllable. . . . I want to get away—to London! I must! I must!"

"Well, why don't you?"

"I can't leave Mother there helpless. Besides, she never lets me have a penny of my own. Don't let anyone else know that, will you, John? I've never let anyone else know except Jimmie. He knew and was awfully generous. He was always giving me money."

I had a sudden impulse.

"I'd like you to have some," I said, "if it would be a help——"

"Oh, no!" She was blushing a little and looked quite young. I thought that one day perhaps if she allowed me I might kiss her. "I wouldn't think of it. It's awfully good of you, but I wouldn't take money from anyone—— Only Jimmie and I——"

I suddenly couldn't endure her. I wanted to get away at once, at once.

I paid the girl.

"I'm sorry," I said, "I promised to meet someone at the shop——"

"Of course," she said, gathering up her gloves and bag.

I come now to the first of the events that were presently to follow. I said at the beginning of my narrative that I am writing all this down to the smallest detail that I may prove to myself, beyond any possible question, that I am telling the truth, the whole truth, and nothing but the truth, as they say in the Law Courts. But, if there ever should be a reader of my story, I want him to realize how sane, composed, undisturbed I am while I am writing this. It is for that reason that I record so accurately many conversations and go often into minute detail. I *am* not mad! I *am* not mad! God, God, Thou knowest. Thou hast given me this trial because of what I have done and I submit. Thou hast the right. I submit! I submit!

I found that, as the weeks proceeded, I frequented the Lower Town very considerably. As I have said already, I had a great liking for it, its silence, its green undisturbed atmosphere, the lapping of the sea waters against the broken pier, and sometimes the sea storming and leaping over the old boards and thundering against the age-stout shore.

I never, until a certain evening, entered 'The Green Parrot.' I found now that I was attracted to it as I had never been in the old days. Attracted and repelled! Something told me not to pass those doors, just as in childhood something had told me not to steal a sweet or read a book that had been forbidden me.

But on one wet, dreary evening the temptation was too strong for me and I went in. 'The Green Parrot' hung, in its upper storeys, over the sea and when you were inside the bar-room you could hear the sound of the waters quite clearly. The room was very bright and cheerful on this particular evening, but as I stood a little uncertainly by the door, I saw to my alarm that Basil Cheeseman, Bob Steele, and a young good-for-nothing called Frank Romilly were seated, drinking together, at a table. They were the very last companions I wanted just then and I would have retreated had I been able, but it was too late.

Cheeseman, lifting his pipe and waving it in the air, called out:

"Talbot! Talbot! . . . Why, who would have thought . . ."

There was a man or two leaning on the bar and talking to the barmaid—Ted Warner, the fat landlord with a round face like a turnip lantern, and a bald head that was always perspiring, looked at me with astonishment.

I went over to the table. They put a chair for me; they were all greatly surprised to see me there.

"What will you have?" Cheeseman asked. "Now, boys, what about another? All of you. The drinks are on me."

"I'll have a ginger ale," I said. They all laughed. Cheeseman was half-way towards the bar. He looked back, his foxy face agrin. "A ginger ale! Nonsense! No one has a ginger ale here, do they, Ted?"

"I'm a teetotaller, you know," I said, with that half-ashamed, half-boasting tone that teetotallers always assume.

"All right," Cheeseman said. "It's your funeral—not mine."

He said something to Ted and they both laughed; then he came back to us.

Frank Romilly was a good-looking, dissipated young fellow whose character was as weak as a spider's web. He was supposed to work in an oil business of his uncle's, but he was supposed also to live on the favours of a rich widow called Mrs. Godfrey, who owned much property some ten miles from our town. I saw at once that Cheeseman had, before my arrival, been turning the screw on both Steele and Romilly. He was in excellent spirits while they were both in the sulks.

Something urged me to continue sitting there; something else pressed me to be gone. I couldn't understand my own mood. But after I had drunk my ginger ale, which I did almost at a gulp, I felt a kind of audacity, a new, bold spirit. It was the best ginger ale I had ever drunk and had a flavour to it that was most agreeable. When I had finished Cheeseman said:

"Now for another!"

"It's on me this time!" I cried. "As soon as you're ready, all of you—it's on me."

Cheeseman took my glass and went to the bar with it.

"So you're wearing Jimmie Tunstall's ring," Romilly said. "Poor old chap! Christ, how I miss him! Do you remember, Bob, how we used to sit at this very table and the songs he'd sing?"

"God! I should say I did," said Steele, who was a little drunk. "Why, old man," he said, leaning towards me and laying his podgy fingers on my arm, "it was that very night you came into my cinema—*David Copperfield*—do you remember? 'Strewth, it was that very same night . . . poor old Jimmie—the best sport, the best . . ."

But Cheeseman had returned to the table with my drink and the effect that he had on his two friends was truly remarkable. It was clear that he had been telling them of something unpleasant.

I drank half of my glass with one impulse: then I put the glass down on the table with a shudder. Cheeseman this time had given me a whisky and soda. I had all my life loathed the smell of whisky and once, given a very small amount as a medicine, had been sick from it. The very thought of whisky made me ill. Now when I had drunk unsuspiciously half a glass of it I was revolted as though I had committed an obscene act. At the same time I was familiar with it. It seemed to me that there was nothing strange in it and that I loved it while I hated it. And yet I was trembling with rage at Cheeseman. It was all I could do not to throw the glass in his face.

He was watching me, grinning at me over the top of his pipe.

"That was whisky," I said.

"As a matter of fact, it was."

"What right had you . . . ? You know I loathe the filthy stuff."

"You can't loathe it, old boy, if you've never tasted it."

The other men laughed.

"Now come—confess—it wasn't so bad."

I got on to my feet. I was about to tell him what I thought of him and go when I did an incredible thing. I drank the rest of the whisky. It wasn't I. Oh, I swear that it wasn't I who acted thus—an action that was to be one of the landmarks in my story. I hadn't known that I had drunk it until I realized that I was standing there stupidly looking at the empty glass.

How they laughed, all three of them! There was I, furious in the very act of saying that I hated the stuff, and I drank it. My body was warm, the room glowed in the light of the fire. I could see Ted smiling at me across the floor.

"No," cried Steele, clapping me on the haunches. "It wasn't so bad, old man, was it? And there's plenty more where that came from."

I remembered that the drinks were to be on me. I sat down. "What are you all having?" I said.

After that a great friendliness seemed to spring up between us. I felt as though I had known young Romilly most intimately although, in actual fact, I had with him a very slight acquaintance. I had always disapproved of him and said so.

After a little time he alluded to this: he had drunk freely by now and his eyes shone brightly, his lips were wet, and he smiled at me as though he loved me. "It's a funny thing, Talbot, but either I'm changed or you are. I've often thought I'd like to know you better, but you've always been so damned stand-offish. 'Who does he think he is?' I used to say, meaning you and no offence meant.

And they'd tell me you didn't like me a bit and used to warn the girls off me. Not that that had any effect, you know!" He threw his handsome head back and laughed like anything. "But now you're a regular fellow. I'll swear he is. Isn't he, Bob? And I'm damned glad we're friends. Always wanted to be friends and now we *are* friends! It's as though your wearing old Jimmie's ring has sort of brought us together. Let's shake hands on it!"

His hand was damp and strong and warm.

I noticed at the same time that something came from under the table. It was Tunstall's fox-terrier, Scandal, the dog that had been down with us on the beach that day. When Tunstall had been there the dog, who had been devoted to him, never paid any attention to anyone else.

He now came from under the table and sat there on his haunches looking at us with large, mournful eyes.

"Why, that's Tunstall's dog?" I said.

"Yes," Cheeseman said, "I've taken him over. Here, Scandal, old boy. Come along, old boy." But the dog didn't move. He stared at Cheeseman with the same intense melancholy. A shiver ran down his spine. Suddenly he lifted up his head and howled.

I cannot possibly describe the effect that that dog's howl had on the warm and brightly-lit bar. It was like what an unexpected gunshot would be in a cathedral!

We all cried out at once: "Oh, drown the bastard!"—"What the hell——"—"We can't have that here, Mr. Cheeseman!" After the rest I said: "What's the matter, old boy?" At once he turned his head to me. He looked at me as though he would stare my face away. Then, very slowly, he came towards me. It was almost as though he crawled. We all watched in silence. He came. He sniffed at my trousers. He sniffed again and again. He raised his head and stared again. Then with a sigh he lay down and stayed stretched out, his handsome head with its short, stiff, white curls resting on his paws.

"He seems to know you," Cheeseman said.

"He's seen me when I've been with Tunstall."

"I can't say he's been much fun since I've had him," Cheeseman said. "Misses his master all the time. And Jimmie didn't treat him over well, either."

"Treat 'em rough. Treat 'em rough," Romilly said, "Women and dogs. Treat 'em rough."

"Well, Jimmie certainly did."

"Jimmie! Jimmie!" Bob Steele suddenly broke out in his thick, mumbling voice. "Why has it always got to be Jimmie? I hated the man personally. Oh, I know he seemed jolly enough but he wasn't jolly really—not by a long chalk. He is dead and there's no one very sorry if you ask me. Yet here we are, always talking about him as though he were still alive. You'd think he was sitting at the very table with us by the way you go on."

I looked at Steele with a grim determination.

"So that's how you feel, is it?" I said to him, and I could see at once how greatly surprised he was both by my look and my voice. "Well, that's pretty ungrateful and you know that it is. Many's the time he's helped you out of a nasty scrape. What about that time in Nottingham and the girl——?"

He broke in. "By God, Talbot, who told you about that? He can't have done. And yet nobody else knew. But you keep your mouth shut, do you hear? How did you know? He can't have told you——"

"Never mind how I know," I answered. "I'm blasted well disgusted with you, Steele, you ungrateful bastard——"

And those are the last words that I clearly and definitely remember. I had never drunk whisky before. I had never sworn before. Whether they were connected I cannot say.

All I can remember is that I went on drinking and while I was drinking I began to disintegrate. I disintegrated before my own eyes. I had always been sure that I had a personality and had suspected that I had a soul to be saved, but now I fell apart—a leg there, ribs and intestines here, blood and muscles and nerves—all tumbling into a golden haze that seemed to emanate from the taproom fire. And if I had no body, what was there to assure me that I had a soul? Why should I imagine that there was any such entity as John Talbot?—a bit of John Talbot, a bit of someone else—a bit of a dog, of a fox, of a bird, of a stoat. I remember that I leant across the table wagging my finger and saying something like this:

"I am nothing. You are nothing. My spittle is as good as your spittle and it is only spittle. Isn't it? Now answer me. You're afraid to. You're afraid because you must have your identity. What's your name? Romilly. Frank Romilly. That's right. Well, Frank Romilly, without your identity you're nothing—see? An empty dwelling-place and seven devils enter in. And the last state of that house shall be worse. See what I mean, Romilly? A devil *has* entered into you. It's looking out of your eyes now. I'll wash him out for you."

And I threw the rest of my glass of whisky and soda in his face. I don't know what happened after that.

I was valiant, standing on my feet singing the indecent song: "My landlady fell down, fell down . . ." I didn't know the song. I had never sung it before. And then I crawled on the floor, imitating the dog Scandal. And then Cheeseman was seeing me home through the cool night air.

I remember Cheeseman saying before we reached my door:

"I haven't heard anyone sing that song about the landlady since Tunstall sang it up at the Spider Club one night——"

I was violently sick and Cheeseman stood there and waited. Then he opened my door for me, led me in and left me.

I sat down in the dark room on the sofa. The fit of nausea had cleared my head and I was cold as though lapped in snow. I was also terrified. I called out at the top of my voice: "Eve! Eve! Eve!" A moment later her step was on the stairs, she had switched on the electric light, and in her primrose-coloured dressing-gown, her hair bound virginally with a silk handkerchief, she stood looking at me.

"John!" Then she added, half-way towards me: "You're drunk!"

"I am." I was too wretched to care. But I was frightened. "There's someone in the room."

She paid no attention to that. She came over to me and sat on the sofa beside me. I put my head against her breast.

"I'm ashamed. . . . It's never happened before. . . . You know it hasn't. . . . Be kind. I need you so."

But she was not at all angry, only business-like.

"I should hope it hasn't. I'm completely astonished. Now come upstairs. I'll help you to undress."

She assisted me upstairs. She helped me to undress. When we were in bed she tucked me up and then lay at some distance from me. I longed that she would take me in her arms, but I was ashamed and I realized that I stank of whisky.

"My head aches," I murmured.

"Here, rub this on your forehead. Now you know how unpleasant the effects of drinking are, you won't do it again."

As I lay there I realized that I was completely my old self. I was not masterful nor roguish nor obscene.

The thought of Cheeseman and his companions, the memory of my chatter, the soft warmth of Romilly's hand—these things repelled and revolted me.

"Where did you go? Who were you with?"

Eve's voice, calm, resolved, unangered, told me that I was in for a questioning. I knew well by now Eve's investigations. There was nothing in the world more definite and relentless. My head throbbed, my body shivered. I was afraid, I knew not why. I stretched out my cold hand and took hers. She let my hand lie in hers, but I knew that she was scarcely aware that it lay there. When she was determined to satisfy some curiosity, she could be ravished and not know her ravisher.

"Where did you go?" she repeated. "And why? It's so unlike you."

I lifted my hand and laid it under her breast, but so unconscious was that breast of any contact that I took my hand away again.

"I'm frightened," I said, and drew closer to her.

"Poor John! What are you frightened of?"

I lay close against her warm, strong side and could feel the calm beating of her heart.

"I'll tell you," I said. "I was in the Lower Town. I pushed open the door of 'The Green Parrot' because it was wet and went in. Cheeseman and Bob Steele and Frank Romilly were there."

"The worst——" murmured Eve.

"Yes, of course, I know. I've always hated them, especially Cheeseman. But something made me. I sat down with them. I had a ginger ale. I think now that Cheeseman must have put something to it, for it was strong, better than any ginger ale I ever . . ."

I broke off. "Eve," I said pitifully, "put your arms round me. I'm so miserable. My head is awful."

"Yes. All right." She put her soft arms around me. I buried my face in her nightdress then timidly raised my head and kissed her soft, warm, enchanting cheek.

"I know," I murmured. "The whisky . . . it's hateful. . . ."

But she wasn't caring for what I did. She said quickly, in the clear, sharp tone of one who is thinking of nothing but the answer to a question: "Yes, yes. He put something into the ginger ale. Gin, I suppose. What happened then?"

"I drank it. I liked it. Cheeseman asked me whether I wanted another. I said yes. Then the dog howled."

"What dog?"

"Tunstall's dog. That nice fox-terrier with the rough curly head. They call him Scandal."

"Why did he howl?"

"I don't know. But it was awful there, quite suddenly, when everything was so cheerful."

"What happened then?"

"I spoke to him and he came over and sniffed my trousers. Then he lay down."

"Well, never mind the dog. What happened then?"

"Cheeseman brought me another drink. I drank half of it before I realized it was whisky. I was furious and began to curse Cheeseman, but while I was cursing him I drank the rest of it. Oh, Eve, that was the awful part! I've always hated whisky. You know I have. Even the smell of whisky makes me sick. You know it does. But now I drank it and liked it."

"Well, that's nothing. Lots of people have thought they hated whisky and found they didn't when they tried it."

"But, Eve, Eve . . . the dreadful thing . . . the dreadful thing . . . I'd drunk it before and liked it. I knew I had. I'd drunk it before. . . ."

My whole body was trembling so that she was aware of it.

"You haven't drunk it before. You've often told me. But that's nothing. I've never drunk port, but I know just what it tastes like. Why, you're trembling! Poor old John! This will teach you not to get drunk again."

I remember it struck me as strange that my virginal Eve should feel little disgust at my condition, should take it indeed as an often-experienced commonplace. How was it, I dimly thought. Had she known drunk men before? But this foolish question was at once forgotten in my surprise at the urgent curiosity in her voice.

"I want to know, John—I've been wanting to know for a long time. What's changed you so completely in these last weeks?"

"These last weeks?"

"Yes—since Jimmie Tunstall fell into the sea."

"I don't know of any change."

"Of course there is!" She gave me a little shake with her firm hand. "I've lived with you for years so I ought to know. Sometimes you're as you've always been, but sometimes——" She leaned towards me. "Are you listening? You haven't gone to sleep?"

"No, of course I haven't."

"Sometimes you've been another man altogether. Bossy. Ordering me about. To tell the truth, I've rather liked it. With Archie, too, you're quite different. He's beginning to look up to you. And your drawing suddenly. And now getting drunk . . ."

My terror had returned, dreadfully, remorselessly.

"Let me alone," I murmured. "I want to sleep. This head-ache——" She was leaning right over me now. She caught my shoulder with her hand.

"I want to know. I *must* know. What's happened? You have some information that has changed you—something about Jimmie Tunstall's death—something that pleases you, puts you above yourself——"

"I don't know anything."

"Yes, you do, John. And I'll tell you what it is. You had a quarrel that night. You struggled and he fell over—something like that . . ."

"I didn't—I never saw him—I was at the cinema."

I pulled myself away from her hand.

"So you say. But, John, I know better. When you came in that night the ends of your trousers were wet. You'd been walking in grass."

"Of course I hadn't. You can't walk in grass in a cinema."

"But you weren't *in* the cinema. Or if you were, you soon came

out again. I've noticed often since how you kept telling people
you went to the cinema, when they hadn't asked you. Guilty conscience."

I sat up. I put my hands to my head.

"And more than that. How about that night when you talked,
pretended you had been asleep? You were no more asleep than I
was, and you were talking out aloud to Jimmie, just as though he
were in the room."

I cried out: "Stop it, Eve, stop it! I can't bear it!"

"I've got to know—I've got to know."

I turned round. I felt for her hand and caught it.

"There isn't anything to know—at least it's all imagination.
You're right this far. Since Tunstall's death I've had a ridiculous
obsession that he isn't really dead. I don't know how he died. That
night I *was* at the cinema and I came back through Cottar's Lane—
that's where I got my trousers wet. How he died, where he died,
I haven't the least idea. But I suppose I hated him so much that
he's obsessed me—is obsessing me now. To-night I began to drink
because he seemed to be there in that pub. Perhaps it's true what
he used to say to me—that death wouldn't separate us. Eve, I'm
frightened. I'm terribly frightened. Be kind to me. Be kind——"

I clung to her, kneeling on the bed, my cheek close to hers. I put
my hand up and stroked her hair.

With an immense good-nature she kissed me, then laid me back
in the bed as she would a child.

"Now you're the old John, the John I married—always imagining
things. Of course Jimmie Tunstall's dead. And a good riddance I
daresay, although I couldn't help a kind of feeling—Now go to
sleep—all right, I'll kiss you. Is that better? Now, John—be good,
go to sleep. There's nothing to be frightened of."

She left me, turned on her side and was soon asleep.

But I lay there, agonizing. For I was empty, empty as a cleaned-
out bin. I was little John Talbot, just as I used to be. But John
Talbot who had been ravished, assaulted, invaded, possessed.
Something—someone?—had been within me that night. Yes—had
dwelt within me and been master of me.

I strained my ears into the dark. The rain lashed the half-raised window-pane and the sea roared and sulked, and sulked and roared.

In my terror as I lay, my heart beating thickly as though it were twisting a muffler round my neck, I waited, wondering whether that something would invade me again. In the dark room it seemed to be waiting, making no sound, its eyes not moving, watching, on the alert. . . . When would it cross the intervening space? Would I suddenly be aware of its naked entry, the thick limbs pushing between my ribs, the brain within my brain, directing, commanding, the wicked will, the lascivious mind . . .

To the falling mutter of the sea I feel asleep.

II

IN THE SPRING I went up to London. I had to see Leila Tunstall.

I went to see her as I might go to a physician. Looking back, I can see now that this journey to London was my first actual admission to myself that I was ill. I said quite simply to Eve: "My nerves are in bits. I know of a doctor in London. Charles Hopping told me about him. He's grand about nerves."

But she answered quite directly: "You're going to see Leila Tunstall."

"I shall call on her probably," I said.

"Are you in love with her?" Eve asked.

"Of course not."

"Because I shan't be in the least bit jealous if you are."

"Of course not. You're the only woman I've ever been in love with—or ever shall be."

"Well—are you afraid of her, then?"

"Afraid of her?"

"Yes—does she know something that no one else knows?"

"There's nothing to know."

I realized then that Eve was eaten up, obsessed, devoured by curiosity. Nothing now mattered to her beside the correct answer to this question: "What connection had I had with Jimmie Tunstall's death?"

His death had wrought some deep change in me. What was it that had occurred?

That last night before I went up to London I behaved to her like the cave-man of the popular novel. She enjoyed it. She responded as she had never responded to me before. For five happy minutes I cheated myself into believing that, after all, she loved me.

When I arrived in London it was a late spring evening, very lovely and delicate with a glistening light on the fresh trees and the pearl-grey stone of the buildings like pigeons' wings. When I had been half an hour in my hotel, however, I realized the apprehension everywhere.

A short while before, in March, Hitler had occupied Prague. Now, what would his next move be? I cared nothing for politics. I was an artist. But I had for years past hated the Nazis almost with hysteria. This evening, as I sat at a little table by myself and listened to an elderly man and woman expressing their horror of the Gestapo, I found myself, to my surprise, almost condoning Hitler in my mind. The two old people were discussing the news. On the day preceding (April 26, I see by my diary, was the date) Conscription had been announced and there had been Simon's new Budget, with its heavy tax on motor-cars, raising sur-tax and so on.

The two old people were saying that it was all Hitler's fault and what a devil he was and when was anyone going to have the courage to put a stop to his bloody deeds? They were very fierce-minded, and I remember that the lady's white-haired head had a perpetual tremble and the old gentleman had large brown warts across the backs of his hands. Only a little while ago how cordially would I have agreed with him. Now, as I studied sceptically my *vol-au-vent* (for this was not an expensive hotel), the thought shot hotly through my body: "Why shouldn't Hitler do his best for his country? It's quite true Germany must have expansion. Everyone denies it her. Hitler is a great man. . . ." And the chicken nearly choked me. I put down my knife and fork. I stared across the hideously decorated room. What had happened to me? This could not be I who was exonerating that band of cruel sadistic toughs? And if not I, who was it?

I could eat no more. I went out and walked the Bloomsbury streets. There were few lights. Only little red patches of colour and the dim swift opalescence from some passing taxi. . . . But in the sky there was a violet glow and a sweet soft air, an almost sacred silence. The British Museum was slumped against the sky, nonchalantly, as though it knew that all the relics of past time held within it made time timeless. But did they? I looked up at the sky, pierced with the sparkle of the stars and with the honied star-dust of countless worlds. From that same violet sky one bomb might one day fall, and where would the mummies be then?

A shiver of apprehension shook me and I realized, as I had never done before, that this world had lost, for the first time in history, all its security.

Then, on the opposite side of the street, I thought that I saw a sturdy, thick figure standing in front of the Museum gates. I thought I heard a chuckle and stayed breath-suspended, expecting to hear: "Hullo, Jacko . . ."

I crossed the street, determined that this time I would challenge him. But of course there was no one there.

I had Leila's address—15, Effingham Road, Surbiton. I wrote to her and she invited me to tea. It was a grey, cold day, with little promise of summer in it, when I caught my train at Waterloo and handed myself over to Suburbia.

I was in a curious state of eager anticipation—as though I had persuaded myself that an hour with Leila would set right all my troubles. I was going to be completely honest with her, and yet I was not going to be honest with her at all—for of course I would not tell her that I had killed her husband. What I *would* tell her was of my own unhappiness and I felt that she would lay her hand on my forehead and heal me. I did not ask myself, as I should have done—how could she heal me when I held back the truth from her?

One thing I learnt during this short journey to Surbiton. There was a short, stout, red-faced, elegantly-dressed man, with a carnation in his button-hole, sitting on the left side of the window. Suddenly his voice snapped at me: "Are you looking for someone, sir? If not, would you mind closing the window? Damned cold day."

Then I realized, as I had not until then done, that as the train started, I had leaned out of the window, peering up the platform as though looking for someone, and that even when the train had left the station, I was still staring up the line. I withdrew into the carriage, apologizing to the gentleman, murmuring something. As I sat in my corner I felt that my face had a furtive look and that my companion looked at me with suspicion.

I realized that I was now doing things without consciousness of them. This frightened me.

I walked from the station to Effingham Road. Rain was threatening and a little chill wind blew fragments of paper about my feet. It was indeed little like summer and I was glad to find a fire in the sitting-room where the maid left me while she went to summon Leila. The room's walls were thickly covered with very bad water colours, painted, I saw from the signature, by Leila's brother-in-law. Leila was staying with her sister. The piano had an old-fashioned air, because, I suppose, the music of Noel Coward's *Bitter Sweet* was open upon it.

There was a clock with a furtive ticking noise and a bird that rustled in a cage by the window. All these things made me feel that I should not get on very well with Leila's sister, so I was glad when Leila came in and said:

"Joan and Forrester have gone to the pictures. Wasn't it tactful of them?"

While the maid brought the tea and for some time after, we talked very conventionally. She was wearing black and it suited her. Her face seemed a little more crooked than it had been, but her eyes were as kind, as tender, as understanding as I had always so gratefully known them. Quite suddenly she said:

"John, what's the matter?"

"The matter?" I asked.

"Yes, you look a sick man."

"I'm not awfully well. I thought it was time I took some kind of holiday. But never mind me. Tell me about yourself."

"Oh, I'm all right! It takes some getting used to, you know—being a widow. If I didn't feel that Jimmie was still around I'd be very lonely."

"Do you like your sister and brother-in-law?"

"Very much. Forrester paints in his spare time, as you can see from this room." She laughed. "How Jimmie hated his painting! We stayed here once and I'm afraid they didn't get on at all."

"No, I know they didn't."

"What do you mean?"

I pulled myself up. "What a silly thing to say! Of course I didn't know. How much longer are you going to stay here?"

She sighed. "To tell you the truth, John, I don't know quite what I am going to do. This isn't like one's own home, of course, and although they are awfully good they don't, naturally, want me here for ever. The fact is—well, I am not very well off nowadays. Jimmie left nothing but debts, I'm afraid. I have a little bit of my own. I like London and I expect I shall take a small flat somewhere."

There was a silence. Then she said:

"How's Eve? And the boy?"

"They're very well. But I don't want Archie to go to school and Eve does."

"Isn't it better for a boy to go to school?"

"I was so miserable there myself and Archie's very like me in some ways—sensitive, you know, and shy."

"If you found the right school——"

"He'd have to go to the local place, where I was. We haven't much money to spare."

"How's your book getting on?"

"Not very well, I'm afraid. I haven't done much at it lately."

She leaned forward and laid her hand on mine.

"John—what's the matter? Tell me."

Then I broke down and did what I hadn't done for a long time—I began to cry.

She was deeply moved but with her great tact and understanding she did nothing to disturb me, only held my hand in her soft small one and waited.

At last I began to talk. I said that I was unhappy, frightened, that I didn't know what was happening to me. I could not get Jimmie out of my mind.

"You must not care what I say. Think that I am not right in my head. For that's the truth. My nerves are all in pieces. I know that

Jimmie is dead and yet I feel that he is not. He is always near me. Sometimes I even think he is inside me. Oh! keep him away! Keep him away!"

At that I fell on my knees at her feet and laid my head against her dress. I held to her as though she were my only anchor. My body shook. Then I felt ashamed of myself. I got up and sat down.

"I don't know why I should behave like this to you. We know one another very little, but I sometimes think you are the only good person I have ever met. I'm in this trouble because of my own sins. . . . I feel as though he—Jimmie—your husband were pursuing me. . . . I have this obsession. Show me, for God's sake, that that is all it is."

"For God's sake?" she asked.

"Yes. You believe in God, don't you?"

"Yes. I do."

"Pray to Him for me. Ask Him to help me. I don't believe enough. I can't believe enough. Soon—if this power gets more hold of me, it will be too late. Pray now. Pray now." Leila answered: "I do pray for you. I have for a long while. I knew that you wanted me to. I pray for you and Jimmie together."

"No. No. No . . . you mustn't. I hated him. I hate him still."

"So you think," she said. "But he needed my prayers just as you do now. He was obsessed with evil too—he wanted to be rid of it but couldn't."

"No, he didn't," I interrupted, fiercely. "He liked to be evil. He was evil. He is evil still."

"He was possessed by a devil. I used to tell him so. 'That's your devil, Jimmie,' I'd say—'not you.'"

"He was possessed by one so long that he became one." I didn't care how much I hurt her. Something inside me was crying out against something else inside me: "So you believe in evil?" I asked her. "A real power of evil in the world, always fighting good. A constant battle. A fight."

"Of course I do," she answered. "Nothing else explains life. If there weren't a fight there'd be no progress. If there weren't evil—strong, active, clever evil—there'd be nothing for good to put its teeth into. God has done us the great honour of giving us our own free will. We have to fight our battle ourselves. But He has given us things to aid us—the love and companionship of Jesus Christ, for one thing——" She stopped with a little laugh. "Now I'm preaching. But you asked me, didn't you?"

"Is it only my imagination that I think Jimmie is still alive?"

"I don't know what death is," she said. "If someone lives on in our minds and hearts, then for us anyway he isn't dead. More than that, I don't know."

"Does Jimmie live on like that with you?"

"Yes. He does."

"Then for both of us he is still alive. But for me he is evil—for you he is good."

She paused for a long time before she answered:

"I wouldn't say this to anyone but you, John. I feel he *is*, at this moment, evil. I have prayed and prayed to see him released from evil, but I can't. I think that at this time he is in the control of an evil spirit. If I have been conscious of any contact with him, it is an evil contact."

There was a dreadful silence in the room, made more menacing by the rustle of the bird in the cage.

"I must tell you something else," she added. "When you are near me, John, I feel that he is near me, too."

I did not answer her. My throat was as dry as sand.

She took my hand and held it tightly.

"You must think of certain things, John. One, that many—indeed most—wise, sensible, intelligent people would think these ideas nonsense. They would say, perhaps quite rightly, that our nerves have been shaken, that we are imagining absurdities. Secondly, that we are together in this, friends, and that whenever you want me I am there for you. And thirdly, that I, at least, believe in God and the love of Jesus Christ, and that the power of good is infinitely stronger than the power of evil. I think that just now the powers of evil are threatening not only us but the whole world, and that however successful they may seem to be for a time, they cannot win in the end. We must take a long view, the longest God allows us to have."

We sat there side by side in that dreadful cold silence.

"Think of me, John," she said, "whenever you begin to imagine anything bad. And don't run away from anything. Anything that is real to you *is* real to you, however absurd it may seem to anyone else. Face it. Face it. Even though you thought that Jimmie was in this very room, face him. Ideas are as real as facts, more real often. You can only get rid of them by facing them."

At that moment, as I now so desperately remember, the door opened. I don't know what, or whom, we expected to see, but in actual truth a mild little inoffensive man stood there, a little man in a rather shabby suit. He gave us a look and a smile, and said: "Oh, I say—I'm sorry," and before we could do or say anything, he was gone, very softly closing the door behind him. Leila laughed.

"That was Richard. So like him, appearing and vanishing like that."

"Richard?" I asked.

"Yes. My brother. You had forgotten I had one, hadn't you? He's been in China for years in a tea business. Now they've moved him to London. He's a darling. He's the human being with most goodness I've ever known."

"He reminds me of someone," I said.

"Well, if it wasn't too silly," she answered, laughing, "I'd say he reminds you of yourself. I'm sure I've mentioned it before. Don't you see the resemblance? At any rate to you as you were a few months ago. For you've fattened out, you know. Your cheeks are plumper. But I'll never forget the day I first saw you—the day Jimmie first brought you to the house. The physical resemblance was extraordinary. I positively thought it was Richard standing there. That's why I think I liked you from the very beginning."

My apprehension was gone. The room seemed normal and happy. I kissed Leila on the forehead.

"I've got what I came here for," I said. "I've been letting myself get foolish. I needed a change. That's what it was. Will you have dinner with me one night before I go?"

She promised that she would.

Part Two

NARRATIVE I

I

I COME NOW to an episode that seems to me, when I consider my past life, quite incredible, and is for me, in all my saner moments, of a peculiar horror. But I wish here to state the truth and omit nothing save the grosser aspects of the incident.

During this stay in London I found that the evenings and nights fascinated me. My little hotel in Bloomsbury was, in any case, not appetizing in the evening and theatres and cinemas seemed difficult. I asked a man at the hotel about the theatres.

"There's a very good piece at the Grand," he said. "I saw it last week. I *did* enjoy it."

"What sort of piece?" I asked.

He scratched his head. "I don't remember anything much about it, but it was excellent."

So even the theatres were veiled in mystery!

However, I was quite happy. I would take an omnibus down to Leicester Square and then walk up Piccadilly. As I have said, I had begun to be uncertain of my own identity. Was there really anyone called John Ozias Talbot? And if there was not, then none of this crowd that passed so dimly to and fro was an entity either. We were all fragments of fragment hanging like the wings of flies to a dead cinder! And yet how alive these ghostly figures seemed! How they laughed and jested as they passed me, making love, discussing food, gossiping about this shadow and that. But I did not feel lonely. I had the obsession that Tunstall now followed me everywhere and sometimes so closely that he and I were one. At other times my brain was completely clear. I knew, as I know now, that I was John Talbot, a separate independent soul, and that the shock following on what I had done had penetrated me as an illness. That this was all imagination about Tunstall and that I must conquer it with my strong, assured common sense.

Nevertheless, walking along these shadowy streets among these dim figures, I had sometimes crazy impulses. Once just outside Lyons' Corner House I almost grabbed a stout man in a waterproof by the arm: "Come inside and have some coffee with me. I will tell you a story. Then *you* can tell *me* whether I am not as sane as you are."

Happily I did not do this.

Then this very horrible thing occurred. I was walking westward along Piccadilly. I was almost opposite the Ritz Hotel. It was a wet night and two women were sheltering under a doorway. One of them said:

"Hallo, darling! Can't I speak to you?"

I walked forward a step or two. My heart was pounding in my breast. I was inflamed with desire. That is a conventional phrase, but it is how I was. Fire licked my loins. I had always felt a shuddering horror of such women. I had never understood how men could surrender themselves to such terrible company. Now, not only was I madly excited so that there was a singing in my ears and my mouth was dry, but I had been so before. This was, it seemed, an accustomed experience to me. I walked back with assurance to the women.

"Did you speak to me?" I asked. They had been chatting eagerly together, but the smaller of the two—she was a little bird-like creature with a face so painted that it resembled a mask—put her hand on my waterproof.

"Of course I did, darling. . . . Coming home with us?"

"What, with both of you?" I said, laughing, for I was bold, masterful, completely at my ease.

The other woman, tall and stout, said in a husky voice:

"You pays your money and you takes your choice."

They both laughed. I called a taxi. The little woman gave an address in the direction of Great Portland Street. Inside the taxi I sat between them, but they paid no attention to me at all. Across my body they continued their discussion about a certain Lucy

and a Mr. Board. How well I remember those names and that
Mr. Board had promised to call on a certain night and Lucy had
waited for him and been furious at losing an evening, for he had
not come and, indeed, was never heard of again and owed Lucy
quite a packet. And Lucy liked him more than a little, and still as
she walked from corner to corner in Piccadilly looked for him,
and things weren't too good for her, anyway, just now, as she was
fined four times last week and seemed to have lost all heart in her
business.

Their voices were compassionate and kindly, but I still burned
with this fire: my cheeks were flaming. The hand of the smaller
of the two women lay coldly in mine. She suddenly cried: "Christ!
but your hand's hot, darling!"

It seemed to me that I had ridden in this cab and heard these
words many times before. I felt big and masterful. My body seemed
to swell as I sat there. It would not be difficult for me to crush both
women in my arms. I felt that I had often crushed women in my
arms.

Then the fat woman said to the other (as though I were the
unhearing, unseeing specimen of some animal product), "He's
quite a little fellow, isn't he?"

They glanced at me, but not for more than a moment. "I don't
blame Lucy," the big one summed up. "I'd bloody well have done
the same myself. After all, if *he* wasn't there to pay she'd a right to
take it out of someone else—that's what *I* say."

"The poor soft!" the mask-faced woman said.

The cab stopped. We all got out. It was raining hard. I paid.

Evil builds up its dour atmosphere, doesn't it? I mean the evil for
which human beings are not responsible—evil like a wet dish-cloth
lying of its own volition on the edge of the table, the drops falling,
the pool assembling, the damp stench smoking in vapour. It was so
now in this house. As we climbed the stairs my nostrils were dank
with corruption, and of course, from above, there came the sound
of a tap dripping.

The big woman unlocked a door. We entered a sitting-room
and stood there.

"Now," the big woman said in a motherly housekeeping tone.

"We won't waste time. It's my room to the right, Molly's to the left—which do you prefer?"

The electric light showed a dusty room, heavy with chill. There was a piano. A pot with a fern. Some shabby bawdy prints in gilt frames. The prints were 'foxed' and the frames chipped.

I went into the room on the left with Molly. She undressed with lightning speed, saying not a single word. I whistled, I sang. I told her a story about Rio de Janeiro.

"How much are you giving me?" she asked.

"Five quid," I answered jovially.

"Thank God, I shan't have to go out again—raining monkeys and coconuts."

I was so wildly excited that my fingers fumbled with my collar-stud. This was only one of innumerable experiences. I sat on the edge of the bed and told her some stories. Aden, Marseilles, Brindisi, especially Brindisi. After that I nearly killed her. She scratched my cheek.

A vast enveloping horror and disgust chilled my poor ghost of a body. Slowly the little room that had been cloudy with a sort of exultation repeated itself to me. The cheap lace curtains, the round, black metal clock, my clothes on the floor, a cheap photograph of Velásquez' 'Rokeby Venus,' all these were symbols of my shame, my humiliation, my self-disgust.

"Tell me some more about Brindisi, strong boy," she said. She was lying on her back staring at me. "You know, to look at you one would never think——"

"I've never been to Brindisi," I said in a whisper.

"What!" she said. "You're a bloody liar! You've just been telling me——"

"I've never been to Brindisi." A strange longing for home pervaded me. To catch Eve's glance as she looked up from the table! But how dare I even think of her? My head hung. My hands were folded on my breast. I was bitterly, bitterly cold. She regarded me with some compassion. "You're shivering, and this room's as hot as hell. You'd better put some clothes on."

I looked at her intently.

"I want you to understand something. That was another man

who was with you just now. *He's* been to Aden and Brindisi and the rest. I haven't."

"You're crackers," she said. She sat up. "I've had 'em crackers before, and I know how to act with them, see? So don't you try——"

"I'm not trying anything," I said, my teeth chattering. I felt the fresh blood from the scratch on my cheek. "I'm only telling you. That wasn't me, that other man."

"What the hell do I care who it was as long as he pays the five quid? Don't forget it, darling, will you? Maybe I'll go out again. The rain don't sound so hard——"

I dressed. I laid a five-pound note on the mantelpiece. I went away.

2

I WAS MYSELF again. I was my complete, real, unalterable self. I was free. I had no thought of Tunstall, nor of his death, nor of his insistent neighbourhood. I had no desire for anything but my own life and the company of my wife and son.

In the train I sat closely folded up in my corner, reading *The House with the Green Shutters*, a novel that had once exerted a great influence upon me. So it did again now. This was the kind of novel that I wanted to write—in my own idiom, of course—but the figures of Bella Scorfield, Cheeseman, and the rest hung before me as starting-points from which my own creations should come. 'The Green Parrot' should be the background, and I saw the start of my novel with the wet, misty evening and the slap of the wave against the wooden skirting of the overhanging walls. I was myself again. I was creative again. I would abandon the novel that I had been writing and follow this new impulse. I sat there hugging my bony knees, thinking about Eve and Archie, feeling that I had been swept clean of whatever corruption had entered me. I was rid of Tunstall. Those odd obsessions had been simply the reaction from what I had done. I thought—how very strange! I have no shame at all because I killed Tunstall, but my cheeks burn if I think of Great Portland Street.

I pushed all such notions from me. I was going home. I would soon be with Eve and Archie again.

Oh, but I was happy when I entered my own home and saw my wife seated quietly reading and Archie at the table doing his homework. I caught her up and almost swung her off her feet. I kissed her again and again. She released herself, laughing:

"Here, here, John! Whatever's come over you? Glad to be home? I think you ought to be!"

Then she stood back and looked at me.

"Why, how you've altered! You're quite fat!"

"No, I'm not. I've not altered a bit."

"Yes, you are. The shape of your face has changed. It has, really! Why, your hair's thicker! That little bald patch is almost gone! And your eyebrows! You usen't to have any! What hair-restorer have you been using? It suits you, I'll admit."

I turned and looked in the glass. I could see no change except that my colour was high with my pleasure at being home again. My eyebrows? I put my hand up and felt one. It *was* a little thicker and I was pleased, because I had been teased about them when I was a young man. I kissed Archie and he seemed to like me, too. I spent a very happy evening with my family.

On the following afternoon, a beautiful day, I took a walk alone to think out the opening chapter of my new novel. I walked on the Common towards Shining Cliff. I had not intended to go that way; suddenly I found myself there. Birds were singing and the sea purred like a cat. At exactly the spot where I had encountered Tunstall on that wet, misty evening I encountered him again. . . .

When I say 'encountered' I want to be perfectly clear. I knew by now that you could encounter someone without seeing his physical body, that, in fact, we are all of us encountering many people every day whom with our physical eyes we do not see. I was aware now of the symptoms in the order in which they occurred. It was always the same. First there was a physical nausea similar to the suggestion of sickness that comes to you when your pipe goes suddenly bad on you. Then there was a quick, almost suffocating beating of the heart and a weakness through all the limbs. After that the certainty of the nearness. All of us have been in a street,

the room of an inn, a theatre, and are aware, with a stab of apprehension, that someone whom one greatly dislikes is drawing near.
One looks quickly round to see whether there is not some avenue
of escape, and if there is not time for that, one submits with the
best grace one may. After that there is the fear of contact, the sickening fear that one's body may be touched in some way. But my
apprehension of Tunstall was worse than this, for it was a peculiar physical fear, the sense that one's body would open and allow
this horrible presence in. When I had been a boy I had thought
that children emerged from the opening breasts of women. This
was the same except that it was an entrance rather than an exit. I
am trying to be exact in my terms, but no words can explain this
dreadful, degrading, sickening fear.

Now with the sun pouring down upon me and the birds singing
above me, I was rooted there, staring at nothing, my body like
water. The contact grew closer. I knew that it was but nervous
hallucination and yet I spoke aloud: "Ah, leave me! For God's sake
leave me! Spare me. Spare me—for pity's sake spare me!"

It is important, I think, that I should record that on this occasion I very distinctly saw a form, although I was aware, with full
conscious clarity, that there was no form there. It is very easy, if
you stare in front of you and then conjure up the physical presence
of someone, clothed or naked, whom you know well, to fancy
at last that that person is present. If you do this at a stated time
in the day and repeat the effort week after week, your imagination will supply all that you need. But to-day my experience was
rather different. I saw standing in front of me the stout body, the
laughing face, the bloodshot eyes, the thick eyebrows of Tunstall,
but I fancied that I also saw—some projection of myself! It was as
though the spectre of Tunstall were transparent, and as through
a glass I saw my own body *behind* his. At the same time, although
I did not move physically from where I stood, I felt as though my
spirit commingled with something—as your breath mingles with
another's when you kiss. This mingling was indescribably horrid,
as though I had been unnaturally ravished. I heard the sharp
metallic singing of a bird and the warm purr of the sea. Then I
fainted, crumpling up on the grass.

I came to myself to find that I was lying on the grass, my face wet and my head against Cheeseman's knee. He had splashed my face with water and was forcing some brandy between my lips. The dog Scandal was roughly licking my limp hand.

I have now, when I look back on the events that followed, no doubt whatever but that Cheeseman had been following me, probably from the town. I suspect that from the moment I returned from London he had been spying on me. It was of the Rat's nature to spy, to ferret out a secret, to discover something that would lead to blackmail. The scene at 'The Green Parrot' had, I don't doubt, excited his intensest curiosity.

In any case there he was, seated on a hard, flat stone, his carroty hair shining in the sun, a pipe between his lips, and his horrid white hands, with the red hair on their backs, resting one on his knee, the other at the flask of brandy pressed to my lips.

I sat up. I looked up at his face. I hated him, yes, but it seemed to me that he had been for years my companion and that we had shared many secrets. And I knew that that was not so.

"How did you come here?" I asked him none too graciously. With some trouble I got to my feet, feeling weak, sat down on the stone.

"I happened to be passing." He looked at me with eager, almost burning curiosity.—"I say—you did topple down! Whatever was the matter?"

"Oh, nothing. I go dizzy sometimes." My only desire was to get away from him. I was ashamed, oh, how deeply ashamed, that he had seen me. But he would not, of course, let me go like that.

"That dog's fond of you, isn't he? Funny. He'd never look at anyone but Jimmie when he was alive. . . . But, I say, what *was* the matter?"

"The matter? With me? Why, nothing at all!"

"Oh, but there was! I was taking a stroll—lovely afternoon and all that. I've been working on my roses all the morning. They're a fair treat, you ought to see them. So I strolled along, smoking my pipe, not thinking of anything in particular, when I saw you standing there as though you were turned into a statue, staring straight in front of you—staring like mad as though there were somebody there. Then you began to speak. I could see your lips moving. I couldn't hear what you said, of course—I didn't want to—I'm not the sort of man to spy on anybody. But you were talking as though there were somebody there. You were, really. And then quite suddenly, all in a jiffy, you throw up your hands and tumble forward on your face. I came up and you'd gone right off—you had, really. So I pulled you over here, splashed some water from that puddle on your face and gave you a drop from this flask. You're not properly round yet. You're as white as a sheet of paper."

"Oh, I'm all right." How I hated him! How I wanted him to go! Well, if he wouldn't, I would. I staggered to my feet, I could just stand.

"Thanks very much, Cheeseman," I said. "It was just a touch of the sun! I must be getting back."

"I'll come along with you."

"No, don't you turn back. It's such a lovely day."

He looked at me, grinning, his pipe clenched between his shining teeth.

"All right. If you don't want me. But do you remember my telling you a good while ago that you knew more about Jimmie Tunstall's death than anyone else alive? And so you do! There's some mystery here. And it's about here he fell over into the sea. I'm certain of it. On his way to Bella's. And you saw him or were close by or something."

I turned on him.

"You think you're clever, but you can't blackmail me, Cheeseman, as you do so many others."

He sprang to his feet.

"That's a bloody, dirty lie, and you shall——"

"Come along, Cheeseman," I said. "You can't put that over on me. Do you remember that you tried it once over what I told you about Brindisi, and how you failed?"

He stared at me as though I were indeed crazy. . . .

"Brindisi? But you've never been to Brindisi! That was Jimmie——"

We stood looking at one another. I picked up my hat that had fallen on to the grass. Cheeseman had to hold the dog tightly to prevent his following me.

No, I had never been in Brindisi. . . . The time had come for a quiet, unsensational, common-sense examination of my situation. And behind the common sense lurked a horror.

That night after Eve had gone up to bed I went to my little room where I worked. It was a hot summer evening. I could hear the lovely sound of the sea through the open window. I locked the door and then I stripped. There was a long old eighteenth-century mirror hanging on the right side of the window. In this I examined myself. Was I physically changed or no? I was stouter, heavier in the chest, the belly, the thighs. My face was fuller and rounder. There was nothing in that. I had always had a tendency to stout-ness. Then as I looked in the mirror I had a crazy hallucination that another naked figure was behind mine, a figure of exactly my height, heavier and stouter, the features of the face coarser and bolder, the hair thicker. And as I looked they merged and became one figure.

I did not faint now. I was absorbed as though I were studying an abstract problem. I put on my vest and drawers and sat down to consider.

The fact was simply this: the crime—or whatever you care to call it—committed by me—had affected my nervous system so deeply that I was the victim of a hallucination. My hallucination was that Tunstall was possessing me. Occupying me body and soul.

It was a crazy, meaningless, monstrous obsession, but unless I could rid myself of it, I was running straight to madness.

I sat there, the perspiration on my hands and forehead and chest. I must do something to prove to myself quite definitely, once and for ever, that this *was* an obsession—something . . . something . . . something . . .

And quite suddenly, as though it were whispered into my ear, I had the solution. I had heard that very morning that Bella Scor-field and her mother had shut up their house and gone away for ten days.

At night there would be nobody there. I had never in all my life been inside the house. I would enter it, walk upstairs and visit

Bella's bedroom. If my obsession were *not* an obsession, everything in that bedroom would be strange to me. If, on the other hand, the furniture and the rest were just as I expected them, then . . .

3

As SOON as the idea entered my head it became a passionate desire. Day and night now I thought of nothing else.

I made the most careful enquiries. I discovered that it was an actual and positive fact that the house was empty. Some neighbour visited it occasionally to make sure that all was well. He kept the keys, but I would tell no one of my purpose. Tunstall had told me once—or had he?—at any rate I knew it as a certain fact—that the window by which he entered was easily opened if you pushed a penknife between the wood that separated the two panes. He had entered in that fashion—how did I know this?—often enough. The period for the execution of my plan was limited. They were to be away for ten days. Their departure interested the town, for Mrs. Scorfield, it seemed, had not left her bed for over a year until now. They had gone to London, apparently, about a will or some legacy.

Eve, of course, noticed my new preoccupation. The relationship between us was now very peculiar. Sexually it was ardent for the first time since our marriage. She seemed to be developing a physical love for me that she had never felt before, and as she grew more affectionate I became less so. I saw several women in the town who were attractive to me. I began to think of women continually. She watched my moods with a passionate interest. I was often very unhappy and would sit brooding in my chair and not speaking. I appeared to have lost all interest, both in the shop and my writing, but my new accomplishment of drawing fascinated me. I had a queer technical facility although I had, of course, never taken lessons. I would make, almost without knowing it, indecent drawings, and then, with shuddering horror, tear them to fragments.

When Eve realized that some preoccupation was obsessing me, she could not let me alone. She had developed now a sort of 'flirting' with me. There was a sexual impulse behind all her words. She did her best to discover my secret and one evening came very near to it.

Looking up at me and smiling provocatively she said:

"You must be fearfully bored, John, now that both your belles are away."

"My belles? I have none."

"Once you hadn't. *I* was your only love. Now there are others and oddly enough I like you the better for it."

It was strange to me when I looked at her how coarse and common she could sometimes be.

"Who are my belles, then?"

"Bella Scorfield and Leila Tunstall, of course."

"What nonsense! You are and always have been the only woman I've ever looked at."

"Nonsense! You are a regular Don Juan nowadays. Everyone is talking about it."

There is nothing more irritating than to be told that 'everyone' is talking!

"What an absurdity! Everyone talking about me! They have better things to do."

"They are, all the same—the change in you. Why, even, they say, you look different. They ask me what I've been feeding you on. Someone the other day said that you were quite gay with women now. I'm afraid they used to think you a very dull dog indeed—and so did I sometimes. Certainly you've changed. I've got a lover now as well as a husband, but I don't want too many other women to discover that you've altered."

I was drinking a mild whisky and soda.

"Perhaps it's the whisky."

"Nothing could be milder." I held up the glass for her to see.

"No, but it isn't always so mild. There's quite a whisky bill nowadays. Until recently you loathed the smell of it. Not that I mind a man drinking a little. It makes him more amiable."

As she had coarsened so had I. I was drawing some other self out of her that through all our years of married life I had not known existed.

"But you must not get too fat, John. You haven't the figure to carry it."

"Everyone says I'm putting on weight. I'm not really."

"Of course you are! Look at that scarab ring that used to belong to poor Jim Tunstall. It's quite embedded in your finger. You can't pull it off."

I tried. She was right. The thing seemed to cling to my flesh, to be part of my body, and as I pulled at it, the green markings were most vivid. The beetle, under the artificial light, seemed to be alive.

The time had come. I dared not leave it any longer. The evening I chose was dimmed with warm, misty rain. I did not wish to be seen by anybody—in fact I must *not* be seen. The misty rain would obscure me.

I told Eve that I was going to the cinema and I started out. It is very difficult for me to describe the mixture of fear and a kind of greedy ecstasy that was in my heart. Partly I knew that my purpose was absurd. I had never entered the house and therefore could not know what it contained. That was clear. On the other hand a wild and exaggerated excitement urged me forward. Something in me whispered that it would be wonderful to be there again. Something else in me—the strongest of these emotions on my setting out—tried to hold me back from visiting Shining Cliff again. I was now *afraid* of Shining Cliff. I had not been. A few weeks ago I would have visited it at any time of day or night without a tremor. But now I wished dreadfully *not* to go. As I approached the place I felt the damp sweat on my forehead. It may have been, of course, the thin rain which spider-webbed the air exactly as it had done on that other evening.

I was walking fast. I was perspiring. The beat of my heart was uncomfortable. There was no doubt but that I had grown stouter, for my body was heavy under my clothes, the clothes clinging to it and yet the body staying separate and apart as it does when it is frightened. In fact I noticed a queer thing, which was that as I approached the Cliff more nearly, physical symptoms arose in my body that did not really belong to me. Any of us who have lived a long time have become accustomed to certain physical properties—a small bone aches in the left wrist; there is a little cough at times that is peculiarly ours; a toe on the right foot burns fierily in certain weathers. I was aware in myself now of new symptoms that were yet accustomed ones. Having been always spare, a teeto-taller and a sparse feeder, my stomach had rarely troubled me. But now I was constantly aware of a sort of heartburn that comes from indigestion. My heart, too, sometimes made me breathless. My neck felt thick and congested. And I noticed on this special evening that the scarab ring dug into my finger as though it bit me.

So I stopped for breath at the very spot on the Cliff whence I had thrown Tunstall over. I was all alone to-night and I longed for company. I would have welcomed anybody, Cheeseman or another. The rain stroked my cheeks with greedy fingers. What a fool I was to pursue this fantasy! And who could say? I might be arrested by the local policeman for housebreaking and what an ignominious thing that would be! Nay—more than ignominious, dangerous. For once they began an enquiry as to why I should enter at night the Scorfield house, their enquiries would stretch further.

My own self, as I stood in my waterproof dismally shivering on the Cliff edge, urged me to go home. Something else in me, hot, lustful, reckless, drove me forward. I went on.

I found, to my intense relief, that I did not know the way. Then, indeed, I might have turned home, for had I not proved my case? I did not know the way. I hesitated at every turn. But as I hesitated I felt as though I were deliberately myself holding back informa-tion from myself, or as though something devilish in me was mali-ciously refusing to tell me what I longed to know—"I could tell you the way. Are you so idiotic as to fancy that I don't know it? I am well aware of every single step and turn, but wait . . . wait . . . I am watching to see what you will do—you poor, pitiable, fright-ened fool!"

Have we not all at times noticed just such scornful bullying voices within our own breasts? At one point I did almost turn home. I had left the sea-path, crossed a little wood and come to the parting of the ways. I was sure that the little rough-stoned path to the left must be the one to take, and yet my feet seemed to drive me to the other. I had to force myself to take the path to the left.

And then most abruptly I came upon the house. It squatted there in sulky, sodden silence. The thin misted rain blew in gusts across my eyes. Dark wet laurels crowded almost to the windows. The ragged drive halted before the steps of the pillared door. To the left was the lawn and I crossed over to this and looked up at the building's other side. How I hated that house with the long dead windows, the beat of the sea seeming to break against their hostile glass, the chimneys appearing to raise insulting ears to me against the dreary sky. No one was there. No one ever had been there. It was a house of kitchen-ghosts and cellar-phantoms!

"Now—do you know the place?" something seemed to whisper to me. But I did not—triumphantly I did not. I could have gone down on my knees on the sopping grass and thanked my Maker.

I was myself. I was myself, and no one else, and had never seen this beastly house before! Ah, but it would have been well for me if I had turned then and run the whole way home!

But already, as I stood on the lawn, it was as though some other quite opposite past-consciousness was approaching my brain. I walked forward towards one of the windows, and as I walked it seemed to me that I had crossed just here a hundred times. I was near to the window. I had pressed my nose against it. Then, like a man obeying a command, I took out my pocket-knife.

I pushed up the lower pane and, bending my back, climbed into the room. It was dark with a sort of musty greenish darkness— or so I felt. The furniture stood about like watching spies, but I realized with a kind of reassurance, as though a friend had laid his hand on my shoulder, that I did not know *what the furniture was*. There were dim pictures on the walls. Opposite me was a portrait, but I could not tell from where I was whether it were male or female. I could not tell! I could not tell! "Can you not?" a voice whispered to me. It was like a physical voice, thick and husky. "Jacko, can you not?"

I dared not move—I felt as though with one step I should advance into some horror from which I should never again escape. And so indeed it has proved. For I am now in that horror—and I shall never again escape! Oh, God! What have I done that Thou shouldst so horribly punish me? Or if my crime is so great—and even as I write these words they mock me by their foolishness. There *is* no God but in the silly superstitions of man's heart. . . . I did not move. I was trembling with a kind of sick disgust. I may have muttered—I cannot tell for sure—"Leave me! I am not yours. . . . I am my own master. . . ."

And then I think I heard the mocking voice—"Jacko . . . Jacko . . . Jacko!"

I only know for sure that wretchedly I knelt down on the floor and took off my damp boots. My fingers muddled with the wet laces.

On my stockinged feet I crept into the hall and began to climb the stairs. A clock began to strike. With agonized certainty I stayed and waited, for I *knew* that before the last stroke there would be a whirr and a grumble as of an old man coughing. I waited. It was so. I moved anxiously lest the boards of the stairs should creak.

In the passage above I moved left. I pushed at a door (I had no doubt now as to *which* door) and entered. I did not switch on the light. I knew exactly how the furniture was. The bed against the wall and on it a pink counterpane. Next to the bed a small table and a lamp with a silver-grey shade. A round tin box covered with an old print of Westminster Abbey that held biscuits. Above the bed two pictures, prints from Hogarth's 'Marriage.' Above the fireplace, two birds in Lalique. A wardrobe of dark mahogany. An easy cushioned chair coloured rose.

I switched on the light. The room was as I have said. I threw off my coat and waistcoat. Then, staring at the bed, breathing fiercely, I pulled my shirt up over my head . . .

NARRATIVE II

I

... The War has lasted two months now and I caused quite a stir at Leila's tea-party yesterday afternoon by what I said. Eve was there, the Parrott, Richard Thorne, Leila's meek-and-mild little brother (who is, so everyone says, the image of what I used to be!), and several pious ladies and gentlemen, the sort that Leila likes to have around her, and Mr. Birthwaite of St. Peter's, a stout, muscular clergyman, the sporting 'Play Football for Christ' clergyman, the kind that I detest.

Well, there we all were, in Leila's little house (she has come back to Seaborne after all), something of the cottage-bungalow variety not far from the sea. There she lives with one little maid most modestly. Her brother Richard, who was in the East so long, stays with her and pays her expenses partly, I imagine.

I think that I disliked that fellow on sight and now I positively hate him. He knows that I do and there is that sort of secret relation between us. Why do I hate him?

Well, I've become a violent domineering kind of fellow lately and I'm proud of it. How I despise that old miserable John Talbot creeping and crawling about, afraid of his wife, afraid of his son, trying to write ridiculous feeble books that no one could possibly want, afraid of a dirty story, of companionship with rough-and-ready chaps like Cheeseman and Bob Steele. Yes—nor am I afraid of Tunstall's ghost any more. I can see that I was altogether wrong when I thought so badly of Tunstall. I can see now that he was only teasing me half the time. I hate myself—or rather my old self—for pushing him over that Cliff, and that is why I think I detest Richard, Leila's brother.

It's almost as though *he* pushed Tunstall over. Physically he's just the man I used to be but, thank heaven, am no longer. Other people have noticed it. He's got no eyebrows and is pasty-faced and

has a thin, poor physique. He won't touch whisky or any intoxicating liquor and is as quiet as a mouse, sitting in a corner of the
room without speaking, just as I used to do.

He gave me a start the other day when he asked me whether I'd
read any of Gissing's novels and whether I didn't like him. I said
that I used to like them once, but had grown out of them.

I added, in that rough way that I like to put on with people who
are frightened of me, that I hadn't much time for reading now
and that anyway Gissing seemed to me a miserable sort of writer.
I liked a novel to have some meat in it. He looked surprised at
that and said he'd asked me because he thought my novels showed
Gissing's influence.

"My novels!" I answered, laughing. "Don't you mention them
to *me*! I'm thoroughly ashamed of them. If I had time to write now
I'd put some meat into them—a bit of skirt, that's what people
want in a novel."

I felt in a sort of rage with him because somewhere deep down
in me I felt ashamed of what I'd said, and I *hate* to be ashamed of
myself and I'd kill anyone who made me feel so.

My fierceness frightened him and he went away without saying
anything.

For one reason, anyway, I like to be with him. Looking at him
reminds me of what I *used* to be. I can estimate it the more truly
because we're about the same height, he and I. How I've filled
out! It's astonishing. It's not only that I'm broader and thicker
altogether, but you'd imagine I'd been using some restorer by the
way my hair grows. On the head, my eyebrows, quite thick on my
chest—everywhere that a manly man ought to have hair! I've got
a chest for hair to grow on, too! *And* a bit of a stomach if the truth
must come out.

I think it is due to the open-air life I lead. None of that skulking
about in that silly shop any more. Eve manages that entirely. I play
golf, I shoot, I fish. You may say it's late for a man to begin all these
things, but Basil Cheeseman, Steele, and some of the others have
shown me the way—yes, and to other things, too!

All in the space of less than a year, and if you ask me I'd say that
it's never too late for a man to learn. Not that I'm always in good

spirits. No one is! And I drink a bit too much. Then I've been developing the devil of a temper lately. There's something in me beyond my control, and when I see red I often wish I didn't. But there! We can only live once and while we live let us enjoy ourselves.

At any rate, whatever else I am, I'm not a hypocrite. What I mean I say!

It was the hypocrisy that made me so bloody mad at Leila's when they were discussing this War. Of course, down in this little place, except for the Black-Out we haven't felt the War yet at all. People are all saying it's a phony war, not like a real war at all.

They were all sitting round as usual, clinking the teacups, nibbling little bits of bread and butter and saying all the usual things— that Hitler and Goering and the others were emissaries of the Devil, and that we were all saints and the saviours of civilization.

I listened for a bit and then I could stand it no longer. I said that what we were was a nation of hypocrites. What right had we to stop Germany from expanding if she wanted to? We had more than half the globe, anyway, and how had we got it? By plundering, thieving, bullying natives. For my part, I thought Hitler was a fine fellow. He had brought his people up from miserable subjection to be a great people again. He was clever and knew what he was about, while we were stupid and decadent. All that Hitler did was to go for what he wanted. After all, he had the strength and was using it.

"I suppose," the parson said in that gooseberry-in-the-throat sort of voice that parsons have, "you'd say that Might is Right—a wicked doctrine and straight from the Devil."

"I don't know about the Devil," I said, in that laughing boisterous voice that I enjoy using, "but I do know that we're a nation of hypocrites and if Germany defeats us we deserve it."

There was a shocked silence after that and only Leila said: "You wouldn't have said that once, John."

Now I like Leila. I have always liked her, but of late that liking has greatly increased. For one thing she is, I think, the only person in the world who really understands me. She is certainly more understanding of me than my wife.

I am not, of course, in the least in love with her. I am keeping this journal day by day, all that remains of my old writing habit, and I may say that at this actual moment of writing I am more at ease with her than with any other human being alive. The feeling that I have for her, queerly enough, is rather as though I had been married to her for many years. I have for her that sense of companionship that comes from long mutual and physical contact, and that is certainly peculiar because we have been nothing more than casual friends. There was, of course, that rather absurd scene with her in London when I was sentimental and wept. But at that time my old self, which I regard now as feminine and ridiculous, was uppermost. It would take something very remarkable to make me weep to-day.

When, however, she said that once I would not have spoken as I did I was abashed. I was angry with myself for being so and left as soon as possible.

My outspokenness about Hitler has been reported and I am aware that numbers of people in this silly little town now look on me unfavourably. Not that I give a damn! When I was meek and mild and took care to offend nobody, they said that I was a milksop. Now that I show some spirit and speak my mind, they say that I was better as I used to be. Well, let them say! If this town is typical of England, then I declare, and I don't care who hears me, that England is finished and done for and deserves to be beaten by the Germans, whose courage and resource and daring I cannot but admire!

I must say something now about my home affairs. The other evening I had a quarrel with Eve and some curious things were said during it.

Eve loves me and sometimes I wish she did not. I know that if once I had written this down on paper I should have been wild with joy, about her loving me, I mean. I am sure she has nothing to complain of me as a husband, but after all, when you have been married for as long as we have, it is only natural and right that the physical part of marriage should take a secondary place. Other things are of more importance. But whereas that side of marriage is of less importance to me it seems to be all-important to Eve. The plain fact is that she is absurdly jealous and would like to make scenes every night if I allowed her to. She is for ever wanting to know where I have been; what I have done; to whom I have spoken.

The other evening after dinner, when I was happily enjoying a whisky and soda, she put her hand over the decanter.

"No, John—you've had enough for to-night."

I could scarcely believe my ears.

"Who says?" I asked.

"I do," she answered. I could see that she was a little frightened and I like her to be frightened.

"Oh, you do, do you?" I said.

"Yes. . . . Oh, John, do listen to me! I've been wanting to say something for weeks!"

She always looks her best when she has tears in her eyes. That excites something in me. She is like one of those old Virginal Priestesses who is suddenly human and pleading.

"Go ahead!" I said, stretching out my legs.

"There was a time," she began, "when I wanted you to be more dashing, more of a man, to go about more . . . but now . . ."

"Well—now?" I asked her mockingly.

"I haven't the right to speak, perhaps. You know what you're doing and I must confess that I *am* much fonder of you than I used to be. You're much more of a man—physically and in every way. But need you—don't be angry with me—drink as much as you do? Need you always be with men like Cheeseman and Bob Steele and young Romilly? Then you offend people by the way you speak to them, swearing and saying you're pro-German and things like that. I know I'm jealous. I never used to be. But then you never used to look at other women—I sometimes wished you did. Sometimes you're so angry with me and over nothing at all. I'm sure it's drinking makes you lose your temper. Sometimes when you're angry you look terrible. I feel as though you weren't the old John at all, your face is so changed. Don't you think—please, please, don't be angry—that if you drank less and went back to your writing again you'd be happier, that we'd all be, you, I and Archie? I'm sure Archie loves you, but he's afraid of you, you know he is. And I'm afraid of you sometimes, too. And you're not really happy—we none of us are."

She ended breathlessly, her eyes beseeching mine, and she put her hand on my arm.

I did what all proper husbands would do. I poured myself out another glass of whisky.

Then I said, quietly:

"Have you quite done?"

She nodded: "Yes—we've always been honest with one another, John—said what we think."

"Yes—well, I'm going to say what *I* think. If you don't like it you can bloody well lump it. That's coarse and vulgar, I know, but then I *am* coarse and vulgar. I wasn't once, and you didn't like it. I am now and you don't like that either."

(It's agreeable to write dialogue again. There's something in me, some remnant of my old life, that sometimes cries out for the novel-writing again. Well, if I ever *do* write another novel it will be a bit more lusty than the earlier ones were!)

"Not that *I* care what you think. For years and years I was your slave, wasn't I? Do you remember our coming away from a party at Tunstall's house once and your being angry with me for not liking him and threatening to leave me? As a matter of fact you were right that evening. Tunstall wasn't such a bad sort, only I was such a damned prig that I took him too seriously. But do you remember that when you threatened to leave me I broke down and said I'd do anything to please you—crawled in fact—and how you graciously forgave me like a queen her slave? Do you remember that, Eve? You had your time, you know, and a grand time it was. But the worm *will* turn—and *when* it turns, it changes. This worm isn't a worm any longer—see? Nothing like a worm. Quite a different animal."

I thought this a good speech and sat back in my chair, pushing my stomach out and feeling thoroughly pleased with myself. I had been drinking quite a bit. But, after all, it was Eve who astonished me, for she didn't answer anything that I had been saying, but asked, very quietly, this question:

"John, what was it you did to Jim Tunstall?"

I can tell you that that astonished me. All the questions and whispers about Tunstall's death had died down by now. No one had mentioned him for months. There seemed to be a sort of conspiracy *not* to mention him.

I myself hadn't thought about it, and the sense that I used to have about his being near to me, the horror, the suspense, the terror—all that had gone—yes, really gone except for some unhappy moments about which I will have something to say in a minute. The *great* change in me now is that I admire Tunstall instead of hating him. By God, I do! He seems to me now the only man who woke this place up a bit. You may say that in a small way I copy him. Basil Cheeseman says, laughing, that I *became* Jim Tunstall as soon as I put his scarab ring on my finger. "Why, you're getting to be the spitting image of him," he said, and we had a good laugh about it. I had an absurd and most dangerous temptation to say: "I can't be Tunstall because I killed him"—a crazy thing to say to the Rat, who isn't to be trusted a yard. Although I like him, mind you. He is damned good company; he knows the hell of a lot about everyone in this place and *nothing* to their credit—and, by heaven, he *can* grow roses!

He said that to me about being like Tunstall yesterday when he handed me over Scandal.

"It's no use my keeping him," he said. "The damned dog is never happy except when he's with you. It's a funny thing. He was just the same when he was with Tunstall. He's a one-man dog, I suppose."

As a matter of fact Scandal was lying at my feet when I had this row with Eve. He's a ripping little dog, his hair curly like shavings and his whiskers as strong and virile as though made of wire. He looks at me with the most loving eyes, and yet he's as sporting a dog as ever I've seen. He obeys me as though he were my familiar spirit. A funny thing, too, that he'll have nothing to say to Eve or Archie. He's quite polite and endures their pattings and strokings, but he's as distant from them as the parson is from me.

I'm sitting here writing and it's late, and I know that Eve is in bed unable to sleep, waiting for me to come to her. That gives me considerable satisfaction.

I must return to my quarrel, from which I have considerably wandered. I didn't answer her question at once. I should have done, but that uncomfortable and maddening consciousness I have (I shall speak of it later) of something unhappy, lonely, desolate (silly words these, and most unfit for a man to use), came up into my throat and choked my words.

At last I said: "What *do* you mean? What did I do to Tunstall? Why, nothing, of course. Do you think I killed him?"

"No . . . not that." I saw that she was picking her words. "But you met him that night. I am quite certain that you did. And it was from that night that you changed, and it was from that night that I began to love you. It was from that night that we all began to be unhappy, Archie and you and I. You have changed more and more. Your face has changed, your voice, your habits—everything. You know it as well as anyone. You don't love me any more, either."

"Of course I do," I said.

"You do?" She caught me up eagerly. "Oh, John, promise me that and I can stand anything. Promise me that you love me, even though it's in a different way. Do you—do you really?"

Everyone knows that there is nothing in the world more exasperating than to be asked again if you love someone whom in fact you love no longer.

I *like* Eve, of course. She is a fine woman, and I admire her when she is brisk and business-like and unsentimental. But love? I don't, I fancy, love anybody—unless it's my son. Yes, I love Archie and must admit that I have a damned funny way of showing it sometimes.

Anyway, I was exasperated and irritated and had been drinking, so I'm afraid I swore at her and said a lot of things I shouldn't have said.

I spoke with great bitterness and I think that I had a right to. I said that she accused me of being changed, but what about herself? Did she realize what her behaviour had been during the last months? That I couldn't go anywhere, speak to anybody, without her wanting to know all about it.

"It isn't true! It isn't true! I haven't . . . I don't . . ." she burst in. Her eyes were fixed on me, pleading, begging me, but I felt no temptation towards mercy. I had better put my foot down once and for all. Every man knows that it's a case of either the husband or the wife. I was master here now whatever I had once been, and I intended to go on being master.

I'm not a sadist (or only as much of one as any real man is), but I have noticed lately that my blood begins to rage and my heart beat thickly over quite small occasions. There *is* something in what Eve says. When I am excited or angry I *know* that my face changes. I can feel that my eyes are bloodshot and a heavy pulse beats in my temples. I like to feel this. I feel masterful and ready to beat the world.

All this about feelings! And I notice that I have repeated the word 'feel' in three adjacent sentences, which the careful John Talbot of a year ago would never have done. Not that I care. I'm not writing this for publication! I simply get rid of my superfluous energy this way. Well, I told her that I wasn't going to be spied on. I should go where I pleased and see whom I pleased. I was answerable to nobody. Did she understand that?

Yes, she said. Oh, yes, she did.

Another thing, I went on—she must understand once and for all that I wasn't a sentimental man. I might have been once, but I wasn't now. Actually it was she who had taught me not to be by being so cold for so long and refusing my advances when I offered them. It would be better, perhaps, if we had separate rooms. She broke out at that and begged, implored me not to do that. As a matter of fact, this had been in my mind for some time and I determined to settle the question here and now. I told her that I could have a bed in my working-room very easily and that I would see about it. There was nothing to make a fuss about—we could see each other when we liked just as we had always done. I was often out late and it was much better not to disturb her.

"I lie awake——" she began.

"Well, you're not to lie awake," I said. "That is just what is so irritating." It's maddening, I told her, coming back at one or two in the morning and finding her waiting for me. Besides, most modern married people had separate rooms, nowadays.

Then there was the question of Archie. How dare she say that I frightened him? The fact was that she had fussed altogether too much over Archie. She would make a regular mollycoddle of him.

I was determined to stop it. It was funny to remember, I remarked, that it was she who had wanted to send Archie to school and I who had wished to keep him at home. Well, I had given in about that, hadn't I? He had gone to school, which was what she wanted, and yet she fussed over him when he was at home, making him quite unfit for being with other boys.

She replied, in a voice so low that I could scarcely catch her words, that all that she meant was that she wanted him to love me and when I was angry——

That infuriated me. If she interfered between Archie and me, I told her, she'd have to look out. She'd get something she wasn't expecting. That was something I wouldn't stand. She'd better look out! She'd better look out!

I'll admit that I was rather excited at this point and shouted a bit.

Then she began to cry. I can't stand it when women cry. It does something to me. It excites me. I got up and stood close to her. I didn't say a word. I saw the chairs and the table in a blur——

She sat there, looking up at me as though she were waiting for something. Scandal, I remember, raised his head and looked at me. I went out of the room.

I've recalled every word and every detail of this little scene because it gives me pleasure to do so.

I have now come to the time when I should write a clear and honest account of my strange affair with Bella Scorfield. Honest? If I'm not that I'm not anything. I'm not ashamed of anything I do or say or feel. Why should I be? I am so honest that I'm not going to deny that something curious goes on in my brain that I don't at all understand. Insanity is a big loose word. I know that for a long time I was afraid that I was going insane, but after that visit to the Scorfields' house when they were away, I threw over my scruples and fears altogether and became the altered man everyone says I am.

But between myself and this paper I'm not altered as completely as I would wish; I wouldn't like anyone to know that, and especially not Eve. The fact is there's something of the old man imprisoned in me still. I have quite unaccountable moods of the old, weak sentimental idiot I used to be—moods when it is almost as though something were imprisoned in me, trying to get out. I crush them quickly enough, of course, and after they are ended I hate myself for indulging them. Just as in the old days I used to hate poor Jim Tunstall for stirring just the opposite in me. I can see now that he was trying to make a man of me. If I'd realized that earlier, we might have been friends instead of enemies. If he was around now we would be friends, I'm sure.

I understand, though, why it is that I dislike Leila's brother, Richard, so much. He reminds me whenever I see him of what I *used* to be! He's for ever apologizing and he's so polite that it makes you sick. When I'm sarcastic with him—as I generally am— he blushes all over—exactly as I used to do.

And that's why I hate him. I don't want to be reminded a dozen times a day of the fool that I must have seemed to other people. And how I loathe that milk-and-water, down-on-your-hams, 'I won't touch you if you don't touch me' kind of attitude. He's so good and virtuous! A sort of saint! He even wears the kind of clothes I used to—rather shabby blue or black. G-rrr! If he doesn't look out I'll twist his neck one day!

Now I must tell the truth—amusing and instructive to me to see it all put down on to paper—of my affair with Bella Scorfield. I confess that I'm proud of the clever fashion in which I conducted it. I was a fool about women once—but now—oh, boy!

Very soon after Jim Tunstall's death, Bella began to take an interest in me. She was lonely, I don't doubt, poor thing. Wanted *some* man's embraces, didn't matter whose!

But that isn't quite true. She loved Jim Tunstall in her own brainless, common, passionate way. Often, after a while, she said that I reminded her of him. It is true that with all my outdoor life I began to thicken out and take on a sort of tan.

She told me only last night that she couldn't ever bear skinny men, and that she had always liked me and admired my brains but had hated the idea of being kissed by me because she'd feel my cheek-bones.

"And now you're quite plump," she said, pinching me just as you would a chicken in a shop. She's pleased, too, that I have hair on my chest. Any proper man ought to have, she said.

Now the odd thing is that from the moment I gave poor Tunstall that push over the cliff, she began to be afraid of me. Basil Cheeseman had told her that I had had something to do with Tunstall's death or, at any rate, knew more than I would say. She wasn't a brainy girl but she told me that from the first I was always reminding her of Tunstall.

I didn't tell her, of course, of the night that I had entered their house. That would have sounded altogether too mad, but I did wonder at the ridiculous fuss that I made over that visit. After all, Tunstall had given me a few details of that bedroom when he had given me also details of certain other things and I had subconsciously remembered them. No, but what fascinated me was that I should go back into that house and do *exactly* what Jim Tunstall had done—repeat one of his evenings in every sort of particular. At the very suggestion of this to myself my brain would grow heated, my heart hammer in my throat. I would grow weak at the knees with desire.

So passionate became my longing for this event that I would lie beside Eve at night thinking of it, going over again and again every detail. Why did I want it so desperately? It was not only Bella, not only the sense of adventure. It was, I suppose, a hark-back to the day when Tunstall had taken me by the arm and whispered in my ear.

It was, also, something, something . . . a reminiscence? What other lives have we lived? Do we not sometimes repeat an experience that we have had in one of them? Who can tell? In any case Bella gradually fell in love with me, but never lost her fear of me. Then came a time when I knew that she was ready to do anything that I asked her. But I waited. I savoured the anticipation. I did not wish to lose a moment of it.

Then came the occasion. I asked her.

"You know that I am in love with you, Bella."

"I like you, too, very much." She went on: "I've been lonely since Jim was killed."

"Don't say 'was killed,'" I said. "Poor fellow, I've missed him a lot."

"And you used to say you hated him! How you've changed—

and it's since you've changed I've liked you so much. You often remind me of Jim. Perhaps that's why."

We were sitting at a little table in the corner of the 'Paradise.' I can't remember what she said after that, but I explained to her exactly what I wanted. She is a girl with a full bosom and high colour and fair hair. She's what a woman ought to be, full of good, warm blood. You could see the blood mounting in her cheeks now. She said—wasn't there something nasty about it? I said, no, of course not. I said that Jim had told me so often about it. He'd understand. Perhaps he'd been watching us and giving us his blessing.

I could see that she didn't care how I made love to her as long as I did it. She had been wanting exactly that for months.

"But what will your wife say?" she asked.

"Oh, she can lump it," I answered, looking her full in her bold eyes. I felt as though I had had her in my arms many times, but not for a long while. Of course it wasn't so. It was only my fancy. But I was triumphant in a wild sort of way as I looked at her. We arranged all the details.

I told Basil Cheeseman about it. I'll confess that I have fallen greatly under his influence of late. There was a time, I know, when I didn't like him at all, even hated him. I seem, when I look back, to have hated him for years. I wouldn't say that I like him now. I don't think anyone could. And certainly I don't trust him. But I don't know a better companion anywhere; he's a wonderful fellow for bawdy stories that really *are* funny; he can drink anyone under the table, and he's ready for any sort of adventure. I am not sure, though, that I can account for his influence over me. He's a great lad for ferreting out people's weaknesses and then making use of them—like Hitler. But, for some reason or other, I'm a proper mystery to him. He knew Tunstall better than anyone else did, and he keeps telling me that being with me is like being with Tunstall all over again. His favourite question is: "How the hell did you know about Brindisi?" It seems that some while ago I said something about an adventure in Brindisi that only he and Tunstall knew. He says that I often tell him things that only he and Tunstall knew—which is, of course, nonsense.

I frighten him sometimes and I'm glad I do, for that keeps up my self-respect. He's such a miserable physical specimen with his little moustache and prominent teeth and red hair and eternal pipe. I could catch him round the throat with one hand and throttle him easily. I nearly do sometimes. He says that Tunstall, when he was drunk, used to threaten him with the same thing. "I always told him," he said, "that he was born to be hanged."

But when I told him about Bella he was for once quite shocked.

"I say, Talbot—she was Tunstall's girl, you know."

"What the hell does that matter?"

"Oh, I don't know—but going to the same room—everything the same——"

"He shouldn't have told me so much about it," I said, laughing.

He looked frightened—a thing he seldom does. I asked him why.

"You look—— Oh, hell! I don't know how you look! I tell you what it is, Talbot—your eyes have the most unpleasant sort of stare in them sometimes."

So, just for fun, I put my hand on his shoulder. I felt him quiver all over, but he didn't say anything and he didn't move.

The evening came all right. It was three nights ago as a matter of fact. There was a thin baby moon and a clear sky. When I got to the house it was as silent as the grave. The lawn was like milk. I'm not going in for a lot of description. I leave that to my old writing days. But I could paint it, I think (I've come on a lot in my painting)—with the house so dark and still and all those beastly laurels. I hate masses of laurel close up against a house. They seem to speak of death. They are so chill and leathery and seem to have a creepy life of their own. I was anything but chill myself. I was burning all over and my hands shook. I pushed up the window, climbed into the room, took off my shoes and went up the stairs. I opened her door and there she was, sitting up in bed waiting for me. I took off my coat and waistcoat and then grinned at her. Didn't I just grin?

Now one thing I want to make perfectly clear—I am not writing all this to justify myself. I write this down, I suppose, for my own benefit because no one but myself is ever going to read it. Why should I want to assure myself that I'm not justifying myself? Am I uneasy? To be quite honest, I suppose I am a little. Everyone in this place, except my few close friends, seems to have turned against me. I have been aware of it, of course, for some time, but it was the Parrott that gave me the full account. With her sharp little eyes and tinny rasping voice she informed me, first, that I was a pro-German by my own confession; secondly, that I kept bad company; thirdly, that I drank too much and flirted with women too much; fourthly, that I ill-treated my wife and son. She ended up: "I used to think you a sissy, John Talbot. Now I wouldn't like to soil my lips with what I think you. You can knock me down if you like." I didn't do that, but I told her in very coarse terms what *she* was, of her scandal-mongering and backbiting, her spying curiosity as to who slept with whom. I told her that if she'd had any sexual experience herself she wouldn't be half so interested, and that she wanted a thorough good raping, but, I said, she'd have the devil of a time in finding anyone willing to rape her. Then I looked at her and laughed and she was really frightened—for the first time in her life, I should think!

However, when I was alone in my room again I was not happy—something inside me was not happy. As I sat there thinking, I felt a great misery rising within me, something apart from myself as though it were quite another personality. I began to wish that I was still as I had once been. I felt as though something within me was imprisoned and was fighting to get out. "Let me out! Let me out!" some part of myself was urging.

We all have moods of this kind and I put this one down to that interfering old Poll Parrott, and a bit of indigestion, I shouldn't wonder, and certainly to my having drunk too much lately. The trouble is nowadays that I don't know how much I'm drinking. Then I get muzzy and drink some more without knowing I'm doing it. Anyway, it's been a rotten week and I'm not happy. It's somebody's fault that I'm not, and when I find out who it is, I'll let them know it.

And this brings me to a little scene I had yesterday evening with Archie.

Archie's a nice-looking little boy but too girlish for my tastes.

He is very thin and fair-coloured and sometimes looks the baby that I'm afraid he still is. The fact is that I myself must have molly-coddled him too much in the early years. And yet I used to be exasperated by him when he shrank from me. I can remember how his shoulder-blades used to shrink when I touched him. I suppose he wanted a more sporting father because I remember how immediately he took to Tunstall and his purple corduroys, and Tunstall promised to teach him to draw.

With me now he is very different at different times. He *is* a bit afraid of me, and because I love him, I like him to be, but I don't want him to be afraid of me all the time. The fact is he's a bit of a prig and doesn't like it when I swear or am drunk or show him a funny drawing I've made. He's very like I used to be, with no sense of humour.

It happened that I was in my work-room, sitting on my bed drawing a bit, when I heard him pass, so I called him in. When I saw him standing there in the doorway, with his fair hair and blue eyes, a great rush of love came into my heart and I caught him to me and kissed him. I suppose my breath stank a bit, for I felt him withdraw inside his skin and that irritated me.

However, I held him between my legs and asked him how he'd been getting on. All right, he said. He really has the complexion of a girl and blushes like a girl. His body is so thin and fragile between my arms that I could crush the breath out of him as easy as nothing.

"How are the games getting on?" I asked. He wasn't awfully good at games and didn't like them very much.

What did he like? I asked.

He liked best drawing and reading.

What did he read? I asked.

Oh, he liked Southey's *Life of Nelson* and a book about Garibaldi and the *Idylls of the King* and a Life of Scott who went to the Pole and *Greenmantle*. He poured out a list of titles—those are some that I remember. Holding him with my arms I gave him a lecture then, how reading was all very well but it was no use being a book-worm at his age.

"You used to read, Daddy," he said. "An awful lot."

"I've seen the error of my ways," I answered him. "What I like is the open air—shooting, fishing, and swimming. I want you to be good at games, see?"

"I'm afraid I never shall be," he said.

"Of course you never will be," I said, shaking him a little, "if you *say* you won't be. You've got to be. That's what you're at school for."

Then I saw that he was frightened. When he's frightened his mouth trembles and I can't bear to see that. It makes me savage. So I said:

"Have you got any of your drawings here?"

Yes, he had, and he ran off to get them. When he returned and showed them to me I was really greatly pleased. He could draw. There was no doubt at all about that. They were drawings influenced, I could see, by his mother's liking for the Pre-Raphaelites. He drew knights and horsemen riding by the sea and Lancelot in front of a tower.

"Now see what I'm drawing," I said. I shouldn't have done it, of course. I think there's a sort of devil in me sometimes. In any case he blushed crimson and he turned his head away.

"Don't you like it?" I said, laughing and half ashamed of myself, too.

"No. No. I don't. I don't!" he cried, and ran from me, actually pushing me with his hand.

I heard him run down the passage, closing the door behind him.

At any rate, whatever anyone else thinks, Scandal adores me. He is a splendid little dog. I know, of course, that you can say about dogs that they love you because you feed them and protect them. I know, too, that they flatter you because they pay no attention to your ill-humours and forgive you any unkindness. But I think there is more than this between Scandal and myself. He knows, I am convinced, what I am thinking and why I do what I do. In any case he prefers me to anyone else and is not ashamed to be seen with me. Indeed, he will not leave my side.

Then he is so clean, so strong, and able to look after himself in any situation. He is sporting and fearless and gives no one any trouble. About how many human beings can you say this?

He was with me two afternoons ago when I had an encounter with Richard, Leila's brother.

I was walking down through the little wood above the town. There was frost in the air and a cold, remote sun, yellow as an orange. I was going down the path, swinging my stick and feeling as fit as anything. Scandal was scurrying and sniffing among the leaves. Richard was coming up the path and with a hurried "Good afternoon" would have passed me. I was in a good humour, though, and was determined to hold him. When I saw his pale, anxious face and his nervous manner I felt a kind of disgust. What right has the man to fear me? I have never done him any harm!

"What are you cutting me for?" I asked him, laughing.

Then, driven by some impulse, I said to him what Jim Tunstall had so often said to me: "You can't escape me, you know."

"What do you mean?" he asked. "I don't want to escape you."

I stood with my legs spread, filling the path and swinging my stick a little to and fro.

"Yes, you do. Look here—I've wanted to ask you for some time—we're alone and I've got you at my mercy, so to speak. Why do you dislike me so much?"

He didn't answer. I could see his mild anxious eyes looking round to see whether he couldn't pass.

"Tell me why. Leila's one of my best friends. She doesn't dislike me. Why should you?"

"I don't know you," he said.

"Don't you?" I laughed some more and came closer to him so that my hand almost touched his waistcoat buttons.

"You soon will. I'm determined that we shall be friends. Leila's brother? But of course we must be friends."

He still said nothing.

"No, but tell me. Is it because of my political opinions?"

He said then, slowly, as though he had realized that there was no escape.

"It's true that I don't like you, Talbot. I like very few people. I've lived so long in the East that I'm not accustomed to English life, perhaps."

"Well, even if you don't like me," I said, my temper rising, "that's no reason why you should be rude to me whenever we meet."

"I didn't know that I was. I might ask you the same. I've seen you looking at me sometimes as though you hate me. I can't think why. I often wonder about it. Why don't you leave me alone? I'm not your sort. I can't be of the slightest interest to you."

"Oh, aren't you?" I answered. "That's all you know. Aren't I a novelist? Everyone interests me."

He said: "I've read your novels. You don't seem to me the man who wrote those books."

"Oh, don't I? Well, I did write them all the same. In those days I was the sort of man you are now—always creeping about, afraid to swear or have a drink. That's why I'm interested in you, perhaps. You're like the man I used to be, and thank God am not any more."

But he had no spirit. If anyone had talked to me like that I'd have knocked him down.

"That's strange," he said. "I don't think people do change. Certain traits develop in people, of course, as they get older." Then he said, almost defiantly: "Would you mind letting me pass? It's cold."

I looked at him then and wanted to knock him down. I can't abide these meek-and-mild little men who are always wanting to get out of your way. I looked at him and he stepped back.

"All right," I said. "I'm not going to touch you. I only asked a civil question. But if you say anything to Leila against me, I'll hear of it and I'll know what to do."

"Of course I shan't say anything to Leila. I never mention you to her. When I said I disliked you, it was perhaps too strong. I simply don't know you. Your affairs are no business of mine."

"All the same," I said fiercely, "you listen to everything that's said about me, don't you? How I drink and womanize and ill-treat my wife and am pro-German. I bet you enjoy it all."

How I hated him then, nervously plucking at his coat, fear in every part of him, looking at the darkening wood, expecting me to murder him then and there, I daresay.

I stood aside.

"Watch out!" I said. "If I hear you've been telling Leila any-thing——"

He slipped up the path like a scurrying rabbit. Scandal came jumping up at me, pleading with me to go on with our walk. I bent down and pulled his ears and he licked my cheek. Then he barked like mad and seemed altogether wild with joy.

2

IT'S ALL VERY WELL, but I must take a pull on myself. I'm afraid of nobody and nothing. Not of the Devil himself. But I *am* afraid of something. I write down what I've written down here pretty often—that I'm drinking too much. Yes, but what good does writing it down do? Of course I can stop it when I want to. Cheeseman says it's because I've taken to it rather late in life that I indulge. But he's the Devil at my elbow. There isn't a thing that I want to do and know I shouldn't but he encourages me.

All the same it's not drink I'm afraid of. Is it the past? He's a poor sort of creature who's afraid of his past. The past's past. The past *is* past.

But I had a look the other day at the earlier journal that I used to keep. It made me sick. I couldn't read more than a dozen pages. All that pious stuff, saying one's prayers, and then that ridiculous hatred of poor old Tunstall. Am I afraid, then, of what I did to *him*? Not on your life! No one will ever know and he teased me into it. Besides, I don't feel that Tunstall reproaches me for it. Oh, the dead *are* dead—every sensible man knows that. Tunstall's physically dead all right, but I can't feel that he's gone, altogether. And if he isn't gone, what crime have I committed? *And*, if he isn't gone, he bears me no malice. I'm quite sure of that. What am I afraid of, then? Well—imagining things—if I'm quite frank with myself. It isn't the pink mice that you see when you've got D.T.s, but it's something very like it. What I keep imagining I see is either Richard Thorne or—myself. Myself as I used to be. That's crazy enough, isn't it? Oh, I know it is! I know it is! This is nonsense that I'm writing. I'll give it up, chuck the thing. But it relieves me putting things down in black and white. The truth is I'm not living the life I ought to. Heartburn simply terrible, and none of those digestive pills do me any good. My eyes are bloodshot. My hands tremble. I'm going to cut out the drink. I'll tell Cheeseman to go to hell. I'll be a bit like the chap I once was, not such a prig, of course, and I'll be damned if I give up Bella. All the same, I've got to get a hold on that temper of mine. I'll be throttling someone one of these days if I'm not careful. But the fact is it doesn't make you happy to let yourself go in every direction. I fancy that there's something in believing in God—even if you *don't* believe, so to speak. It puts you in touch with something or someone. . . .

Well, then—what is it I think I see? A thin, weak figure in a worn blue suit beseeching me with its eyes. It's the eyes that seem so real. They cut right into my gizzards. What is it that he is asking me? To let him go—to release him. Release him from what?

Now see where this is taking me! Plumb crazy! Cut out the drink, Johnny, my boy. Cut out the drink! Oh, Jacko—— Isn't that what Tunstall used to call me? Just for fun I'll call it out here in this room in the laughing, teasing voice that Tunstall used—"Jacko! Jacko! Jacko!"

By God, it makes me feel queer—I seem to have caught Tunstall's very accents. A pity the old boy isn't here. He could sing out 'Jacko' as often as he pleased. And *that's* a funny thing to say about the man you murdered!

But now I must get to facts. No nonsense now. Write down things as they are.

Well, two nights ago I was with Bella. I left her about three in the morning. We were neither of us very happy. When I had finished dressing I sat on the edge of the bed and held her hand.

"You were crying in your sleep," I said.

"Oh, no, was I? . . ." Then she added: "Go along now, Johnny dear. It's always depressing when it's all over. At least that's how I feel."

"That's how many people feel," I answered. "That's the time you ask yourself why the hell——" I stopped just in time.

But she was quick.

"Why are you so unhappy?" she asked.

"Unhappy?"

"Yes—Jimmy wasn't. He was sulky and cross sometimes. And

often he was as savage as anything. But he wasn't unhappy like you are. At least——" She puckered her forehead. "I don't know. Are *all* men unhappy when they've made love—unhappy or so damned sleepy they don't know what they are?"

I looked at her gloomily.

"I don't care what Tunstall was. Why are you always bringing *him* up?" Then I kissed her. "We don't really love one another, Bella. I don't think I love anybody but my dog."

"I tell you what it is, Johnny," she said, "you're drinking too much. You don't mind my mentioning it, do you? But you are, really."

I suddenly caught her arm.

"Wait," I said. "You don't hear anybody, do you? It's like some-body crying."

We both listened.

"It's only the clock, silly," she said. So I kissed her and left her.

What I am going to describe now is exactly what *seemed* to happen, but I don't say that it is at all what happened in actuality. In the old days when I fancied myself a writer I thought myself a handsome dab at what the professors call 'psychology.' That earlier journal of mine is full of the stuff and of things I fancied that I saw or heard. I remember that I even fainted on the cliff one after-noon because of what I thought I saw. I've shaken myself out of all *that* nonsense, which makes my other fancies on this particular morning all the more peculiar. And that is why I want to be minute and exact. Because I won't deny to myself that I was frightened, and I won't allow myself to be frightened. Do you hear that, you miserable, pitiful-looking, lamblike scarecrow? I don't believe in ghosts or shadows or anything that is dead. When you're dead, you're *dead*. Do you hear? DEAD.

The odd thing was that I had drunk nothing but water since lunch on the day previous. I never touch anything intoxicating before I pay Bella one of my visits because she doesn't like it. One wants to please her when one can. It's a little thing to do—yet it's damned difficult sometimes. So it wasn't that. It wasn't liquor.

Anyway, the fact remains that when I stood outside her bedroom door in my stockinged feet I didn't like it. Didn't like what? I don't know. We had both been pretty depressed, and as I stood there hesitating, I wondered how long it would last. It wasn't real love, of course, on either side. I knew what real love was because I had once loved Eve. The real thing is as unlike the sham thing as a diamond is to a piece of glass. Is that sentimental? I don't think so. Ask the roughest tough in Dartmoor Prison and he'll tell you it's true enough. The worst of the other thing—the thing that isn't love, is that if you go in for it, it's just like drink. The more you have the more you want. You want that freshness, that newness. The bloom's off as soon as you touch it. I suppose that that was why we were both sad the other morning—because we knew that once again we had been deceived. It wasn't the real thing. One more experience, and we were further from the real thing than ever. Now this is the sort of thing I *used* to write, and despise even thinking—so let me get to the facts.

When I had been sitting on Bella's bed I fancied that I heard someone crying. That gives you a sort of a shock in a house that is as silent as the grave, when everyone is asleep at three o'clock in the morning. And certainly when we both listened we heard nothing. I can tell you also that there is something *very* uncomfortable when two people listen together in the middle of the night. The sudden silence filling the room you're both in thrusts on you all sorts of sounds that you didn't hear before. If I ever write novels again (which I won't) I'll write something about that.

I stood outside the door and listened and again I seemed to hear someone crying. It was very faint and it might have been the drip of a tap or the wind blowing through the wall. No, it certainly wasn't a tap and there was no wind that night. Not a breath. The crying—if it *was* crying—was a hopeless sort of whimpering. But it was not the crying of a child. There was a mature despair in it. In concert with it was the ticking of the clock on the stairs, with that drunken whirr every now and then. Because of the clock I couldn't be sure there was any other sound at all. I decided that there wasn't and I started down the stairs. I was always very careful going down, for, after all, the old woman, Bella's mother, might be awake. Bella had told me that she was sure that she knew all about Jim Tunstall, but she mightn't be greatly pleased if she knew that her daughter had taken another lover so soon after Tunstall's death.

But a stair creaked and I stopped. Against the clock and the beating of my heart (which races madly sometimes) I seemed again to
hear that crying. I seemed even to hear words—"Let me go! Let
me go!" but that was, of course, nonsense.

I got into the dark room, crossed without touching anything
and opened the window. Outside there was a misty, moony grey-
ness.

Here I must be exact as though I were surveying the whole
scene with a painter's eyes. While I had crouched down on the
room floor, putting on my shoes, I had listened with all possible
intensity and had heard no sound at all save the ticking of the clock
on the stairs and the mouse-like scratching of a clock in the room
where I was. But when I stood on the edge of the lawn and looked
about me I was frightened—once again I had that sense of moving
outside myself. It is the most grisly feeling in the world, for—if
you are not sure of yourself, what are you sure of? I was standing
there, looking about me, as though I had never been there before.
The laurels made me feel sick. In that misty pallor they looked
like a mass of moving fungi advancing on the house. You could
swear that they were alive and that they turned their cold, leathery
leaves upward as you move your hand. As I stared at them I felt
that they might close in on me and their chilly palms move up and
hang about my throat and then flap like the fins of fish about my
cheeks and against my eyes. I would be blinded then and dragged
to my knees. They would tower above me and I would be suffo-
cated under their bloodless, boneless touch.

I write this down to prove to myself how overwrought I was.
Not a bit myself. So it was natural, considering the state that I
was in about those laurels, that I should fancy that I saw someone
standing in front of a tree on the right corner of the lawn. I stared
and felt sure that I was not mistaken. It was Richard Thorne
standing there and looking as much like what I used to look as
was possible! He was even wearing the silly bowler hat that I used
to wear. The hat that Eve was always trying to persuade me to
destroy, one of those bowlers with a large crown and a narrow
brim. An awful thing that to-day I wouldn't be seen dead in!

As a matter of fact, I have seen Richard Thorne wearing a bowler

—nothing as old-fashioned as I used to wear. But still—bowlers *are* old-fashioned, aren't they?

There he stood, staring at me, his hands hanging at his sides. It was, of course, only the shadows. When I moved forward on to the lawn, he was gone. Only shadows—but when I moved back to my old place near the house, there he was again!

It was time I went home. It was damp and chilly, anyway. For some reason I loathed, that night, the house and everything about it. I even hated the thought of poor Bella. I wanted to be in my own warm bed in my own cosy house. I had a sick feeling that I was never going to reach it. The distance, at that moment, between myself and my home seemed enormous.

So I started off. But when I had reached the end of the untidy drive and started towards the Common I felt sure that someone was following me. There was gravel on the drive, and after my step there was an echo of my step. I stopped and the echo stopped, which was natural enough. I went on and then, half-way along the path, I heard that beastly crying again. By this time I could catch the rhythmic beat of the sea and, when you hear the sea, you often hear many other sounds as well. But I stopped and looked back, my heart hammering like a drum. Oh, I may as well confess it! I was as frightened as hell. I was tempted actually to take to my feet and run! I could see no figure, but the light was so uncomfortable, like the fluorescence you see sometimes on the surface of a watery soup, and you couldn't be sure of anything. But as I looked back I seemed to catch again, through the steady beat of the sea, that thin, pitiful voice crying: "Let me go! Let me go!"

I pulled myself together. What I had got to do was to reach home, to throw off my clothes, climb into bed and sleep, sleep, sleep. I was suddenly infinitely weary and my legs hurt like toothache.

I walked quickly and reached the Common with Shining Cliff at the end of it, poking up its wicked sharp head, razor-edged sheer to the sea.

I almost ran (but not quite) to the cliff edge. "Now, no nonsense," I thought, and I formed the words (or did I?): "Come on, you dirty coward. Face me if you've got any pluck!"

There *was* a figure there! I'll swear that there was. Alone, isolated on that misted turf, and it seemed to me that now the crying came to me most clearly, so desolate and unhappy. The figure was outlined—the bowler hat, the dark suit, the hanging hands—myself as I used to be, or Richard Thorne—not a penny to choose between them.

Of course it wasn't so. I have said already that the whole thing was, as I saw clearly later on, a hallucination. But through my fear (for I was still afraid) a rage beat up. Here I was at the very spot where I had thrown Jim Tunstall over. Poor Jim! Why had I done that cruel thing? For I felt it now to be cruel. For the first time I was filled with rage for what I had done—or what my earlier self had done. If Jim were here now we would be friends. I would understand him now, his jokes and jollity and indifference to what people had done to him. And I knew now, with a sudden revelation, why it was that I detested Leila's brother. He reminded me, with every look and movement, yes, and whenever I thought of him, of that miserable, pious, prayer-making, murderous John Talbot I had once been. I had the fantastic notion that if I met that earlier self of mine here and now, I would catch him and hold him and squeeze his miserable, bony throat until there was no life left in it and hurl him over that cliff just as once I had hurled Tunstall. I was mad with fear and rage and violence. I cried: "Come on, you dirty swine! Come on if you're not afraid!"

Then I heard that miserable wretched crying again—and I took to my feet and ran.

3

SINCE the morning that I have just described, things have changed for the worse. To hell with the lot of them!—and it gives me considerable satisfaction to write it down. If we are to have air raids over this country (and I must say there are no signs of them as yet) this wouldn't be a bad little place for them to start with. They could destroy the lot as far as I'm concerned—with the exception of Leila and one or two more—and little harm would be done.

Harm? What harm have I ever done *them*? And yet you would think by the way they cold-shoulder and avoid me that I carried cholera germs with me. I'm sure I've tried to be jolly with every-one—especially the women. All right. Be damned to the lot of them. If they don't like me jolly they can have me savage. It's true that I was drunk in 'The Queen's' the other night and made a bit of a noise, but what harm did *that* do anybody?

I understand now something of what Hitler must have felt, ill-treated and spurned and spat upon. A few concentration camps wouldn't do *this* country any harm, if you ask me.

I acknowledge that I am pretty easily irritated these days. Then I have a lot to annoy me. Wherever I go that miserable brother of Leila's is on view. I see him everywhere, always silent in a corner, watching me. One day I shall make him sorry for himself. I've told Cheeseman about him. He agrees that he's a wretched specimen. "The sort of fellow you used to be yourself," he said. But none of this is the real trouble. There is something in me, savage, fierce, that won't let me rest. Is it anger with myself that I killed Tunstall? I think it is in a way. I feel it now with a kind of self-pity, almost as though I had done myself in. But how am I to explain that to anybody? They won't understand! They won't understand! Even Leila doesn't, although I think she knows more about me than anyone else. Strange the notion I have that makes me feel that we have been together for ages. She's plain enough and yet her face is comforting to me. I detest all her silly talk about God and good-ness. God? I hate that superstitious nonsense—and yet I listen to her.

Which brings me to Eve. Last night I behaved badly to her. Oh, I know it! I'm sorry. But was there ever any woman so aggravating?

After Archie had gone to bed she said: "Please, John—don't show Archie any more of those drawings."

I said: "What drawings?" although of course I knew.

"You think them funny, I know—and I daresay they're all right for a grown person. But he's only a little boy and—he hates it."

That made me angry. As though I'm not as well able to look after Archie as she is!

"Who says he hates it?" I asked.

"He's very loyal to you. He wouldn't say anything. But I know he does."

"Oh, you know he does, do you?"

I was sitting near to her. I dropped my paper and took Scandal on my lap to hide the trembling of my hands. He can't abide to be petted, but he'll let me do anything to him.

She answered at last: "I think we'd better go away for a little, Archie and I. We're all very miserable, aren't we? Perhaps it will be better if we go away for a bit."

"I see," I said. "You'll take my son away from me, will you?"

"Only for a little while. A week or two. When the Christmas holidays begin."

"Well, you won't, do you see? I'm not going to have everyone saying I've driven my wife out of the house. They say bad enough things already. And I'm not going to let you put Archie against me. That's what you want to do, isn't it?"

"No—of course not. What terrible things you say now, John! You'd think we were enemies."

"Well, we are enemies," I shouted. "If you separate me from Archie—if you do that—look out, look out, I tell you!"

I was trembling all over. I tried to pull myself together. Something inside me warned me. Something was praying me not to go too far. But I could see from her face that she was frightened of the way that I looked. Cheeseman said to me the other day when I was angry in the High Street when someone pushed me: "By Jove, Talbot, you looked like the Devil just then."

"I can't help my looks, can I? When a man's angry, he looks angry."

I put Scandal down and got up. She got up, too.

"Oh, John!" she said, "I can't stand it! I can't stand it!" She began to cry. She ought to have known that that's a thing I can't endure.

I struck her. I struck her on the breast. She fell back almost on to her knees. She got up slowly and, still crying, went out of the room.

I shouldn't have done it, I know that. Something in me was very unhappy. I sat there for a long time with Scandal on my knees.

4

SINCE my night at Bella's and my last quarrel with Eve, things have been moving faster and faster. I feel as though I were being hurried along towards some climax. I dream horrible dreams at night. One especially seems to recur, although I may have dreamed it only once and thought about it afterwards. I am in a prison deep down in the bowels of the earth, naked, chained to a wall sweating with damp. Rats fight their way over my bare flesh. Tunstall, grinning, looks down at me through a grating—"Jacko!" he says softly. "Jacko!" But then, suddenly, he too is in the prison naked and tied to the wall by the same chain as I. We are so close that it is almost as though our pallid and corrupting flesh mingles. He has the blue tattoo-mark on his right arm. He tries to kill me and I try to kill him. We are bound so closely together that we can hug one another, that we may crush one another. Then slowly his bare chest opens and I begin to be drawn, struggling, screaming, crying, inside. I wake trembling.

It is indeed a vicious circle, for I drink to escape my apprehension which comes from my nerves, and the drinking makes me more nervous and more nervous. I would be better if that spy and murderer Richard Thorne were not watching me at every step. For I have now the conviction that Richard Thorne has somewhere murdered a fellow human being—out in the East perhaps. He has just that skulking hang-dog look. He suspects that I have discovered his secret. Perhaps also he knows mine. But I will put a stop to his plots and his secret following of me and spying upon me. He's the kind of man that poor Jim Tunstall would have despised. He would have been for ever teasing him just as he once teased me.

And this brings me to something that happened yesterday, something of importance. Just after breakfast a letter was brought by hand. It was from Leila. She asked me whether I would come to tea that afternoon as she had something important to say to me. I sent back the message that of course I would.

So in the afternoon, about four, across to her little house
Scandal and I walked. I hesitated at first about taking Scandal with
me because he always hates Leila's brother. All his hair goes up.
He refuses to have anything to do with him. But I had a kind of
hunch that the little pipsqueak would be out. Certainly he would
not be there if he knew I was coming, or not there for me to see.
He might, of course, be hiding behind the curtains or peeping
through the keyhole!

The sitting-room—light and shining, gay with chrysanthemums,
Leila's touch over everything—was quite empty when Scandal and
I came into it. Scandal went at once and lay down near the fire,
his beautiful head, with its snow-white paper-shaving curls and his
military whiskers and his bright, burning, loving, intelligent eyes,
raised a little, listening to every sound—I ask you where among
any human beings will you find anyone as beautiful and modest,
as intelligent and unboring, as vigorous and unassuming, as loving
and as unsentimental? In the firelight he shone roughly as though
he were made of some precious metal. I thought to myself—if
people trusted and believed in me as this dog does, how temperate
and amiable I would be! Then Leila came in, still wearing black for
Jim, and once again I felt as I always do when I see her, as though
I had known her always, as though we shared a deep intimacy, so
deep that no words need be spoken.

While the little maid brought in the tea we spoke common-
places. She mocked me for my growing stoutness. "Why, you'll
soon be fatter than Jim was! I'm afraid Eve feeds you too well!"

At that moment my scarab ring bit into my finger. I have
grown much stouter, there's no doubt of it, and the ring now is so
embedded in the flesh that only if it is cut with an instrument shall
I ever be able to get it off. Lately I have fancied that the growing
flesh has caused it to split where the join of the gold is because on
several occasions it has been exactly as though the ring were biting
into my finger. I have, however, looked carefully and I can see no
split. The pain is very sharp and sudden, like the bite of an animal.

I held up the finger now. "Look, Leila," I said, "I'm afraid you're
right. Poor Jim's scarab that you gave me is deeply embedded."

While she talked, lightly, pouring out my tea, I could see that she was examining me. We had not been alone together for a considerable time. I could see, too (for I have become very observant—suspicious perhaps), that she was shocked by what she saw. I know that I am not very well just now. My hands tremble, my complexion is pasty, I am a bit flabby. I would have been furious enough if anyone else had looked me over like that, but with Leila it is different.

As soon as the maid had left the room, she said:

"John—why are you persecuting Richard? He's never done you any harm."

"Persecuting," I said sulkily. "That's a strong word—and it's nonsense." (I translate the drift of all this into dialogue. I cannot, of course, claim the exact words.)

"Now listen to me," she said, leaning forward and looking at me intently. She held her thin, blue-veined hand forward to protect her face from the fire. I could see the half-deformity working in her face.

Scandal had looked up and was gazing at her with great intentness. "John Talbot, you have been making a fool of yourself for the last six months—rather in the way Jimmie used to do, only worse. I won't say what you've been doing, you know well enough without my telling you. What you do, how you choose to behave, is your own affair. But we're very old friends and I'm sorry at all this.

"When it comes to Richard, though, it's quite another thing. Now that Jimmie's dead I love him more than any other human. He's in my care. He wouldn't hurt a beetle or even a slug. You are frightening him and I won't have it. And I want to know why you're behaving as you are."

"Frightening him?" I tried to speak scornfully. "How am I frightening him?"

"He says you are following him, seeking him out wherever he is. If you are in a room together you stare at him, look at him insultingly. He says you stopped him in Carfax Wood the other day and were very rude to him, and he thought you were going to knock him down. He can't understand it—nor can I."

Her voice was softer as she said urgently: "John—John—please—tell me why you're doing this."

I paused before I answered.

"For one thing, Leila, he's greatly exaggerated everything. He must be a pretty nervous subject if he takes alarm because I look at him or speak to him."

"It's more than that," she broke out warmly, "you know it is! Besides, Dick isn't a coward. He's simply one of the finest human beings alive—warm-hearted, generous. Sometimes he's gay and sometimes not so. He's shy, of course, and retiring, but I should think he's never been frightened of anybody before. But he *is* of you. It's making him ill. Tell me, John—dear John, we've been friends for so long. Tell me at least why you dislike him?"

"Yes, I do dislike him," I said. "I can't bear him."

"Why? Why?"

"For one thing because he's so like what I myself used to be—and I hate what I used to be—pious and frightened and sensitive. What I did to Jim——" I pulled myself up with a jerk.

"*What* did you do to Jim?" she said quickly.

"Oh, nothing—except that I was so silly about him. Poor old Jim—I see now that he was only good-naturedly teasing me and I *wanted* teasing. But I told everybody I hated him and ran him down——"

"No," she said quickly. "Wait. It wasn't a case of 'poor old Jim' at all. During those last years Jim was bad. It was as though he were possessed with evil and hated it but couldn't escape it. He was dreadfully unhappy and I could do nothing for him. Oh, I know because I lived with him! He was bad—or at least something in him was."

"Now, Leila," I said angrily, "don't you of all people go running Jim down. He was very fond of you, even though he did go after women a bit. I misjudged him. Everyone did."

She was looking me through, and I stared down on to the strong curly hair of Scandal's coat.

"It's strange, John; you spoke then just as Jim used to do. He would defend himself just like that. 'I'm misjudged,' he would say. 'Everyone's down on me. I'm not a bad fellow really.' But he was—he was terrible to live with towards the end."

"But you loved him always, didn't you?" I said eagerly.

"Yes, I loved him always."

Something impelled me to say: "All that nonsense about evil—you don't really believe it, do you?"

"That there's evil in the world? Of course I do."

"Poor old Leila! You're a thousand years behind the times. What do you mean by evil?"

She spoke then sensibly with no sensationalism, and I was compelled to listen, although it was all nonsense and anyone else but Leila I would have laughed at.

"I believe—and, more than that, I know—that there are powers of evil as well as of good. They fight together eternally and we—all human souls—share in the struggle. Indeed, it is about *us* that the battle rages. If we are weak and submit we can be possessed with evil. It can enter us and own us just as good can. God has given us complete free will. We are our own masters. Why, John," she went on, her voice rising, "it's never been clearer than in the present War, Hitler and Himmler and the rest of that wretched crew don't matter as individuals, but they are the strongest instruments of evil the world has seen for hundreds of years. Their doctrines are completely evil—against God, goodness, kindness, freedom, love. They believe in cruelty, atheism, slavery. And we've been so lazy and selfish and idle that we have given them the weapons they wanted."

"Now, Leila," I said tolerantly, "I'm not going to start a war discussion with you. There's a lot to be said for Hitler as a matter of fact. The Germans have been villainously treated—ruined, deprived of livelihood, spat upon."

"They needn't have been," she said quickly. "And anyhow I'm not hating anybody. Not even Hitler and his crew. We are fighting something much more terrible than any *men*. And we've got to win, or we lose—not only our bodies but our souls."

I laughed. Then I got up, stood in front of the fire, stretched my arms and my legs and said: "Never mind all that. What you say is sentimental woman's nonsense. What did you really ask me to come and see you for?"

She looked at me sadly. She said, as though to herself: "I can do nothing . . . I see that . . . nothing at all." Then she went on quickly: "First to tell you, John, that you *must* leave Dick alone. If you don't,

I shall protect him. We have been friends so long—I have been so fond of you—but this is closer to my heart than anything in the world. I don't know why you are doing it. Nothing that you have said explains it. What you have said about your past is true. You *are* changed—terribly. But what has Dick to do with that? He *is* like what you were. I often thought of it when he was abroad. But he is stronger than you ever were, much, much stronger.

"But the other thing I wanted to say"—she leaned forward with her urgency until she almost touched me—"is that you are in terrible danger—terrible, dreadful danger. You are moving, John, to some awful catastrophe. Those words aren't too strong. You are possessed as Jim was possessed. It is the same evil. Dear John—I beg you, I implore you, whether you believe in God or not, to take a chance—implore Him to help you. Beg Him to make you strong enough to fight this. Throw the evil spirit out. It's not too late. But almost—almost . . ."

Her eyes were filled with tears. I had an impulse to go on my knees to her, to confess everything, to implore her to help me. And directly after that I was angry. What right had she, with all her silly chatter about God and evil and the rest of it, to talk such exaggerated stuff? Wasn't I a grown man? Didn't I know what I was doing?

"All right, Leila, if that's all you have to say." I looked at her with contempt, for that was what she deserved. "Come along, Scandal," I said, and I left her.

5

LEILA made a mistake in talking to me about Richard. Somehow it increased my anger against him. To think that she should be protecting him. Why shouldn't she be protecting *me*? I needed someone to look after me very much more than did Richard. And what a miserable skunk he must be to hide under his sister's petticoats! It was the kind of way in which I used to hide behind Eve in the old days. And imagine a grown mature man going to his sister and complaining because someone in the town frightened him! Frightened him! A man of mature years! It is true that I myself used to be frightened of Tunstall, but then what a shameful ass *I* was in those days! How I despise that old self of mine!

In any case, this thought that Richard was hiding behind his sister made me want to get at him and do him a mischief. I'd give it him for complaining to Leila.

He could be seen every day driving about in a little maroon-coloured Morris. He'd stop in the High Street to do some shopping. He'd draw the car up at the side of the street, then very cautiously step out and look about him and nervously put his hand to his collar. His face had an anxious peaked look and it irritated me that he had almost no eyebrows. It amused me, though, to stand near the shop door and watch him go in. "Good morning, Richard," I would say suddenly, and he would jump inside his collar. I would tease him just as Jim Tunstall used to tease me. I would touch his arm. "You can't escape me, you see, Richard," I would say, smiling.

Then a wonderful chance came to me—a real opportunity for teasing. It was a lovely, soft, gentle evening—the sky was pale white-blue with pools of light green in it. I can't describe it, but I think I could paint it.

I went down to meet Cheeseman at 'The Green Parrot.' I stopped on the rough grass-grown little jetty to look at the way in which the green and blue sky, now turning, under the influence of two glittering sparkling stars, into grey dusk, reflected its delicate shades in the gently-heaving water.

Someone came towards me. I looked—and behold, it was Richard.

"Why, Jacko!" I cried—and then, as I caught his arm, laughed because the parallel of Tunstall's stopping me on this very same spot was so close that I had actually used his old jesting name for myself. And realizing that, I had an idea.

I caught his arm and felt the slender weakness of it and saw the terror—yes, real, true terror—in his eyes.

"What is it, Talbot?" he said almost hysterically. "What are you going to do? Let me go!"

"This is a very good little place," I said, "for us to have a talk. I've seen you a lot of times lately, as you very well know, but there have always been people about. There is no one in sight now."

"What do you want to speak to me about?"

"For one thing you've been complaining about me to your sister."

"I haven't. . . . Complaining? Of course not—what should I complain about?"

I could tell that he was frightened, but I could feel also some real resistance rising up in him, a secret, unseen stiffness that came partly from his very loathing that I should touch him. Just so had I loathed that Tunstall should touch me!

"I'm not angry," I said, smiling and almost caressing him with my touch. "Why should I be? I don't mind whether you complain to Leila. I'm only sorry that you should dislike me so much."

"I don't dislike you," he said. His face stiffened. "Why should I lie? I do dislike you intensely. I hate you even to touch me." I knew that he was trembling.

"That's all right," I said cheerfully. "Come in and have a drink on it." I jerked my finger towards 'The Green Parrot.'

"In there? . . . Oh, no! Besides, I don't drink!"

"Now don't be so unkind—one drink to show there's no ill-feeling. It will do you good, Jacko. It will indeed!"

"Jacko! That's not my name. Why do you call me that?"

The sky was white now—white with a faint green shade. The water could scarcely be seen.

"Silly of me. Someone used to call me that once. A pet name."

"Let me go. I want to get home."

"No—no. One drink with me. The 'Parrot's' a jolly place. You'll like it. I won't keep you."

I had my arm round his shoulders. He hung his head as though he were ashamed. But he didn't resist. I led him. I touched for a moment his hand and it was as chill as the green sky. I took him in with me.

The room was warm and smoky. The stout landlord stood behind the bar, and Cheeseman was alone at a table. I was amused to see the Rat's look of surprise. He was smoking his pipe, of course, and he looked over the top of it, his nasty little eyes narrowing and the red hairs standing out on the back of his pale fish-scale hand. Part of me loathed and hated him, the other part of me welcomed him as an element in the jolly gross side of life—the warm, juicy, odorous mud in which everyone, sinner and saint, likes at times to wallow. Oh, yes, they do! In the secrecy of the dark forest they play their games . . . or would if they had the courage. I'm writing fine words. What I really mean is that there is the jolly friendly nuzzling hog in the best of us. Well, the Rat is a hog all right, *and* a nuzzler!

He was polite to Richard and greatly amused to see him there.

"Now—what will you have?" I asked him.

"Oh, I don't know," he answered. "A ginger ale if you like. I'm a teetotaller."

"Don't tell me," the Rat remarked. "Out in the East all that time and a teetotaller?"

"Oh, there's a lot of nonsense talked about the East. Plenty of fellows are teetotal. As a matter of fact, I hate spirits."

He seemed remarkably at his ease. I suddenly realized that he was afraid of me no longer and that annoyed me. I wanted him to be afraid of me.

"How's your car going, Thorne?" Cheeseman asked. "Nice little Morris that."

"Just like any other Morris," Richard answered quickly. I could see that he detested Cheeseman. He finished his ginger ale and I had an idea.

"Have another," I said, and before he could answer had gone up to the bar with his glass.

I had it filled with a strong whisky and soda. I brought it back.

"Here you are," I said, grinning.

He picked it up, then put it on the table.

"That's whisky," he said.

"All right, old man," I cried jovially. "Try it—you'll find you like it."

He picked it up and for a moment, an exciting, stirring moment, I thought he was going to drink it. Richard drunk would be quite an experience. But it slipped from his fingers and shivered on to the floor.

"I'm so sorry," he said. . . . "Good night," and before either of us could answer him, he was out of the door.

"Well, I'm damned!" Cheeseman said. "Very different from the way you behaved once, Talbot. Remember?"

Quietly I vowed to myself that I owed Richard one for that. *And he would pay!*

We sat on there and quickly Cheeseman swathed me with the veil of his influence. It was like that. It wasn't at all that I was ever afraid of the man or trusted him. I certainly did not admire him. Once, when I was in love with a girl, oh, years ago, I remember walking up and down the streets of Glasgow, Bute Street and Sauchiehall Street, in a sort of mesmerized trance. One Sunday I especially remember. It was years ago—long before I married Eve. One of my very rare trips to Scotland. I was young and that soppy, contemptible kind of ass that I once was. It was a wet Sunday, but she and I, hands interlocked, walked regardless of all other human bodies, houses, vehicles. We said little, but I remember the strong, cool clutch of her fingers and her generous, kindly eyes. With Cheeseman there was disgust rather than love, but he spun something of the same kind of web around his fellows. Was it mesmeric?

There was something in those evil, hot little eyes. . . . Mind you, I like the fellow. There is no dirty thing he hasn't done, no filthy sight he hasn't seen. I admire him for his honesty and his persistence. If he's after something or somebody he will go on quietly for years tracking it down. So to-night he caught me.

"Whatever did you bring him in here for?"

"I like him. He reminds me of my old, good, simple self."

"You don't. You hate him."

"Yes, I hate him. I'd like to do him an injury. I will, too. The damned cheek. He dropped that glass on purpose."

"Of course he did." Cheeseman picked his protruding teeth. "Still you never know, for all his saint-like conduct. You'd be surprised at the things that good quiet people do! I've caught them out many a time and then don't they just squirm! Your good citizen has one pet vice and no one knows of it—but if you discover it you are taking away from him the *only* fun he has. He isn't like you or me, Talbot, who have our eggs in several baskets." He chuckled. "Don't you hate the holy men, Talbot? The bloody hypocrites!"

Something made me say, "Perhaps they are not all hypocrites."

"Of course they are. There's not one righteous man anywhere."

"I wasn't a hypocrite before I killed Tunstall."

There was a long pause. Cheeseman leaned forward. "Before you did—what?"

So I had told him. I didn't care. He would have got it out of me sooner or later.

"I pushed Tunstall over Shining Cliff."

"You didn't? . . . My God!"

No. I didn't care. And yet I felt as though I were bound to him from now on. And yet I didn't care.

The room was very deserted. There was nobody near us.

"You guessed—long ago."

His little eyes stared into mine. "Well—I wondered. I didn't think you had it in you—not then. Now you might. Why did you do it?"

"He teased and taunted me all my life. He was making love to my wife—or I thought so. I fancied a lot of things. It was mad, crazy. I wish I could have him back. I'd tell him how sorry I was. We'd get on like anything if he was here now."

"I believe you would. Poor old Jim! Although he never liked me. Do you remember how you knew that, although no one ever told you? And how you've changed since that night! I suppose a thing like that *does* something to you. I've known one or two murderers. . . ." He paused reflectively. "I might even be called a murderer myself. . . . Somehow, what with the last War and this one, you can't take killing anyone very seriously. And poor old Jim was going down hill fast——"

Yes—I was tied to Cheeseman for the rest of my days. Something inside me gave a sort of lurch of nausea.

"Don't go telling other people," he said.

"What do you think?" I laughed.

"Have another whisky; I'm going to."

"Thanks."

I could see that he was thinking hard. It was as though, in his mind, he was going over the list of his prisoners and captives. Now he had one to add.

"How did you do it? I wouldn't have thought you had the strength—not at that time."

"We were on the edge of the cliff—I pushed him over."

I could see the Rat's white hands clench sadistically. The knuckles stood out like a dead animal's bleached bones.

"Yes. Did he cry out?"

"Once."

Cheeseman drank his whisky:

"Here's how."

6

I AM WRITING with the tears drying on my cheeks. I am writing because I must—to rid myself a little of the sorrow and rage in my heart. Soon I will be quiet. To-morrow I go up to London to return tit for tat. Tit for tat. TIT FOR TAT. The revolver that I got last spring is on the table beside me. When I wangled the license I wondered whether I should ever use it. I don't wonder any longer. I have been crying, I who have not cried for so long. They shall be the last tears I shall ever shed—the last tears for the last friend.

Yesterday afternoon Scandal and I had our last game together. He was a regular baby for a dog as old as he was—or at any rate he would be a baby with me. He would be anything with me if I wanted him to be. I have an old leather bedroom slipper that was his especial property. People sometimes say that dogs have no imagination. Ignorant people that don't know anything about dogs. Scandal certainly had plenty. He knew that the old shoe was an old shoe, but he also knew that, when he wanted it, that old shoe was a rat, a rabbit, a cat, and then, after that, something more—all his longing for glory and adventure and romance.

When I brought it out from its drawer and showed it him, at once our two selves were drawn close together. We were one romantic longing and desire. I don't believe any more in romance or sentiment or any kind of weak, silly slop, but there was nothing silly in *our* alliance. And now he is gone—the only friend, except Leila, that I had in the world.

I was proud, too, of the disregard that he had for everyone else.

He never gave Eve and Archie a thought. He was polite to them, of course. He was a proper little gentleman and had beautiful manners, but they meant nothing at all to him. Nor did anyone else anywhere.

Everyone in this damned place thinks that I'm going to perdition—or have gone there already. But Scandal didn't. He thought I was simply the most perfect creature in the world, silly little fool. If I was sharp or violent to Eve he thought it was Eve's fault and would give her a nasty look. If I had drunk a drop too much, he would grin at me as much as to say: "Drink all you want to. We can only live once."

How physically beautiful he was! There was never another dog to touch him! The bright strong curls on his coat seemed to promise that he would live for ever. He was utterly fearless, but he wasn't one of those dogs that just fought any dog he saw. Many dogs were not worthy of his attentions. He had a wonderful dignity although he could play like a baby if he wanted to. I can't believe that he's left me. I can't believe that I shall never hear his quick excited bark again.

After luncheon yesterday I took Scandal with me for a walk in Carfax Wood. The high road passes on the north of the town. I was about to cross it. Scandal ran ahead of me. A maroon-coloured Morris car turned the corner and approached us. I saw the driver and was certain that it was Richard Thorne. The car caught Scandal, drove swiftly on. When I ran up to him he was already dead. I picked him up in my arms and rushed down the road, shouting I know not what.

This morning I went to Leila's house. The servant told me that she and her brother had left for London.

When this afternoon I told Eve that I was going to London, she kissed my cheek and said that she would be waiting for me when I came back.

I buried Scandal in our little garden under the rose-bush in the right-hand corner near the road.

While I have been writing this a strange urge has been strengthening in me to take revenge on this filthy crowd of human beings who have insulted and derided and tried to murder me—who have killed the only friend I had.

NARRATIVE III

I

I FRIGHTENED him all right. I certainly frightened him. I've begun to write again because it tranquillizes me. What am I writing? Anything. What does it matter? Except that I'm telling the truth and the whole bloody lot will be astonished when they hear it; they think that there's only this phony War on—this War in which no one does anything but creep about in the dark. They don't realize that there's another war on too and that's *my* war. First to deal with Mr. Richard Thorne and then settle all the others—the nasty, mangy, creeping, crawling crew.

I return to Facts. Facts are tranquillizing. I will report to my friendly Demon *exactly* the Facts. Is that Demon Cheeseman? For he is with me. We arrived last evening at 5.30, just before the Black-Out; it was raining and we discovered this boarding-house standing in a puddle of water.

The taximan asked us where he should drive us and I said: "Bloomsbury. And go on until we stop you." But, turning the corner by the Museum, I saw this boarding-house before it saw me. I knew at once that it was the very place for us. To begin with, it is painted a liverish colour like a piece of underdone beef and all its windows are ugly like old maids looking through keyholes. All the old women with sooty glass faces stared down at us as our taxi halted, and I could hear them whispering: "Here comes the very man for us. If we watch him we'll see something."

Yes, there were two bedrooms and everyone had meals in common amity. Mrs. Foxborne her name was, and she is dressed like the British flag in red, white and blue and has the coldest, chilliest eyes I've ever welcomed. Her hands are like claws. She has a large pink-and-white brooch with the Three Graces carved upon it.

I gave myself the best bedroom, of course. Cheeseman doesn't mind what he has. He is so deeply excited about what is going to happen that he has no thought for anything else. And he knows that it will not be for long.

All I said to him was:

"You know that Richard Thorne killed my dog."

"Oh, did he?" he said.

"He's flown to London because he's frightened and I'm flying after him."

"I'll fly too."

That's all we said, but in my mind's eye I saw two big black birds feasting just outside the Leicester Square Tube in a dark and empty London on somebody's carcase. I showed him my revolver.

"I'm going to chase him first," I said.

There's a jerry under the bed, a large tear in the carpet, a picture on the wall of Christ blessing the Children. There is a clock, too, that stopped at four-thirty years and years ago. Last night before I went to bed I painted a little. It was a fanciful picture of London like a spider-web and two eyes where the spider ought to be. There is dried blood stiffening the corner of the web, and the eight-day clock ticks although the web is strangling it.

I tore it up and jumped into bed. I was very cold but my head was hot as hell. I didn't sleep very well. I lay there remembering how once, after leaving that girl in Glasgow whom I loved so much, when she didn't write I was hot and cold all day long and trembled when the post came. But at supper I had a good meal— roast beef and apple-tart. There were half a dozen of us at the table, one thin, one fat, one round, one straight, and one with a hare-lip. Who was the other? There was an empty chair. I ate because I was hungry, but as I looked at them sitting round the table and mincing their words I thought how pleasant it would be to tie them to their chairs with green window-blind cord and shoot them, slowly, quietly, one after the other. You would gag them first with their soiled table-napkins. How their eyes would stare as they realized that death was coming to them after all—real posi- tive death that is never real until it is actually upon you. No escape for them as they stare frantically at 'The Fighting Téméraire' and 'Christ Leaving the Temple' and the beef congealing on the plate

and two flies digging into the sugar-dish. Then I aim, with what
a jolly, friendly smile I aim at first one then another. Their arms
are bound backwards on to the sides of the chairs so as they are
hit their bodies bound forward. How delightful for the others to
watch while their friends depart!

I leave one to the end. I think it should be the young man with
no eyebrows. It is indecent not to have eyebrows.

And I should say to him:

"Have you ever loved a dog?"

He will be too sadly terrified to reply.

"Have you ever been thrown into the sea?"

Still no reply.

"Have you ever been mocked and taunted by all the citizens of
your filthy little town?"

Then I shall fire.

2

I HAVE bought two pairs of shoes with felt soles. I love to walk in
the dark without sound. I will jump upon Richard before he can
hear me coming.

I love this darkness. I adore it. I belong to it. It is what I have
always wanted.

There are still many theatres open in London and the crowds
move in Leicester Square, in Piccadilly Circus, in Regent Street,
in thick moth-like throngs, laughing, loving, moving adroitly out
of the way of one another. But these are not the places where I at
present resort. I am only at the beginning of my pursuit with my
dark soft hat pulled over my eyes, my face pale if someone flashes
a torch, my little revolver in my pocket, my soft, soundless tread.

Once the darkness falls I find it difficult to stay indoors. But
I like first to have my evening meal with the boarders. They are
afraid of myself and Cheeseman. I know their names now—Miss
Lucy Bates, Mr. Henry Bates, her brother (he has the hare-lip),
Mrs. Constantine, Mr. Floss, and very old Mrs. Taylor.

In the first place they dislike my silent approach. I come upon them in the passages, in the bathroom, in the sitting-room, on the stairs before they are aware of it. I am very polite and courteous, and especially so to my landlady Mrs. Foxborne. Then when they speak to me they become uneasy under my stare. Yesterday evening I walked down the stairs behind old Mrs. Taylor huddled under her shawl and looking at every step cautiously with her blind, red-rimmed eyes.

Before she took the last step I said gently:

"Good evening, Mrs. Taylor."

She gave a little shawl-muffled scream.

"Tell me, Mrs. Taylor, why don't you have a little dog—a Pekinese, for example?"

She held her hand on her heart. "Oh, dear—I never heard you coming."

"Why don't you have a little dog, Mrs. Taylor?"

"Oh, dear—I don't know."

"I had a dog that I loved very much. It was killed by a motor-car."

I opened, with a little bow, the door of the dining-room.

During the meal I like very much to silence the conversation. It begins very briskly and soon they are all talking gaily about the War, the Black-Out, the theatres, and what they have done during the day. What I enjoy is to look at them one after the other. There is something about my face that they dislike. I have a strange feeling about my face. I feel it to be a mask, a mask through which my eyes burn. Behind it what thoughts and fancies burn! It would never do if they should see my real face, for passions rage in it—passions of anger and violence because I am in this world now for one purpose only—to be revenged on just such miserable cattle as these who have spoiled my peace and attempted to destroy me.

And so I look at first one and then another. I look at them one by one and they look at me and their eyes drop. Gradually a silence falls.

When the meal is over I put on my hat and coat and go out. If it is a dark night without moon or stars, it is as though you walked in a vast underworld where the little red lights, whether in the

air or just above the ground, are like the eyes of animals. I walk,
making no sound, through the streets. The darkness is doubly,
trebly enfolded, layer upon layer. You can put out your hand and
feel it. Suddenly you are on the edge of plunging into some abyss.
You pull yourself up sharply and your heart beats at the escape of
some fine danger. My gloved hand closes round the revolver in my
coat pocket. I love to feel it there.

There are not many people in these streets, but what I love is to
touch them suddenly, coming up upon them before they know it.
I put out my gloved hand and for an instant rub their arm, or push
against their back, or even touch their neck. They flash their torch
perhaps and sometimes cry out. I apologize very politely, raising
my hat. But I cannot help thinking how pleasant it would be to
turn a neck and twist it or throw them down and stamp upon their
silly meaningless faces.

But of course those are things that I must not do.

When I am accustomed to it, the darkness has many colours—
purple and dark green and opalescent grey. It moves like blown
water and you can feel its waves upon your face. It contains also
many odours; the acrid tang of smoke, the stifling thickness of
petrol, the damp of wet towels, the thin clamminess of human
breath.

The buildings, filled with invisible human beings, which they
hold like prisoners, contemptuously, share gladly in the darkness.
At last, after so many years, they are truly themselves and can
pursue their own purpose unwatched by men. You can tell by the
sounds they make—the gurgling of water-spouts, the straining of
boards, the creaking of doors and windows, that they are alive and
busy.

These are only the preliminaries. My great purpose here is
to find Richard. And very quickly I have found him. I remembered that once Leila had said to me that Richard, when he was
in London, found much pleasure and solace in the Coffee Club.
When I asked her what was the Coffee Club, she told me that it
was a little place off Jermyn Street, a small club for gentlemen who
had been in the East, or were interested in the East. That Richard
could have a meal there and talk with friendly and congenial souls.

Two days after my arrival in London, on a fine and sunny afternoon, I went along to Jermyn Street. I walked from one end of
it to the other, down to St. James's Square, along King Street, up
St. James's, back along Jermyn Street. "You'll be getting it one of
these days," I thought to myself, "you swanky, leather-smelling,
school-club-tie sycophants and snobs with your nice smart little
church where there are royal services for Royalty, and your rich
Turkish baths with a nice blue plate on one of them to that King
of Snobs, Walter Scott, and your shoe shops and your hat shops
and your picture shops, and your Orleans Club where there is the
best food and drink in London, and your grand St. James's Theatre
where Sir George Alexander of the crooked smile and creased
pants once had his famous first nights and Oscar Wilde received his
grand bouquet of cabbages. Oh, all you ancient, leather-stinking,
stuck-up guardsmen and harlots," I thought to myself, "the time
is coming, and is not far distant either, when the bombs will be
raining down on you and the holes where the window-panes ought
to be will be hot with roaring fires. You can pile your sandbags up
one on top of another! A lot of good they will do you!"

I must say these thoughts give me the greatest of pleasure,
because I detest all those conceited stick-to-yourselves, we-are-the-
best-people-on-earth kind of Englishmen. What a lot of good a
few nice bombs will do them!

As a matter of fact I could see, even as I walked about, how they
looked down on me and took care that the hems of their garments
should not touch me! I felt spasms of rage contract my fingers as
I saw them sneer at me! What harm was I doing them? In fact, I
spoke to one man, an elderly pompous fool with watery eyes and
a white moustache. I said: "You'll know me again, won't you, sir?"
and walked on, leaving him pretty astonished. But what right had
he to stare at me as though I were a criminal? I must confess that
when I saw a shop-window in Jermyn Street with all the regimental
ties laid out in patterns, and gloves as elegant as any dandy could
wish, and silk handkerchiefs with initials embroidered on them, it
was all I could do not to fire my revolver into the middle of them.
They positively sneered at me, those things in that window. As I
write those words down I know that they are true. Why, there

was one tie of red and green and purple that spoke to me, saying:
"How is little Scandal? Ha! Ha! Nice little dog, wasn't he?"

However, to get on with my dear Richard.

At length, at the corner of St. James's Square, I asked a chauf-
feur standing beside his elegant car whether he had ever heard of
the Coffee Club. He scratched his head and asked another chauf-
feur. I could see that they were laughing down their sleeve at me,
the parasites, but I didn't care. At last the fellow came to me and
said that he thought it was opposite the women's Turkish baths,
to which he pointed up the hill—somewhere there, in any case.
He was staring at me as though he didn't like my face. However,
I had more important business, so I went up the street, and there,
on the right-hand side, sure enough was a little brass plate, 'The
Coffee Club.' I drew a deep breath of satisfaction. I agreed with
Cheeseman that we should divide our time in watching. The most
likely time for Richard to be there would be luncheon and he
would come out, in all probability, somewhere between half-past
two and three. If days passed and I didn't catch him, I should go
into the Club and ask for him. All that I wanted for the moment
was that he should know I was in London.

Well, two days later out he came—just as though I had
summoned him. It was exactly three-fifteen of a chill, foggy afternoon. It was not at all a fog of the old pea-soup variety—I fancy
that they are vanishing as a feature of London life. It was rather
wispy and straggly and grey-white with a kind of thin drizzle at
the heart of it. The lights were already in the shop-windows, and
as the fog blew in the breeze, everything seemed to move, the
buildings, the lights, the shadows of St. James's Square. I was just
thinking that I would go home for the day when the door opened
and out stepped Richard, almost into my arms.

"Good afternoon, Richard," I said. For a moment he didn't recognize me, for my hat was pulled down over my forehead. Then
he stepped back. After that he didn't speak and he didn't move.

"I only wanted you to know, Richard," I said, "that I am in
London and you will be seeing me very soon again."

3

THE PURSUIT has begun. I am in a state of exultation. I am obeying the will of my Master who tells me what I must do.

I cannot remain still and I hate to be alone. If I am not in pursuit I am wasting my time. If I am alone I am aware of something within me that is struggling not to obey.

I remember reading somewhere in Memoirs by a contemporary that Napoleon once told the writer that he had always been compelled to make his decisions 'against the sometimes absurd and cowardly remonstrances of his weaker self,' or words to that effect.

I often feel in Hitler's speeches that his oratory is loud and powerful not only to convince his audience, but also to silence something inside himself—something that he knows is weak and sentimental, something that would betray him altogether were he to give way to it. So it is now with me. When I am alone in the boarding-house, especially at night in my room, I am conscious of an urge to get something free in myself. I envisage this as a prisoner whom I have subjected. Were I to listen even for a moment, I would be betrayed and by myself. I can hear sometimes a weak, pitiful voice in my ear, and sometimes I fancy, as I have done in the past, that a figure lingers beseeching in the shadows of the room. This condition is undoubtedly due to this nervous ecstasy that I now experience. The thought of settling my debt with Richard once and for all is a deep sensuous delight to me. I will revenge upon his miserable body all the miseries that I have suffered and the contempt that has been poured on me. Hallelujah! Hallelujah! Upon this town that has rejected me shall be showered hailstones of fire—huge bursting hailstones like flaming, destroying angels.

And now I must say something about my visit to Leila yesterday. I went to the little house where once I had tea with her and, pitiful fool that I was, wept at her feet. I rang the bell, asked whether Mrs. Tunstall was at home, and before the maid could answer me, brushed past her and opened the sitting-room door. She was sitting on the sofa, her feet up, reading. I stood in the doorway, like the avenger from God, and I felt my power to be so great that I could, with one hand, command this house to be ashes. I felt my eyes burn through the brick and mortar and look into eternity.

She was not afraid of me. Unlike others, she has never been afraid of me. She said:

"Oh, poor John!"

That would, in another, have been so insulting to my pride that I would have wrung their neck, but Leila has always had an influence upon me. Yes, for many, many years.

She said quickly: "Richard isn't here." Then she got up.

"Poor John, come and sit down. You look exhausted."

Exhausted! When I am at the height of exultation.

I didn't move from the door. "It doesn't matter," I said, "where Richard is. I shall get him when I want him."

The sight of her kind face with its tenderness and slight deformity always moves me. I was ashamed of myself, but I said almost beseechingly:

"Richard killed my dog; Scandal was my only friend."

She gave a real cry of sympathy. "Oh, poor John! Is Scandal really dead?"

"Richard rode over him in his car."

"I am sure that he did not. When did it happen?"

"The day before you left for London."

She stood for a moment thinking. "Richard never used the car that day."

But this is the important thing—the words that I now spoke. I don't know why I said them.

"Richard isn't your brother," I said. "He is John Talbot."

She only gazed at me. She has always been very kind to me.

"I am Jim Tunstall, your husband. Talbot tried to kill me and now I am going to kill him. That's fair, isn't it?"

I felt an immense relief. It was all so right and so just.

Leila spoke very quietly and slowly, as though she were trying to explain something to a child.

"Listen, John. You are very ill. You have been ill for a long time.

You killed Jim and after his death the evil that was his curse has been your curse. I have known it a long time. My brother has nothing to do with this, nothing at all. Before it is too late, you must be rid of this evil, destroy it, throw it away. I will help you. Stay here with Richard and me. You and I, with God's help, will destroy it together."

I remember thinking what a silly conversation it was between two grown people. I knew, as I looked at her, that we had lived together and slept together and eaten and drunk together for years and years. At the same time something in me wanted to surrender to her and feel her strong, cool hands on my forehead (I know the touch of her hands so well) and stay with her and, above all, sleep without dreams.

So, lest I should listen to that ridiculous voice inside me (we all have these ridiculous voices), I spoke loud and fast.

"You tell Richard that I'm after him and I'll follow him everywhere and at last I'll get him and he can't escape me. Do you hear? He can't escape me." And I went out of the room and out of the house, breathing as though I had been running fast.

Two nights ago I had Cheeseman to sleep with me. Nothing could be more disagreeable than this, and yet I am beginning to avoid being alone. When Cheeseman was undressing I asked him suddenly whether he saw anyone in the corner of the room. He walked in his shirt and in his bare feet (his toes are bent and red like the claws of crabs) and examined the room from end to end.

"There is no one here," he said. And yet, even then, I could see, I fancied, a thin figure with bent head, shadowy and yet real.

Cheeseman, I am happy to say, is, in spite of my confiding my secret to him, afraid of me. . . . I was acutely aware that last night he wished desperately not to sleep in the same bed with me. He would give almost his life not to do it, but does not dare to refuse me. The Rat does what I tell him. At last he has found a power stronger than his own.

While I was undressing I looked at the upper part of my arm and it seemed to me that I detected a tattoo-mark faintly blue. I made Cheeseman examine it and with all the more pleasure that he hated to touch my body. He could see nothing. I fancy that I can trace a design.

In bed the Rat lay withdrawn, dreading with all his flesh lest I should touch him. I reached out my hand and laid it on his thigh. He trembled from his ears to his toes. This gave me great pleasure and after that I allowed him to sleep.

But last night I refused to surrender to any absurd panic. I had had a wonderful walk in the darkness and I had heard news of Richard. Cheeseman reported to me just before supper that he had that afternoon seen Richard and Leila leave a taxi and enter, each carrying a bag, a little hotel off Soho Square.

I have indeed great powers from my Master, for consider the coincidence that the Rat, passing through Soho Square, thinking of his own affairs, watches idly a taxi-cab draw up outside the shabby hotel and sees Leila and Richard emerge from it! Such things do happen, of course. Everyone can recall astonishing coincidences. But does not this one convince me that I am indeed assigned this especial task of punishing my fellow human creatures and that I have been granted especial powers? Even a wretched creature like Cheeseman can feel something of this especial divinity in me. When I look at him he lowers his eyes. When I speak the tips of his ugly ears are crimson. When his teeth protrude and his head crouches into his shoulders he is indeed like a rat caught in a trap.

However, last night I slept alone. I awoke abruptly at one-fifteen. Someone was in the room, and, sitting up in bed, I heard once again that pitiful sobbing that had exasperated me so outside Bella's room.

I switched on the light and, staring a little breathlessly, was certain that in the far corner between the looking-glass and the window I saw that thin, shabby, bending figure.

When I write down the dialogue that follows, it is for my own reassurance that I may realize its absurdity. But it seems to me that I talked with the Figure, who answered me.

And yet it may be that I still slept and that I talked to myself in my dream.

MYSELF: *"Stop that crying."*

"Let me go, then! Oh, for pity's sake let me go! If I did you once a great harm, I have been punished enough."

MYSELF: "I don't know what you are talking about."

"You do; you know you do. Ever since we were small boys together you threatened me. You said we were the Siamese Twins —that nothing could separate us."

MYSELF: (chuckling) "You wouldn't listen. I warned you. What was it I used to call you?"

"Jacko."

MYSELF: "Yes, Jacko. That was it. A silly name."

"Let me go now. Please, please let me go. And this other man whom you are pursuing has nothing to do with us. He may be like me a little, and so the sight of him infuriates you, but he is not us."

MYSELF: "I am not so sure."

"You are carrying me along with you in your dreadful purposes just as you have always done. How ashamed and unhappy you make me—just as you have always done. My poor wife and boy. You struck her and showed Archie indecent drawings. They thought it was me. Oh, the shame, the shame!"

MYSELF: "And so it was you, Jacko! For you are me and I am you!"

"I am not! I am not! You said that when we were children together, and it wasn't true then and it isn't true now. Every man's soul is his own, and if he is strong enough, no one can touch his inviolability. But I am not strong enough because of the one evil thing that I did."

MYSELF: "Poor Jacko! The one brave, downright thing you ever did, and see how you are punished for it!"

"Leave me. Leave me. Go your own evil way and meet your own evil destruction. Let me return to my wife and son and beg their pardon and Leila's pardon, too, and show the town that I am just as I used to be. . . ."

MYSELF: "Oh, no, Jacko! That would be far too easy an escape. We go on together to the end. One's acts are irrevocable, you know. After all, you were paid the compliment of free will. You really can't blame anybody but yourself. Now stop crying like a baby, Jacko, and let me have some sleep."

Dreams! I don't know. As I write down this nonsense I can see myself years and years ago trembling at Jim Tunstall's touch, even as Cheeseman trembled the other night at mine.

4

I HAVE ESCAPED. For a moment only perhaps. Oh, God! Give me time! I know that someone is praying for me and has given me this extra power. I, in my turn, pray to God to keep me free and allow me time for my penitent submission.

Everything is so quiet here. It is as though I had been fighting under turbulent waters. With a dreadful din in my ears and a drive of waves beating at my throat and heart and eyes. Now suddenly I am floating in a blessed silence and the steady beating of my heart. . . .

This room is so still. Why did it seem to me so mocking and sinister? The clock on the stairs has struck two. I went to bed in a kind of madness. A furious hatred of mankind. I was planning some dreadful act. In my dreams it seemed that someone called to me again and again as friends do when they are trying to wake you!

"John . . . John . . . John Talbot, John Talbot . . ." And I struggled as Lazarus must have struggled. It was as though I had to lift a great burden. I was fighting someone and I heard his chuckle: "Down, Jacko! Down! Keep down!"

In my nightmare I knew that I could never beat this off unless great help was lent me, and I called out, as one does in dreams: "Help! Help! . . . In God's name help!"

I felt the hands on my shoulders keeping me down, and I felt the hands under my armpits lifting me up. New strength came to me. I cried out—and it is the first time for so long that my voice has been heard—"I am free!" Then I woke. I was sitting up in bed. I switched on the light, put on my dressing-gown, and now I'm sitting, writing this on the dressing-table, writing as once I did, happy, tranquil, quiet. . . .

Early to-morrow morning I will go back to Eve . . . I will catch
the first train. . . . Oh, God, forgive me my sins. I have sinned. I
have sinned. I will give myself up to justice.

Oh, God, Thou hast punished me enough. Release me now
from the possession of evil. Make abhorrent for me these vices
that I abhor, but am a servant under. Deliver me from Evil. Oh,
God—Deliver us from Evil. Raise my head from under this possession.

Oh, God! He is returning—my heart sinks with fear. My breath
thickens on the glass. He looks through my eyes again. There is the
stink of his breath in my nostrils. Oh, save me, God, save me. . . .

5

So you thought you had escaped, old fellow, did you? You thought
you had escaped? I have read that nonsense. But *was* it, like my
fancied dialogue a night or two ago, an imagined dream? Memory?
When I dream—and I have dreamed much of late—who am I?

My handwriting does not change. That is simply a trick of habit.
But have we not all an imprisoned self? In any case, *my* imprisoned self is a wretched creature with his weeping and wailing
and appeals to a God who does not exist. I heard the other day
of an old Jew in one of the German prison camps, and when they
threatened him with torture he prayed to God. So they beat him to
death with hose-pipes and between every blow they cried: "Now,
Jehovah! Help Thy servant." The thought of those beatings stirs
my blood. So, Jacko, say: "Now, Jehovah! Help Thy servant!"

My hand trembles as I write. This writing is almost illegible.
That does not matter, for no one will ever read it. This is in all
probability the last time I shall ever write anything. From words to
deeds . . . I feel a conqueror. My heart beats in my breast like the
heart of a king. What I did last night I will do again—and again
and again. I will terrorize this whole city. I am Hitler's forerunner
of vengeance. Maybe I *am* God. Who can deny it? I stretch my arm
and it seems to reach into infinity. I stare with my eyes and, as in
that pub last night, they are turned to stone.

Last night the wind blew with a fury and all the houses seemed to bow to me. I walked into the darkness like a king.

And to-night, when I have settled my debt with that pitiful murderer, I will begin my campaign of vengeance. The winds of the air, the stones of the streets will aid me.

Well, about last night.

Cheeseman watched and saw him leave his Club off Jermyn Street. He followed him then to a little eating-place at the Knightsbridge end of Sloane Street. Then he met me where we had agreed to meet, at the coffee-stall at Hyde Park Corner.

Strange, isn't it, that I thought by my confession that I had yielded myself into Cheeseman's hands, and it has turned out the exact opposite from that! Cheeseman, the great Cheeseman, the blackmailer and terrorizer, who has held so many men and women at his mercy for so long, strange that he should at last be in the hands of someone else! For he is terrified of me and with every day his terror grows the stronger. Yesterday in my room I asked him: "Why are you frightened?"

"You look like——"

"Like what?"

"Like the Devil."

"You are not frightened of a man's looks, Cheeseman. Come here." And he came. "Kneel down." He knelt down. "Raise your hands and touch my arms." He could not do it. "Hold my arms, Cheeseman."

At last, his body trembling, his head averted, his hands lay on my arms, those pale hands with the thin, red hairs.

I bent forward and cupped his chin, forcing his head upwards. His eyes closed.

"Look at me, Cheeseman."

He would not.

"Look at me, Cheeseman."

He would not.

"Look at me, Cheeseman."

His face trembled like a face under moving waters. Then he looked at me.

I feel a deep pleasure as I describe this remembered scene.

I went and stood outside the little restaurant. After a while Richard came out. There was a strong wind now rushing in and out of the restaurant. There was no light from the door of the restaurant, but I flashed my torch. He saw me. For an exciting moment he stared into my eyes. I thought he was going to speak, but he did not. He crossed the road and walked quickly along Knightsbridge. I followed him.

My pleasure was now so intense that I could have suspended it into eternity. I knew what terror there must be in his heart. I wondered whether he would stop at Hyde Park Corner and take an omnibus. But he knew that that would not save him. He knew that there must be that last walk from Piccadilly to Soho Square. If he took a taxi-cab there would be that moment when he stayed on the pavement to pay his fare. Or, perhaps, he wished to end it. Whatever he did, wherever he went, he could not escape. If he appealed to the police, that would not save him, for no one save Leila had heard me threaten him, and in any case the police could not save him for ever. But, Richard, you are only the first. After you there will be many, many others.

As I walked through Knightsbridge, I felt an exquisite, a sensuous pleasure. To feel the revolver in my hand and to know that my power, my great, great power, stretched far beyond my revolver. I could have shouted with joy at my power, calling out, "Rain down your hailstones of fire, Revenger!" And so they will rain down and a great fire roar to heaven, and these puny buildings come crashing to the ground.

The wind blew through the darkness, making it vocal. The power of the wind met my own power. We were great together.

By the coffee-stall at Hyde Park Corner he paused. He looked about him, the poor miserable fish. He was considering, I fancy, whether he would not take a taxi. I would be there before him if he did. There was a little crowd round the coffee-stall, which was dimly lit. There was a cheerful hum of voices and laughter. I stood, robed in my darkness, and thought: "Aye, you may laugh. Soon you will be crying to heaven"—a grand thought that made my heart beat almost to suffocation.

He decided to walk and I followed him down Piccadilly. While

I was behind him I was also with him. My hands were on his neck and I had twisted his head round so that his eyes were staring pitifully into mine, begging for mercy.

Along Piccadilly the wind, blowing across the Green Park, was raging. Pedestrians had difficulty in standing steady, and as the wind blew against them I knew that it was my power and I had only to command and the wind would rise until it lifted them off their feet and blasted their bodies against the walls, and then the walls, too, would crash to the ground, buildings, old, beautiful buildings that had been the country's pride and pleasure for hundreds of years, reduced to dust and rubble.

At Half Moon Street he turned up into Curzon Street. Why he did this I do not know. I followed him up that dark little street. By the Christian Science Church he paused and then struck right. And then—I lost him.

I made a mistake. There is a little public-house on the right and I thought he entered it. I pushed open the door and looked in. The room was brilliantly lit. There was a man behind the bar, a girl serving drinks, some people at the tables.

As I stood in the doorway they all turned and looked at me. Some power compelled them. Some power also held them so that they seemed turned to stone, all staring, not moving. But he was not there. I was out in the street again and began to run. I collided with a man hurrying in front of me. I was enraged at his stopping me. I caught him by the neck. He cried out. I hit at his face with my fist. I hit again and again. He fell to the ground and, with an exultant pleasure, I stamped on him, on his face, on his belly. I kicked him, bent down and tore at his face with my hands. Ah, but that was a pleasure, a great exultant happiness. I felt his flesh under my hand, I felt his belly quiver as I turned my boots upon him.

I felt all the power of the wind and the darkness in my soul as I ran on, ran till I could run no more, ran until I reached the steps, and there, laughing because I was master of the world, knelt down to tie my bootlace and then stayed to wipe the sweat from my face and steady my beating heart. I had lost him. For this moment I had lost him, but not for long.

This will be, I fancy, the last time I shall write. . . . Deeds now.
Not words.

The little tinny bell has rung for supper. Through my open door
I can hear them scurrying down to their food. I will sit with them,
eat with them, drink with them. How wonderful that at last, at
last, this long-postponed hour has come!

6

Letter from Leila Tunstall to Eve Talbot

MY DEAR EVE—By now you will have received my telegram. We
must wait for the inquest, and as soon as that is over Richard and
I will bring John down to you. I want to give you an exact account
of what occurred so that you may understand, as though you had
been there, just what happened.

First I must tell you that poor John killed Jim by throwing him
over Shining Cliff. This he himself told me, but I knew it long ago.
Perhaps you also had guessed it.

A simple explanation of all that occurred after that is that John
brooded so deeply on what he had done that he became insane.
Nothing more is needed than that, although I think the real explanation is a much more complicated one. You do not know perhaps
all that I suffered during my last years with Jim, although you can
understand it possibly by all that *you* suffered during these last
months with John. We all watched the change in John. It seemed
to eat him up, bit by bit, like a disease. I know how you suffered,
but I suffered in my own way too, for I loved John—like a mother,
a sister—but I loved him always and I love him now. I was not,
however, more directly concerned until I found that he hated
Richard. Richard is, and has always been, my particular care. When
we were children together I tried to look after him and protect
him. Physically, Richard resembled very closely what John used
to be, and in some curious way this physical resemblance exasperated John. At first Richard thought that he must be imagining this
hatred. He had never had anything to do with John, bore him no

ill-will although the John of these later months was antipathetic to him in every way, but he knew how fond of him I was and he put up with him for my sake.

However, during this last summer, matters became serious. John insulted him in every possible way, followed him about and once in Carfax Wood nearly assaulted him. I invited John to come and talk to me about it, but when he came he only talked wildly of hating him.

You know how John's face had changed during these last months, how terribly it had changed. He reminded me often, by his looks and speech, of Jim as he had been during those last years. In that talk I had with him I felt certain that he was in the possession of some evil power, as Jim had been. Here I must ask your patience, for you may consider the power of evil and its possession of human beings as a piece of old-fashioned nonsense, not seriously to be held in these days by any mature, sensible person. It seems to me that if you believe in God you must also believe in Evil and in a constant battle between good and evil. But I am not pretending that I am putting forward here any belief but my own. I am not attempting to force it on to anyone of a different belief. We have each of us our own explanation of the great mystery, an explanation that must come from our own experience of life. No one has the right to say to us that we are speaking falsehood as *we* see truth, nor have we the right to challenge the belief of anyone else.

However, this persecution of Richard by John became so incessant that Richard's health (he has never been very strong) became affected by it and I decided that we should go to town. We went but had been there scarcely any time when Richard was met by John outside his Club. Quite suddenly John appeared at my house. He stood in my doorway and, Eve, I looked at someone so terrible that I shrank as from the presence of the Devil himself. It was *not* John with whom I spoke, but something I had never encountered before, save in my most terrible dreams. Something not only incredibly wicked but something also quite dreadfully sad.

I did not know what to do. To inform the police, to insist that John should be medically examined, was hopeless, for what would they, who knew nothing of the inside of our story, see but a quiet, sad-faced man who would talk to them with perfect coherence and deride my fears? But the danger to Richard was most urgent. He felt it himself and yet could not believe in it.

We moved to a small hotel off Soho Square and began to make our plans for going to some other part of England for a time. Richard was against this. He felt it a cowardly surrender to an absurd fear. I on my part was sure that this was no solution.

We had scarcely settled in at this little hotel before John found us. When we were out someone—John or another—would enquire for us. John, of course, had quickly found the number of my brother's room. I cannot describe to you, dear Eve, how strange this experience was. Someone was following us in the dark, drawing ever closer and closer. Wherever he went, whatever he did, Richard felt that he was followed. Sometimes he saw John staring at him out of the darkness.

An evening came when Richard returned to the hotel, his nerves gone, trembling and begging me to protect him. Richard is a brave man and has faced many perils in the East. I had never seen him like this before.

We sat up late that night and decided, after much discussion, that we would trust in God and face the climax of this whatever it might be. I told him that we must be together from this time on and take whatever was coming side by side. I knew that I had some power with John.

We had not long to wait.

On the evening following Richard's collapse, at about half-past nine, Richard went up to his room and I went up with him. I was sitting in an arm-chair, Richard on the bed. The door opened and John stood there.

I think my first feeling was one of relief that we had all met at last face to face. But at once I, who am not, I think, a nervous or cowardly woman, was stricken with fear. Dear Eve, I want you to understand exactly what followed, but it is far from easy to explain this dreadful moment as I saw and felt it without your feeling it to be exaggerated and false. And yet I fancy there must have been moments in your last weeks with John when you realized some-

thing of the same kind. This was John and was *not* John. You know
how, when someone you love and have lived with for a long time
falls into a sudden tempestuous rage, how the face, the body even,
changes and you feel you are encountering a stranger. It was not
that the figure in the doorway was in a rage. It was calm and controlled with a horrible coldness. I am exaggerating nothing when
I say that the room seemed to chill around us. Richard himself
acknowledged this to me afterwards. The figure looked at us both,
and from those eyes came a gaze so cruel and at the same time so
distant that it belonged to no time, as we recognize time. Isn't it
the worst thing that we feel about Hitler that he has no human
passions, no love, no lusts, no sensuous weakness, no bowels of
compassion? We are human beings bound all of us together by our
common human experience, and we can imagine nothing more
awful than encountering someone who has had none of our experience and is bound in no way by our laws, to whom no appeal can
ever be made that he will understand.

This figure that faced us was evil because it was not human.
The black hat, the dark coat, the gloved hands were a symbol
expressing the whole power of inhuman impersonal evil.

At once, for this that takes so long to tell occupied a very brief
time, I felt, rising in my breast, beating down my fear, an immea-
surable overwhelming pity for John. Something infinitely greater
than myself filled my soul. At the same time I felt a disgust, a sickness of revolt as though I were seeing some appalling cruelty to
children or animals.

I prayed to God. I implored Him to give me strength to fight the
force confronting us. I knew then, Eve, in a swift impulse of revelation, that everything I had been, done, and suffered was to count
now. Had I suffered that much less in the past—mental, spiritual,
physical suffering—the less strong would I be now.

I rose and cried out as though I were summoning the dead:
"John! John! John!"

The figure moved forward into the room. In its gloved hand was
a revolver. I saw that and Richard saw it, too, but I think neither
of us felt the least fear of it, for as the figure stepped further into
the light, its face was quite dreadful to see. It was not the cold,

passionless stare of the eyes, the pallid, swollen, bag-like folds of the flesh, the mouth slightly parted, but sharp like a trap—it was rather the absence of all humanity and the sense of horrible time-lessness as though, for ever and ever, it had been exactly thus and would continue for ever so.

Then I fought it. There was, of course, no physical contact. I should have died, I think, had there been. I don't know, Eve, what I said or even if I spoke. But my spirit saw John's spirit struggling to be free. With all that was good in me, with everything that had ever been worthy in my life, I fought for that spirit. My spirit said: "John, John, I am with you. Don't be afraid. You are escaping! You will soon be free! You will be free, John! Be brave! I am with you!"

The figure raised its hand. There was no other motion. Into that evil, timeless face there came movement. A fearful struggle. I seemed to have John's body in my hands. It was as though, between my hands, I felt the battle to be free. I cried out to God, and in myself I realized a power I had never known before, like the sun breaking on to a sullen plain, a warmth, a heat, a consciousness of resurrection. The face with which my whole soul was battling broke up. The eyes dulled. The mouth trembled.

A deep, bitter, heart-breaking sigh trembled on the air.

The figure turned on one foot, seemed about to fall, then, with bent hand, directed the revolver into itself.

We heard the report as though from a great way off.

At last Richard came over to the body, and very gently, rever-ently, turned it over.

There was lying there, Eve, the old John, the face thin and drawn, the eyes staring with a peaceful happiness—John, as you and I for so long knew him and loved him.

I can tell you only, dear Eve, that I have spoken the truth as *I* found it.

We are in God's hands now and always.

Your affectionate friend,
LEILA TUNSTALL

ALSO AVAILABLE FROM VALANCOURT BOOKS

MICHAEL ARLEN	Hell! said the Duchess
R. C. ASHBY (RUBY FERGUSON)	He Arrived at Dusk
FRANK BAKER	The Birds
WALTER BAXTER	Look Down in Mercy
CHARLES BEAUMONT	The Hunger and Other Stories
DAVID BENEDICTUS	The Fourth of June
PAUL BINDING	Harmonica's Bridegroom
CHARLES BIRKIN	The Smell of Evil
JOHN BLACKBURN	A Scent of New-Mown Hay
	Broken Boy
	Blue Octavo
	A Ring of Roses
	Children of the Night
	The Flame and the Wind
	Nothing but the Night
	Bury Him Darkly
	Our Lady of Pain
	Devil Daddy
	The Household Traitors
	The Face of the Lion
	The Cyclops Goblet
	A Beastly Business
	The Bad Penny
THOMAS BLACKBURN	A Clip of Steel
	The Feast of the Wolf
JOHN BRAINE	Room at the Top
	The Vodi
JACK CADY	The Well
MICHAEL CAMPBELL	Lord Dismiss Us
R. CHETWYND-HAYES	The Monster Club
ISABEL COLEGATE	The Blackmailer
BASIL COPPER	The Great White Space
	Necropolis
HUNTER DAVIES	Body Charge
JENNIFER DAWSON	The Ha-Ha
FRANK DE FELITTA	The Entity
A. E. ELLIS	The Rack
BARRY ENGLAND	Figures in a Landscape
RONALD FRASER	Flower Phantoms

OLIVER ONIONS	The Hand of Kornelius Voyt
J.B. PRIESTLEY	Benighted
	The Doomsday Men
	The Other Place
	The Magicians
	Saturn Over the Water
	The Thirty-First of June
	The Shapes of Sleep
	Salt Is Leaving
PETER PRINCE	Play Things
PIERS PAUL READ	Monk Dawson
FORREST REID	The Garden God
	Following Darkness
	The Spring Song
	Brian Westby
	The Tom Barber Trilogy
	Denis Bracknel
GEORGE SIMS	Sleep No More
	The Last Best Friend
ANDREW SINCLAIR	The Facts in the Case of E.A. Poe
	The Raker
COLIN SPENCER	Panic
DAVID STOREY	Radcliffe
	Pasmore
	Saville
MICHAEL TALBOT	The Delicate Dependency
RUSSELL THORNDIKE	The Slype
	The Master of the Macabre
JOHN TREVENA	Sleeping Waters
JOHN WAIN	Hurry on Down
	The Smaller Sky
	Strike the Father Dead
	A Winter in the Hills
HUGH WALPOLE	The Killer and the Slain
KEITH WATERHOUSE	There is a Happy Land
	Billy Liar
COLIN WILSON	Ritual in the Dark
	Man Without a Shadow
	The World of Violence
	The Philosopher's Stone
	The God of the Labyrinth

WHAT CRITICS ARE SAYING ABOUT VALANCOURT BOOKS

"[W]e owe a debt of gratitude to the publisher Valancourt, whose aim is to resurrect some neglected works of literature, especially those incorporating a supernatural strand, and make them available to a new readership."

Times Literary Supplement (London)

"Valancourt Books champions neglected but important works of fantastic, occult, decadent and gay literature. The press's Web site not only lists scores of titles but also explains why these often obscure books are still worth reading. . . . So if you're a real reader, one who looks beyond the bestseller list and the touted books of the moment, Valancourt's publications may be just what you're searching for."

MICHAEL DIRDA, *Washington Post*

"Valancourt Books are fast becoming my favourite publisher. They have made it their business, with considerable taste and integrity, to put back into print a considerable amount of work which has been in serious need of republication. If you ever felt there were gaps in your reading experience or are simply frustrated that you can't find enough good, substantial fiction in the shops or even online, then this is the publisher for you."

MICHAEL MOORCOCK

TO LEARN MORE AND TO SEE A COMPLETE LIST OF AVAILABLE
TITLES, VISIT US AT VALANCOURTBOOKS.COM

CPSIA information can be obtained at www.ICGtesting.com
Printed in the USA
LVOW10s1406230315

431661LV00002B/36/P